I DIED
for
BEAUTY

Also by Amanda Flower

Because I Could Not Stop for Death

I Heard a Fly Buzz When I Died

I DIED *for* BEAUTY

An Emily Dickinson Mystery

AMANDA FLOWER

BERKLEY PRIME CRIME
New York

BERKLEY PRIME CRIME
Published by Berkley
An imprint of Penguin Random House LLC
1745 Broadway, New York, NY 10019
penguinrandomhouse.com

Library of Congress Cataloging-in-Publication Data
Names: Flower, Amanda, author.
Title: I died for beauty / Amanda Flower.
Description: First edition. | New York: Berkley Prime Crime, 2025. |
Series: An Emily Dickinson mystery
Identifiers: LCCN 2024031770 (print) | LCCN 2024031771 (ebook) |
ISBN 9780593816462 (trade paperback) | ISBN 9780593816479 (epub)
Subjects: LCGFT: Detective and mystery fiction. | Novels.
Classification: LCC PS3606.L683 I35 2025 (print) |
LCC PS3606.L683 (ebook) | DDC 813/.6—dc23/eng/20240712
LC record available at https://lccn.loc.gov/2024031770
LC ebook record available at https://lccn.loc.gov/2024031771

First Edition: February 2025

Printed in the United States of America
1st Printing

The authorized representative in the EU for product safety and compliance is Penguin Random House Ireland, Morrison Chambers, 32 Nassau Street, Dublin D02 YH68, Ireland, https://eu-contact.penguin.ie.

For Emily Dickinson

Who lived and died for Beauty and Truth

I died for Beauty—but was scarce
Adjusted in the Tomb
When One who died for Truth, was lain
In an adjoining Room—

He questioned softly "Why I failed"?
"For Beauty", I replied—
"And I—for Truth—Themself are One—
We Brethren are", He said—

And so, as Kinsmen, met a Night—
We talked between the Rooms—
Until the Moss had reached our lips—
And covered up—Our names—

—Emily Dickinson

I DIED

for

BEAUTY

CHAPTER ONE

I'D NEVER BEEN this cold. Despite the three pairs of stockings on my feet, I no longer felt my toes. Nor could I feel my hands with two pairs of mittens on them. I looked down at my hands from time to time to reassure myself that I still held the market basket. It was not as heavy as I hoped nor as full as my employers would have wished.

The trains had stopped running days ago. Snowdrifts up to ten feet high blocked their path. It was the worst winter in my memory or in the memory of anyone I knew. We all felt the pinch from the Cold Storm of 1857.

December had been snowy, but it seemed that January was taking it upon itself to prove it could surpass the very worst of weather the last year or even the last decade had to offer.

Here in Amherst, the mercury was twenty degrees below zero, but I also heard that the same temperatures were crippling points as far south as Washington. The cold was torture here, but at least we expected harsh winters. It must have come as a shock to the Southern belles and fine gentlemen in the capital.

I was grateful Horace, the Dickinsons' grounds keeper, had shoveled a path from the street to both the front and back doors of the homestead. Without that cleared path, my skirt would have been soaked through in no time at all. Even so it was narrow, just wide enough for one man to pass, so I had to grip my skirts and hold the market basket out in front of myself like I was making some sort of offering to the winter gods that caused this weather. The way I held my arms out reminded me of the mummy illustrations in the volume of ancient Egyptian history in Mr. Dickinson's library.

Margaret O'Brien, the head maid at the homestead, met me at the back door that led into the laundry. She took the basket from my hands so quickly I felt a sharp pain in my stiff fingers. "Get in here before you let the heat out," she said in her Irish lilt.

I stepped into the laundry and made sure the back door was firmly closed behind me. I placed the heavy blanket back in its place at the foot of the door to keep out the draft. I removed my bonnet, cloak, mittens, boots, and two pairs of stockings, which I tucked into the boots. When I was out of the boots, I changed into my house shoes. It was a relief to not be buried under so much fabric, but much of the cold that the cloak held at bay hit me like an icy wave crashing into Boston Harbor.

In the kitchen Margaret unpacked the basket. "Where is my molasses? And where is the cinnamon I asked for?"

Emily Dickinson came into the kitchen just then, quietly and lightly as she always did. She moved around the place like a house wren that popped up here and there on an unexpected branch in the garden.

Emily was the eldest daughter in the house and the most puzzling of the Dickinsons. While her sister, Miss Lavinia, was straightforward and direct, Emily tended to weave her thoughts into verse and she felt no need to explain in common language their meaning or purpose.

"Willa," she said with a smile. "You're back. You must be frozen to your very bones. Margaret, set a stool by the stove, so she can warm herself."

Grudgingly, Margaret started to walk to the stool.

I hurried on unsteady feet stiff with cold. "There is no need. As soon as I start working, I will warm up quickly."

Emily eyed me as if she was not so sure of that, but to my relief, she didn't argue with me. It was my wish not to annoy Margaret any more with my unusual friendship with Emily than she was already. The more special treatment that Emily gave me as her friend, the more Margaret O'Brien resented me.

I knew a second maid claiming an upper-class educated young lady as a friend was unexpected to say the least. However, over the last two years that I had worked in the Dickinson home, Emily *had* become my friend as much as she could be, considering our stations in life, and I was appreciative for the bond. She was there when I lost my brother, Henry, and I would always be grateful to her for that.

Emily looked over the items that Margaret unpacked from the basket. "Where is my coconut?"

I started to boil water on the stove to wash the breakfast dishes that I had left undone to run to the market. Usually, the market boy delivered to the homestead. With the harsh weather, all deliveries save the milkman had stopped. That was a blessing as it was so cold that our cow had stopped producing milk.

"I'm sorry, Miss Dickinson," I said. "But the grocer told me that there was no coconut in all of Amherst. With the cold, the trains can't make it in. The rails are too icy for clear passage, and the ones that are not icy are blocked with fallen trees or feet of snow."

Emily sighed. "I suppose there go my plans to make a coconut cake for supper in order to raise all of our spirits. I was very much looking forward to doing that. Baking is the very best way for me to let my mind wander and discover new poems that are waiting to be written. Baking and being in the garden at least. It seems with this weather that option is off the table as well."

"We have the ingredients for your black cake," Margaret chimed in. "I believe there is just enough molasses left. You can bake that and let your mind wander to your heart's content." She added this last bit with a touch of disapproval in her voice that Emily either didn't notice or simply didn't care about. I guessed the latter as there was very little that my mistress missed.

"Are we nearly out of molasses too?" Emily asked. "What is the world coming to?"

Margaret shook her head. It was times like this when I longed to be able to read her thoughts. I was certain that she had a few things that she wished she could say about Emily's comment.

Emily clicked her tongue as if in dismay. "What will become of us when there is no molasses or coconut?"

I bit the inside of my lip to stop myself from saying many people live without these luxuries. In fact, I had never even known of coconuts until I began working at the Dickinson home. They were so exotic to me. Having grown up with nothing gave me a perspective that Emily didn't have. I did not hold it against my friend, but it was a painful reminder of the vast chasm between our life experiences.

"I'll make some sort of pound cake instead," Emily declared. "Something simple, yet bright and festive. We should save the molasses as there is no telling when we will get more."

"Surely, this cold can't go on for more than a day or two more," Margaret said.

"You have said that for two weeks, Margaret, and it has given no indication of stopping. The papers say it could go into March. Father has been watching the barometer in his office and makes doom-filled pronouncements about the weather to come."

Margaret sniffed. "I don't know how that gadget of gears and dials can predict the weather. Only a well-aged farmer can do so accurately." She said this like that was all she had to say on the matter.

"It's science, Margaret, and is much more reliable than an old farmer licking his finger and holding it up in the wind. Father sounded quite confident about the weather to come."

Margaret crossed herself. "Let's all pray that it doesn't come to that."

Margaret would have never made that gesture in front of any other member of the Dickinson family because it would only be a reminder that she was Irish Catholic at heart. It would make their Calvinist sensibilities most uncomfortable.

As Emily had no interest in organized religion and followed a belief system of her own creation, it had no effect on her. She didn't even mind that I was raised Baptist, which some members of the Dickinsons' church found appalling.

Margaret caught me listening to their conversation. "Willa, get on with the dishes and when that is done, dust and polish in the parlor as long as the family is not in the room."

I nodded and set to work. The hot water seeped into my frozen skin, and it was both painful and welcome.

Shortly after Margaret and I returned to our daily tasks, Emily left the kitchen, saying she would be back in the late morning to bake her pound cake, as they did not take as much time to make as her coconut cake would have.

When I finished the dishes and had dried them and tucked them away, I went through the dining room into the parlor. I was happy to see that everything in the dining room was polished and put away. Typically, that was my task, but Margaret had taken it upon herself when I was at the market. I would thank her for it later even though she would outwardly scoff at the gratitude while inwardly enjoying it.

I was just stepping into the family parlor when the terrifying scent of smoke tickled my nose. I hurried inside the front parlor to find an ember from the fireplace had made its way through the screen and smoldered on the edge of the carpet.

I stamped it out with my shoe with my heart beating out of my chest. Had I not been there at that very time, there was no telling what would have happened.

I pulled my foot away from the spot and there was the faintest of burns no larger than a penny on the colorful carpet. I wondered how I could remove the stain without anyone being the wiser.

My hopes to keep the incident quiet were dashed when Mr. Dickinson stormed into the room. "Do I smell something burning?"

Emily and Miss Lavinia were just steps behind him.

Mr. Dickinson was not a large man but formidable all the same. He had a receding hairline, and what hair he had on the sides of his head stuck out in triangular tufts. His brow was heavy and thick as were his sideburns. His nose was pointed and sharp, almost like a beak. He was the very last person that I would have wanted to find me in this current state.

The urge to place my foot back over the burn spot was overwhelming, but I stopped myself. I did not want to look like I was covering something up as though this was my fault.

"Willa, are you all right?" Emily asked.

"Yes, miss," I murmured, and kept my eyes pointed at my shoes.

"What has happened here?" Mr. Dickinson asked. "Have you burned a hole into the carpet, you careless girl?"

I could feel my body quake, and I willed it to stop. I was about to be sacked. I just knew it. Honestly, it was a miracle that I had lasted two long years. I thought most of that had to do with Emily's intervention when it came to her father.

She came to my rescue again. "Father, please. Willa would never do that!" She nodded to me. "Willa, tell us what happened."

"Thank you, miss." I took a breath and was determined to keep my voice steady. "I had just come into the front parlor to start the dusting when I smelled a hint of smoke. I saw an ember had come through the gate and fallen to the carpet. I stamped it out with my foot." I held up the toe of my shoe as if that was proof in some way. "It must have just happened as I was coming into the room. I was grateful I was here, miss. Most grateful."

"As are we," Emily said. "The whole of the house could have been lost!" She turned to her father. "See, she saved us all!"

"When was this hearth last cleaned?" Mr. Dickinson asked.

It took me a moment to realize that he was speaking to me. The father of the home rarely addressed any question to me. If he wanted information from me, it was relayed back and forth through Margaret and at times, Miss Lavinia.

"Yesterday morning, sir."

"But not today?" he roared. "Why not?"

"The fires were made in haste, sir," I admitted. "I had to go to the market as there is no delivery due to the cold."

"That is not acceptable. Every hearth must be cleaned every day until this weather breaks. I will not lose this house after I spent a lifetime earning it back. More people die of fires than the cold," he snapped. "Remember that."

I swallowed. My throat felt swollen, but I managed to speak. "I can clean the hearth now, Mr. Dickinson, if it is your wish."

"I expect you to," he said, and left the room.

Miss Lavinia, who was dark-haired and petite like Emily, if a bit thicker, made a move to leave the room and stopped in the doorway. "Don't let Willa cut corners, Emily, simply because you think of her as your *friend*," she said snidely, and left.

Emily patted my arm. "Do not worry about them, Willa. I still believe that you are a heroine."

"I don't feel like one," I said.

"You cannot put a fire out a thing that can ignite," she said, and left the room leaving me to wonder what fire she meant.

CHAPTER TWO

WHEN THE FAMILY left the room, I began to roll up the hearth rug and set to work. As there was already a fire in the hearth, I would have to snuff it out before cleaning. The fire's remnants would be hot, but I didn't believe I had any other choice in the matter but to set it to rights. I had to clean it quickly and set the fire again before the room grew too cold to stand.

In an hour, I scoured the hearth from top to bottom and front to back. I'd never done such a thorough job cleaning a fireplace before, but Mr. Dickinson's mention of fire scared me. In my mind's eye, I could still see that ember smoldering on the carpet.

Emily's large brown dog, Carlo, wandered into the room when I was in the middle of cleaning. He flopped in the family parlor in front of the piano. The pocket doors between the two rooms stood open. Until I was done with the task, no member of the family would come into the parlor for fear of getting soot on their clothes.

I was grateful for Carlo's company.

Finally, I finished and rolled the hearth rug back into place. I had just gathered up all my brushes, cloths, and buckets when there was an authoritative knock on the front door. I stood there holding a jumble of items without a spare hand and with soot on my face and my apron. I wasn't in a presentable state to greet any of the Dickinsons' fine neighbors.

I was more than a little surprised that someone would come out in this terrible cold to make a call. It wasn't Mr. Austin Dickinson or his wife, Susan, who lived in the Evergreens, the house next door to the homestead. Either one of them would have walked in without knocking.

The knock came again with an irritating *rat-a-tat-tat*.

I thought it was best if I made a dash for the laundry and came back to answer the door when I was more presentable.

I was making my way into the kitchen when I heard Mr. Dickinson bellow, "Would someone answer that confounded door?"

Thankfully, Margaret wasn't in the kitchen when I arrived. She wasn't in the laundry either. I guessed she was cleaning the bedrooms on the second floor. That was good for my sake. I quickly put all my things down in as orderly a way as possible in my haste, removed my apron, and ran a clothing brush over my dress. It helped. But anyone who saw me would know right away that I had been cleaning a hearth.

Back at the front of the house, I straightened my skirt and opened the door. "Good morning, may I help you?"

A stout woman with wide shoulders and an enormous hat that only made her appear larger glowered at me from behind her fox fur wrap. "You can help me by allowing me to come inside before I freeze to death."

I glanced over my shoulder, hoping that someone was there to provide me with guidance as to whether I should let her in or not. No one was there, and a frigid gust of wind that blew snow into the house around her was the deciding factor.

I stepped back. "Please come in. I will have you wait in the front parlor if you don't mind."

She handed me her wrap and her large hat. "That will be fine. I am here to call on Mrs. Dickinson. It is a matter of extreme importance. Please tell her that so she will deign to talk to me. I know that the lady of the house is selective as to whom she will see."

I promised her that I would. I stifled a yelp as I saw the poor fox's head was still attached to the wrap with unseeing eyes, pointed teeth and all.

I showed the woman to the parlor and pointed at the velvet settee where she was welcome to sit. "Who should I tell Mrs. Dickinson is calling?"

Even as I asked this, I knew full well that Mrs. Dickinson would not speak with the woman. The guest was quite right that she was selective as to whom she spoke to. Other than family, Mrs. Dickinson kept her interactions limited to Mr. Dickinson's law clients and dignitaries from Amherst College across the road from the homestead. She spoke to these only as a good hostess and wife for her husband, not because she wished to converse with them. So, if it was someone that her husband did not ask her to speak to, she chose not to.

She handed me her calling card. "I am Mrs. Gertrude Turnkey."

The card read, "Mrs. Gertrude Turnkey. Ladies' Society of Amherst, President."

I had never heard of the Ladies' Society of Amherst, but that was little wonder. It sounded like a social club, and I would certainly never be accepted at any such place. If Mrs. Turnkey thought she was here to recruit Mrs. Dickinson for the club, she was to be sorely disappointed.

"Thank you, ma'am," I murmured. "Please wait here while I see if she has a moment to speak with you." I went to the entrance of the family parlor and closed the pocket doors into the family parlor behind me, but it was not before I noted that the woman seemed to take in everything that she could spy in the room and make a mental note about where the item was and, dare I say, its value.

In the dining room, I turned the card over in my hand, wondering what I should do. I could not leave Mrs. Turnkey in the parlor for long alone. At the same time, I knew that Mrs. Dickinson would be resting at this time. I didn't want to barge in on her if she was sleeping.

I opted for a third choice and one that made the most sense but was going to be uncomfortable. I would ask Miss Lavinia. In many ways, Emily's younger sister was the unofficial woman of the house. Even though their mother was alive, and Emily was the elder of the two sisters, Miss Lavinia had the practicality and purposefulness to run the large household that her mother and sister lacked. Such domestication didn't come naturally to Emily, and Mrs. Dickinson was ill more often than not, making it difficult for her to run the home.

I went through the dining room and up the stairs and, as I expected, I found Miss Lavinia in her room. She leaned against the headboard of her bed with a book in hand. Four of her cats slept in front of the fire. They were all tabbies and snuggled together so tightly it was difficult to see where the first cat stopped and the next began.

A fifth cat—Baby Z, Z for Zeus, not that anyone called him that—Baby Z had seemed to stick the most as Miss Lavinia coddled him like he was still a newborn kitten—was the one in her lap. He was all black and easily missed, but his large personality and talkative nature made him known.

I knocked on the doorframe. Miss Lavinia looked up from the book that she was reading. When she saw it was me who was standing there, she sighed. "What is it now, Willa?"

I didn't know how I had gotten the reputation from Emily's sister to be such a nuisance, but to her I was. I thought many times that it was jealousy of Emily paying attention to anyone else other than Miss Lavinia herself. At times, I had seen her have the same reaction to Miss Susan, the sisters' sister-in-law, to whom Emily was particularly close.

I cleared my throat. "A woman is here to call on Mrs. Dickinson. I thought it best considering your mother's delicate nature, to consult you about the matter before I went to your mother."

"Who is the woman?" she asked with a bit more interest than she had a moment ago.

I stepped into Miss Lavinia's room and handed her the card.

The cats near the hearth all turned and looked at me as one. It was disconcerting to be sure, and I loved cats. However, I didn't know how these cats perceived me as their loyalty was fully with their mistress.

As she took the card from my hand, I backed into the doorway.

"Mrs. Gertrude Turnkey. The Ladies' Society of Amherst," Miss Lavinia read, and then sniffed. "I know what this is about. She's here to ask for money. Do not bother my mother about this issue. Send Mrs. Turnkey away and ask her not to come back." She made a gesture as if she was returning to reading her book.

I hesitated. "Shouldn't someone from the family speak to her? She came all this way in the cold. Whatever it is she has to say it must be of some importance."

Miss Lavinia glared at me. "Are you, a second maid, questioning my decision?"

I shook my head. "No, miss—"

"I will go down and speak to her," Emily said from behind me.

I jumped, for I hadn't known that she was there. Emily had a way of sneaking up on someone that could make a person feel ill at ease.

She stood in the hallway in a brown-and-cream-gingham dress, which was different from the white morning dress she wore earlier in the day. It was apparel she wore for social calls. Had she expected Mrs. Turnkey's arrival and not mentioned it? Usually, she would tell Margaret or me of such an event so that we could prepare for a guest properly and have tea service at the ready.

Miss Lavinia waved her hand as if she was done with the conversation. "Do whatever it is you wish, Emily. You always do, with or without permission."

Emily didn't look the least bit offended by her sister's words; in fact she simply nodded as if Miss Lavinia had made a statement that was quite right indeed.

Emily and I found Mrs. Gertrude Turnkey in the front parlor, and she was looking at the bottom of an empty vase that was on the mantel.

"If you are interested in the cost of the vase, Mrs. Turnkey," Emily said, "I would be happy to call my father for you in order to estimate its value."

Hastily, the visitor put the vase back in its place. "Miss Dickinson, you should not creep up on others like that."

Emily lifted her chin. "And you should not touch something that is not yours. I would say that we are even in rudeness, no?"

Mrs. Turnkey sniffed. "I'm here to speak to your mother about a matter involving the Ladies' Society of Amherst."

"Yes, Willa has told me as much. Unfortunately, my mother is not available at the moment. However, you can share your message with me, and I will relay it to her."

Mrs. Turnkey pressed her lips together as if she didn't like the conditions but had little choice but to accept them. She glanced at me. "I will not speak on the matter in front of a maid."

"Willa is my trusted confidant and friend. If you do not wish to speak to me in front of her, this conversation is over."

Emily perched on a chair by the fire and invited Mrs. Turnkey to sit across from her. I stood by the door. I don't know if I chose to do that because I thought Mrs. Turnkey might run or so I could make a hasty exit if need be.

Emily arched her brow at Mrs. Turnkey and waited.

The visitor cleared her throat. "As you know, this terrible cold has been difficult on all of us. Classes have been disrupted at the college and the trains have been delayed. Everyone has been inconvenienced." She settled into her seat as she became more comfortable with her speech. "But inconvenience is fleeting. Those who have truly suffered are the less fortunate. Just three days ago, two people died of exposure because they could not afford wood for their fire. Those of us with more means must step forward and help."

Emily nodded. "I read about the young men who died. It is quite terrible."

"I am glad that you feel so because the Ladies' Society of Amherst would like to help, but with so much suffering we are reaching out to those who are not members of our group to increase our impact."

"How so?" Emily asked.

"The idea behind it is every well-to-do family would take on one that is less fortunate to help them through this dreadful time. Almost all the college professors' wives have signed on to help, and I would love it if your mother would join that number. It would include making sure the family had everything they needed to survive this horrendous winter: food, tea, warm blankets, and wood for the fire."

"It is a wonderful and noble idea, but my mother does not have the strength for such an endeavor."

Mrs. Turnkey was undaunted. "What about you and your sister? Surely, during these times when there is little to do in society because of the cold, it would be good for the mind and body to do something to keep you alert and fresh."

"I do not need outwardly activities to keep me occupied. I

have many thoughts within that could sustain me for hours upon end."

Mrs. Turnkey frowned as if she didn't have the faintest idea what that meant.

"I do see the value in what you suggest," Emily went on. "But I will have to ask my father before we commit to anything, and speak to my sister as well."

"Please don't delay making the decision. I have a family that is in desperate need that lives not far from you in Kelley Square. As most of my volunteers are overcommitted already, I don't have anyone to take them on."

"Who is the family?"

"The Boyles. They are a family of four, a father and mother and two young children."

I gasped.

CHAPTER THREE

EMILY LOOKED AT me. "Willa?"

I blinked at her as I pulled myself out of memories from my childhood that flew across my mind.

Emily tilted her head and her auburn hair caught the light from the flames in the hearth, making it glow fiery red. "Willa, is something wrong?"

I swallowed. "No, miss. It's only I haven't heard that name in a very long time. If it is the same family that I am thinking of they were our neighbors when I was a child. My brother, Henry, played with the oldest boy, Danny, when we were all small."

I didn't add how many scraps the pair of boys had gotten into together. Until I was nine years old, we lived in Kelley Square, the Irish community close to the railroad tracks. We weren't Irish, but it was where my mother could afford to rent a room in a boardinghouse for us. Henry and Danny were in trouble often, and my mother had so many nightmares that Henry would be hurt on the tracks. Finally, when I was able to work, too, we were able to save up enough for us to rent a little house in the woods.

"Daniel Boyle is the name of the head of the household," Mrs. Turnkey said.

I blinked. The last time I had seen Danny Boyle he was about fourteen, I guessed. He had been in and out of trouble, much like Henry. However, he didn't have Henry's charm to get himself out of scraps. The last I heard was he went off to Boston. I had taken a sigh of relief at that time. Henry got into enough trouble on his own; he didn't need Danny's help.

Emily seemed intrigued. "Were they friends?"

I didn't meet her eyes. "They were, miss."

Emily nodded. "Well, that settles it, then. Mrs. Turnkey, the Dickinsons will take the Boyle family on as they are friends of Willa's. A friend of Willa's is a friend of ours."

Mrs. Turnkey narrowed her eyes as if she didn't quite believe what Emily was saying. "I thought you needed to ask your father before you commit."

"I need to tell my father, yes, but when my heart is set on something, he has very little choice in the matter."

Mrs. Turnkey stood. "I am very glad to hear it." She reached into her satchel and produced a piece of paper. "Here is their address. I will get a message to them that they should be expecting you tomorrow. I imagine as it is still early in the day that it will be enough time for you to put your plans in order as to how to help them."

Emily took the piece of paper from her hand. "Yes, that will be fine."

What have I done?

It wasn't that I didn't want to help the Boyles and their children, but in many ways I blamed Danny, who had been a few years older than Henry, for setting my younger brother on the path of mischief. I had hoped to never see him again.

"Well," Mrs. Turnkey said, "I am pleased to hear it. As you will be at the Boyle home in the morning, I will stop by and see how you all are faring. I also have some donations from the society that I can present to them. You and your sister will be going I assume."

"And Willa," Emily said.

Mrs. Turnkey glanced at me. "I don't know if that is a good idea, as Willa was once at their station and she rose above it. It might cause envy and ill will."

"Or," Emily said, "it will give them hope that they can rise above their circumstances."

Mrs. Turnkey stood. "In my experience, this is not the case, but as I see your mind is made up on the matter, I will say no more about it. But please note that I heartily discourage it."

As I got the signal that Mrs. Turnkey was about to leave, I hurried from the room and gathered her fox wrap and hat. I waited by the door, holding them for her.

In the parlor, Emily said her goodbyes to Mrs. Turnkey, and the officious woman came into the entry. I helped her into her wrap.

As she set her hat on her head, she stared at me. "You and I both know that it would be better if you stayed home. The residents of Kelley Square will not look kindly upon someone who rose above them."

I gasped.

Emily came to the parlor door. "Is something amiss?"

Mrs. Turnkey glanced at her. "No. All is well. I will see you in the morning." She went out into the frigid cold.

I closed the door after her.

"What did she say to you?" Emily asked.

"It was nothing." I doubted that I could bring myself to say more to Emily on the matter.

Emily studied me as if she thought I might have spoken in a riddle and was trying to decipher what I had really meant when I spoke.

Just when I thought she would press me more on the topic, she said, "Dreadful woman. It almost makes a person want to withdraw from society completely rather than run into a person like that."

I could not help but agree.

The rest of the day Emily locked herself in her room to write. I knew the next day there would be random bits of paper all over her bedroom floor, full of discarded verse. They were meant to be thrown into the rubbish, but since I could not bring myself to do that, I would collect them and take them to my room where I had a growing collection of Emily's bits of poems, which is how I thought of them.

Margaret and I didn't have such a leisurely afternoon. The Dickinsons would be hosting a dinner party that night for dignitaries from the college. The college president, a donor, and one of the professors would be coming to the homestead with their wives. Emily's brother, Austin, and his wife, whom Margaret and I continued to refer to as "Miss Susan" even though she had been married to Austin for months now, would also join the dinner, which set the party at twelve. It was one of the largest gatherings that we had hosted and the first party since the foul turn in the weather.

Miss Susan and Austin came to dinner often, and even though they were family, their arrival always put an extra bit of pressure on Margaret and me to present the very best meal and service. Mrs. Dickinson was an accomplished hostess, but she did not have the flare and zest for it that Miss Susan did. Her daughter-in-law thrived in company and entertaining while Mrs. Dickinson would much rather stay in her own room quietly reading. Because of this, Mrs. Dickinson's nerves rose whenever her son and daughter-in-law came to dinner. At times, I thought they made her even more nervous than the gentlemen and ladies who Mr. Dickinson invited over from the college and his days in government.

Unsurprisingly, since their home, the Evergreens, was on the same property as the homestead, the younger Mr. and Mrs. Dickinson arrived first. I met the younger couple at the door, and they quickly handed me their outer garments. Emily hurried down the stairs to greet them.

"Sister!" Emily cried, and kissed Miss Susan on the cheek. "It seems like ages since I have seen you."

Miss Susan smiled and shared her own greeting in kind. She was a very pleasant-looking woman with chestnut-colored hair divided down the middle and set in knots on either side of her head and an oval-shaped face. Like Emily, she was in her late twenties. The two women were not just close in life but close in age as well as they were born only nine days apart. Miss Susan's face lit up anytime Emily was in the room.

"What about me?" Austin wanted to know. Austin was a

handsome young man. He was a bit taller than his wife and had thick brown hair and dark eyes. His sideburns were as full as his head of hair, but the rest of his face was clean-shaven. He wore a dark suit and the chain of a pocket watch peeked out of his vest pocket. However, there were creases beside his eyes I had not noticed before and deep lines about his mouth. I imagined proving himself to his father was more difficult than he thought it would be.

Emily laughed and patted her brother on the arm. "I have seen you much more often than Susan as you have come to the homestead to work with Father. In the meantime, Susan has locked herself away in the Evergreens making a home for you like a dutiful wife. It has been an agony for me not to see her, as even walking across the yard in this temperature causes great pain."

Austin snorted. "The drama that you are able to spin with your words, Emily, cannot be discounted."

Emily held out her skirt and bowed as if she were an actor on a stage. "You are most welcome." She straightened up. "Our other guests will be here at any moment. I wish it was just a simple family meal. I do hate these overblown affairs. Father has been pacing all afternoon."

Austin grimaced. "I know President Stearns and his wife are coming. There are more?"

"The Westons as well. I do not know them at all. Dr. Weston was recently added to the college faculty in late fall. I have not met his wife. Verona, I believe her name is, but it seems that Olive Stearns has it in her mind to begin taking her around to make friends with those in the community. I like Olive very much but it's simply dreadful if you ask me, that I must chatter about nonsense when I have poems clamoring in my mind to reach the page."

Austin paled. "The Westons are coming? I did not know that."

Susan looked sharply at her husband as if she was trying to decipher why this would be such a great concern.

There was a knock on the door again, and I opened it to find all three men and two women waiting on the front steps.

"Please come in." I held the door open widely for them.

"Thank you," Mr. William Stearns, the college president, said. He was an austere man with deep-set eyes, wire spectacles, and thick white sideburns that ran the length of his face. He was no stranger to the homestead as Mr. Dickinson was the college treasurer and they had much to discuss about the finances of the college.

I took the visitors' coats and cloaks and showed them to the front parlor where the family was already waiting.

Mr. Dickinson stood when they entered the room. He greeted the ladies with a polite nod and gave all the men a firm handshake. When he came to the youngest man of the group, he said, "Kelvin, where is your lovely young bride?"

Mr. Ward pushed his glasses up the bridge of his nose. "I told her to stay home in Holyoke for this visit. I did not want her to come out in his weather in her delicate condition. I'm sure she is being spoiled by her mother as we speak."

"Then, congratulations are in order. When is the baby due?" Mr. Dickinson asked.

"Next month," Mr. Ward said with a smile. "I am eager to

return home to Mount Holyoke, but it is better for my dear wife that I am gone now instead of after the baby is born. I am here for a few days to consult with Weston."

Dr. Weston was a young man with a thick middle and a black mustache that reminded me of the bristles of a broom. "I am grateful that you could come. I think we will make great progress."

Mr. Ward nodded. "It could be a breakthrough."

Emily cocked her head. "A breakthrough in what?"

Mr. Ward looked at her as if he did not expect her to be paying attention to their conversation. "In seed germination. With my funding, Weston is working on drought-resistant seeds to be sold out west. As the country expands, the need for more crops grows, but not all places in the country are as lush as Massachusetts."

"I would not say Massachusetts is lush right now," Austin said with a laugh. "As we are buried deep in cold and snow."

Emily cocked her head. "You live in Mount Holyoke?"

Mr. Ward turned to her. "Yes."

"I went to college there for a year. What is it you do there? Something with the college?"

He laughed. "Dear me, no. I'm a landowner and have some part in the mills there. I lease land to farmers, that sort of thing. My main interest is melding agriculture and industry. I believe there are so many ways that we can make machines and science work better for us if we can just apply the right minds and resources. Weston and I met at a conference on the matter and found we knew the Stearnses in common. The commonwealth is small, as you must know."

"I couldn't agree more, Kelvin," the college president said. "It is my hope that Dr. Godard Weston will ring in a new dawn of advances in this area set forth by Amherst College."

Emily looked as if she had more questions to ask, and I wasn't the only one to notice. Her father did, too, and swiftly cut her off. "Shall we go into the dining room?"

That was my cue to skirt into the hallway and beat them there. Margaret was already in the dining room, fussing with the table settings. Everything was lovely and perfectly in place, but she was never completely satisfied.

Everyone took their seats. Emily sat between her father and Dr. Weston.

Of the two women, I recognized only Mrs. Stearns, as she often came to the homestead with the college president, although as the president's second wife, they had not been married long. She was a petite, middle-aged woman who wore the very latest in fine fashion. Not that I saw her too often, but I had never seen her in the same dress twice. Tonight was no exception. She wore a blue-and-white-pinstriped dress with a ruffled collar and cuffs. It was perfectly fitted to show off her nice figure to the best advantage.

The second woman, whom I took as Dr. Weston's wife, sat across from Mrs. Stearns. Mrs. Weston was much younger and one of the prettiest women I had ever seen. Her features were small and delicate. She had sparkling hazel eyes and shiny raven-colored hair. She wore a purple-and-green dress with lace at the collar.

She looked around the room in the same way that Mrs. Gertrude Turnkey had that morning. It was almost like she was assessing the value of every last item within view. Her eyes stopped on Austin, who was next to Mrs. Stearns.

He must have known that she was looking at him because his face turned red from the base of his neck to his forehead.

A small frown settled on Mrs. Weston's pretty face, but it made her no less beautiful and me no less curious.

CHAPTER FOUR

I SERVED THE FIRST course, which was a hearty potato soup.

Mrs. Stearns nodded at me as I set the bowl in front of her. "This is just what is needed on these cold nights. The weather is the worst I have ever seen, and I'm just heartbroken hearing of those two young men from Kelley Square who got caught out in the elements during the storm. If the weather doesn't break, I am afraid that we are going to hear more stories like that very soon. I'm trying to organize a warming station at the First Congregational Church for those who are struggling due to the cold."

President Stearns shook his head. "My wife is determined to be a saint by any means that she can."

"It is interesting that you mention that," Emily said. "Because Mrs. Gertrude Turnkey was here this morning from the Ladies' Society of Amherst and shared their plan to help those who don't have the means to combat this weather."

Mrs. Stearns pressed her lips together in a thin line. "Yes, I am aware that Gertrude is going door-to-door making such a request, but I truly believe it is the role of the church for such charity. The Ladies' Society is not attached to a congregation."

"What does it matter who helps if help is offered?" Emily asked.

Mr. Dickinson cleared his throat. "I did not hear about this visit, Emily."

"I meant to tell you, Father, but a poem came to mind, and I had to turn my mind to it before it was lost."

Dr. Weston looked at Emily as if he had never seen a person quite like her before. I was certain that not many people had.

I left the dining room to collect the second course.

"Willa," Margaret said the moment I stepped into the kitchen, "will you focus on the task at hand? You dawdle too much."

"I'm so sorry, Margaret. You are right." I couldn't tell her that I dawdled because I was hopelessly eavesdropping on interesting dinner conversation. I was eager to return to the dining room and hear more. But I also knew Emily would fill me in on anything that I missed.

The second course was lamb and new potatoes. It was one of Margaret's specialties and smelled divine. I hoped that there would be a serving or two left by the end of the meal for Margaret and me to share when it was our turn for supper.

I stepped into the room just as Miss Susan was saying, "Gertrude Turnkey came to our home as well. She must have come here first because by the time she made her call she said that the elder Dickinson home had already committed to help the Boyle family."

"Is that right?" Mr. Dickinson asked. "I do wish I had been

consulted before this was settled by you both. One headstrong daughter is more than enough in this family. Now, I have two."

Across the table dutiful Miss Lavinia frowned. She was not counted in her father's number of headstrong daughters and appeared to take offense to that.

"Father, what choice did we have?" Emily asked. "We must help the less fortunate during this trying time. Is that not true? Is that not part of your Christian charity, to care for the poor and suffering?"

The patriarch pressed his lips together. "It should be part of your Christian charity, too, Daughter."

"If I were a Christian, sir. But since I don't claim such beliefs, I do it out of my own goodwill, not obligation."

Mr. Dickinson scowled at his elder daughter.

There were several nervous glances exchanged among the guests. Few people dared to denounce religion in such a public way.

I served Mrs. Dickinson first and then the ladies in descending rank: Mrs. Stearns, Mrs. Weston, Miss Susan, Emily, and Miss Lavinia. I had to concentrate on not dropping a single dish as I listened with all my being to their conversation about Mrs. Turnkey.

My hand shook as I set Miss Lavinia's plate on the table.

"Careful," she hissed.

I went on to the gentlemen.

"And did you agree to help a family as well, Susan?" Austin asked.

"I did." She dipped her wide spoon into the soup but did not raise it to her lips. Instead, she rested the handle on the side of the bowl.

"I was not aware of this. You did not consult with me first," he said.

"Do I need your permission to make decisions when it comes to the household budget? We can make do with less for a few weeks to help a family that is less fortunate."

"I am the man of the house." Austin pulled on the collar of his stiff shirt.

"That may be, but I run the house. You spend more of your time reading and searching the countryside for landscape paintings than concerning yourself with domestic matters. If I am the one to run the household, to make sure everyone is well-fed, comfortable, and content, should I not be able to make the decisions about the household funds? We have enough now to keep us quite comfortable and still share with a family that is not set as well-off. Unlike you, dear husband, I do know what it is like to struggle and wonder where your next meal will come from. Unless you have felt that for yourself, it is difficult for you to relate."

My eyes were wide as she said this, and I was in complete agreement with Miss Susan. It was hard for most of the Dickinsons to relate to those who straddled the edge of poverty. Like Miss Susan, I knew how it felt to not have enough and scrape and scrimp just to make it to another day.

No matter how true her words were, I was surprised that she would be so candid in front of Mr. Dickinson's guests. The family was quite open with one another in private, but it was another thing entirely to speak so in front of mere acquaintances.

I stood next to the door, waiting for the family to complete the main course before clearing away their plates to make room for the next course. It was only a four-course meal, for which I was grateful.

Emily sat across the table from Susan and Austin and watched their exchange with an odd expression on her face. I could not tell if she was upset or somehow relieved that her brother and his wife were quarreling.

"Who is the family you are helping?" Miss Lavinia asked eagerly, as if she would say just about anything to stop her brother and sister-in-law from publicly arguing in front of their parents.

Miss Susan looked to her. "The Doolan family."

With some relief, I didn't recognize that family name. I wasn't sure what I would do if there was another family from my past that came and reared its head.

"Oh, I know them in passing," Mrs. Dickinson said, speaking for the first time.

Everyone turned to look at her as the lady of the house rarely made such a strong statement at dinner or at any other time of the day, to be frank.

She hesitated. "They live in Kelley Square, closest to the college."

Emily cocked her head. "Then, they must live close to the Boyles. That's quite convenient. Sister Susan, we can make our run with alms together."

"That would be very nice," Miss Susan agreed.

Austin watched his wife with a dark expression on his face. I didn't believe that he agreed, not one bit.

Mrs. Weston cleared her throat. "I can understand why a

husband would want his wife to at least consult with him before making such a commitment. Mrs. Turnkey came to my home too."

Mrs. Stearns gasped. "You didn't tell me that, Verona."

"There is nothing to tell, Olive dear," Mrs. Weston said in return. "I politely explained to her that I was already committed to helping you with the warming mission at the church. Of course, I had already spoken with Godard. I would do nothing without consulting with my husband first." She gave a pointed look at Austin as she said this. I felt like she held Austin's gaze a little too long.

It seemed that I wasn't the only one. Miss Susan looked from her husband to Mrs. Weston and back again several times, as if there was a riddle there that she couldn't quite parcel out.

"I am glad to hear that, Verona," Mrs. Stearns said.

"Yes," Dr. Weston said. "Verona is nothing if not a loyal wife." The way he said that, there wasn't a ring of truth in it.

Mrs. Dickinson smiled at the party. The smile appeared a little forced, but she pressed on. "Mr. Ward, where are you staying while you are visiting Amherst? I do hope it's someplace nice as you might be here for a few days longer than expected."

He sipped his water. "Yes, I expect to stay a few extra days with the hope that the weather will break. The Stearnses have very kindly welcomed me into their home. It has become a bit of a stopover for wayward travelers."

"What do you mean?" Mrs. Dickinson asked.

"There is another guest staying with us too," Mrs. Stearns said. "Her name is Lucy Stone. She was lecturing nearby and was stranded in the snowstorm. Of course, we opened our home to her."

"You should have brought her with you," Mrs. Dickinson said.

"Oh," Mrs. Stearns said. "That is very kind, but Lucy is an old childhood friend. We met at revival when we were young and have kept in correspondence ever since. She is just a handful of years younger than me but quite different in her thinking."

"I do insist that if we have another party while she is here, please bring her. I do not like guests to be left out," Mrs. Dickinson said.

Mrs. Stearns sipped from her water glass. "If that is what you want, I will."

It might have been my imagination, but that seemed to come out like a threat.

CHAPTER FIVE

I WAS ON A walk with my brother, Henry. It was a bright summer's day. His blond hair shone in the sunlight that came through breaks in the tree canopy above us. He ran ahead of me and then would run back, just like he had done when we were children. He was always the more adventurous of the two of us, but he always came back for me. Always.

He ran back along the pine needle–covered path a third time, and I spoke. "Say something."

I was eager to hear what he had to say.

He smiled broadly and a cacophony of bells rang from his mouth. There were no words, just the chiming of bells.

"Can't you speak?" I asked. "I want to hear your voice. Please. Say something. Anything."

He opened his mouth again and the sound of bells came again.

Tears came to my eyes. Why wouldn't he talk to me just once? Just once say something that I could hold—

"Willa! Willa! Wake up! Those are the church bells." Margaret O'Brien held me by the shoulders and shook me so hard my teeth clanked together.

I awoke to find myself in my little room over the laundry with the Dickinsons' first maid standing over me. Her dark hair with the finest streaks of silver was down and tangled and she wore her nightdress. In these long two years that I worked for the family I had never seen Margaret with her hair down or in her nightdress. I found that more disconcerting than her shaking me awake like I was a night watchman who had slept through his shift.

"Church bells?" I asked in wonder. "Is it Sunday morning? Did I sleep through services? I'm so sorry. It must have been the cold that would not allow me to awake."

"No, you fool! It's fire," Margaret said. She could barely hold the panic from creeping into her voice.

Fear wrapped its cold fingers around my heart. Little else than the threat of fire to home and hearth could cause such immediate terror.

"Here?" I managed to squeak.

"No, get up. It is near the railroad station, and Mr. Dickinson is heading out. We must be on call to assist." With that, she left my room.

I got dressed as quickly as I could and tethered my hair at the back of my head in a haphazard knot. I hoped that the Dickinsons would not look so closely to see how disheveled I appeared. However, I supposed that everyone would look a little less than composed considering the hour and the incessant ringing of the church bells.

Church bells all over Amherst rang. It was not just the

Dickinsons' congregational church across the street, but even my Baptist church that was tucked in the woods. Everyone was called to help with the fire, and this was even truer if the fire threatened the college because the people of Amherst glorified the college whether they attended there or not. Maybe I took pride in living in an overly educated town, too, as an education was a luxury I never had but could appreciate from afar.

By the time I made it downstairs to the kitchen, Margaret was already in a housedress and her hair was perfectly drawn back in a bun at the nape of her neck. She was in the midst of packing a hamper of food. It seemed she was determined to give all the bread that we had left to those who fought the fire.

She closed the hamper's lid and shoved the hamper into my hands. "Here. Take this to Jeremiah to take with them. I can't do much for the men going to help but give food. Jeremiah should be out front by now with the carriage."

Jeremiah had been Henry's dearest friend and the one who found my brother's body when Henry was killed. After the incident, Emily convinced her father to hire Jeremiah for the homestead stables as they were moving here to the homestead from North Pleasant Street. She rationally told her father that they were coming into more land and space overall and would need someone who worked full-time for the family to care for the livestock as it was a much larger menagerie than it had been at their old home.

I grabbed my own cloak, bonnet, and mittens from the laundry. I put everything on and was about to go out the back door when Margaret stopped me.

"Don't go that way," she snapped.

"You want me to go out the front door?" I asked in shock. I never went in and out the front door. I was a servant, not a guest of the family.

"The snow is too high again, and you will be soaked through," Margaret said gruffly. "Go out the front." She narrowed her eyes at me. "This one time."

I nodded and took the hamper to the front of the house. In the foyer, Mr. Dickinson was hastily putting on his heavy wool coat and gloves. His wife stood in a nightdress and cap and wrung her hands. "Edward, you are no longer a young man. Leave it to the younger men to put out the fire."

Mr. Dickinson glared at his wife. "As the college treasurer I must go. The air is cold and dry. In these conditions the fire could spread quickly even to the college. I must go."

Mrs. Dickinson looked as if she might be ill as he said this, but as a good wife, she kept any other opinions to herself.

Emily slid into the foyer in her winter wool frock, cloak, bonnet, and sturdy boots. Carlo, her beloved dog, was at her side. "I'll make sure Father is safe, Mother."

"Emily Elizabeth, you are not coming with me," her father snapped.

"I am and I will, and if you don't take me, I will simply ride with Austin. The stable hand said that he was getting his carriage ready to depart as well."

"I don't have time to argue with you on this matter. You and Carlo are not coming."

"That is where you are wrong." She flung open the door and a rush of freezing air and blowing snow flew into all of our faces. Emily didn't seem to be the least bit bothered by it. She looked over her shoulder. "We will be in the carriage. Don't delay. We don't want to miss what's happening."

I tensed when Emily said that. We knew what was happening to someone's home, their whole life was being dissolved into flames. I could not imagine what it would have felt like.

Emily went out the front door with Carlo walking behind her. Before she closed the door, she glanced over her shoulder. "Willa will be coming too."

I stood there unsure what to do.

Mr. Dickinson scowled at me as if this were somehow my fault. "Get in the carriage," he barked.

I didn't hesitate and carried the heavy hamper out of the house.

A path had been shoveled from the front door to the driveway. The carriage and the Dickinsons' horse, Terror, stood at the ready.

The large black horse stamped his hooves on the gravel, and hot steam rose from his nostrils. He didn't want to be out in the cold any more than I did.

Outside the relative safety of the homestead, the pealing of the church bells was deafening. As the congregational church stood just across Main Street, it rang the loudest to my ears. I knew that Horace must have been ringing the bell with all his might. He would have been the first one to the church as he was the sexton and had lodgings behind it.

Emily was already in the back of the carriage when I slipped the heavy hamper inside. Carlo lay across her lap like a warm blanket.

"Ride inside with us, Willa," she said as I stepped back.

"No, miss, your father wouldn't like it, and he's already upset."

I could tell that she wanted to argue with me more about it, but her father appeared. I slipped to the front of the carriage.

Jeremiah closed the carriage door after Mr. Dickinson was inside. He climbed up in the driver's seat, and I followed him. Jeremiah was as bundled up from the cold as I was. All I could see were his dark eyes, and I supposed with my scarf wrapped tightly around my own face that was all he could see of me. Even with all the layers, it was freezing, and I didn't know how long I would last in this cold. I didn't know how long Emily would last. She was far smaller than I was. It was like throwing a songbird out into the snow.

"What are you doing here?" Jeremiah hissed and flicked the reins. Terror shook his head and then started down the drive at a careful pace as there was a thick layer of ice over the gravel.

When we reached Main Street, I said, "Miss Dickinson insisted that I come."

"Why?" he asked.

That wasn't a question I could answer, and as the road was bumpy with ice and snow, I didn't say another word and held on to my seat with a firm grip.

Jeremiah pulled the reins so that Terror would turn left on Main Street, which was away from the college and toward Kelley Square. We had traveled only a few yards when the smell of smoke engulfed us. Just on the edge of Kelley Square a burning house came into view. My heart was in my throat at the terrifying scene before my eyes.

The fire licked the sky. Men ran back and forth with buckets of water from the college well, but it didn't seem to make much difference. Another group of men splashed water on the nearby college buildings, to deter the fire from engulfing other buildings.

We were still three homes away when Jeremiah stopped the carriage, but it was as close as the carriage could go. Police officers blocked the road and didn't let anyone pass. I searched the faces of the officers for any sign of my friend Matthew Thomas. I hoped to see him on the street and prayed he was safe. However, I knew he would be with the men fighting the fire. He was always the first to help.

Jeremiah jumped down from the carriage seat and then held out his hand to help me down. He opened the carriage door and Emily and Carlo came out.

Emily stared at the flames. Her gaze held that faraway look that she sometimes had, and of which was I so familiar. "A thing that can ignite," she murmured.

Mr. Dickinson came out of the carriage. "Heaven help us."

"Father"—Emily looked over her shoulder—"will you go and help the men fight the flames?"

Mr. Dickinson cleared his throat. "The college has plenty of good, sturdy young men who are already here and will do better to put on the fight than I ever would. I will supervise."

A man with a full silver beard and a black felt hat walked over to us. He wore a long black overcoat, but as the hat did not cover his pronounced ears, they shone red in the light of the fire.

"Dean Masterson," Mr. Dickinson addressed the newcomer. "Tell me what has happened."

"Mr. Dickinson," the man said in turn. "It is a dreadful sight, but I can assure you that the fire will be contained. I have been told that it is no real threat to any of the college buildings. I assume that is why you are here."

"Of course," Mr. Dickinson said. "Losing one of our austere academic buildings would be a great tragedy and a concern for me as treasurer, as I would have to appropriate the funds to rebuild it."

The dean nodded. "We have been told by the volunteer firemen here tonight that there is no need to be concerned. We're taking every precaution."

"Very good," Mr. Dickinson said by way of approval.

Dean Masterson saw Emily and me standing a little bit behind Mr. Dickinson and scowled. "This is no place for gawkers. A home is lost. Don't make a mockery of it."

Mr. Dickinson's back stiffened. "That is my daughter to whom you are speaking."

"You brought your daughter with you?" the dean asked, glancing at Emily.

Mr. Dickinson cleared his throat. "I believe that it is important for young women to know what the true risk of fire can bring. If she sees it with her own eyes, she will be more careful with her candle in the future."

Dean Masterson wrinkled his brow as if he didn't know what to make of Mr. Dickinson's statement.

Another man joined the pair and had the same academic look about him that the dean did. I wanted to hear what he had to say about the fire, if anything, but Emily grabbed the edge of my cloak and pulled me away.

"Come," Emily said. "There is no time to waste."

I let her lead me away but wondered what time she was referring to.

Emily moved closer to the fire and stopped behind one of the small homes to watch. Unsure why we were there, Carlo and I stood with her.

Men shoveled snow on the flames that they could reach. It seemed like such a futile act as more of the flames came out of the roof. A fireman stood on the top of the fire wagon, spraying all the water he could from the hose onto the roof.

I glanced at Emily, and her dark eyes glowed in the light of the flames. Her reddish hair, which peeked out of her bonnet, shone as if it were always meant to reflect the blaze.

"It is magnificent," Emily said. "Horrible, but magnificent all the same."

I looked at the fire and tried to see it through her poet's eyes. I don't believe that I managed it. There was very little that I could see through Emily's eyes. I was far too removed from musings like she had. I was far too cynical and practical as a result of my hard upbringing and a life of hand to mouth.

"I wouldn't be calling that fire magnificent for all it cost," a man with a slight Southern accent said.

I was surprised by the accent. I hadn't heard someone speak like that since I had accompanied Miss Dickinson to Washington two years ago. It took me back to some happy and also terrifying memories from that time.

Emily looked up at the man and even though she was a head and a half shorter than he was, she seemed to be the more commanding force. "What did this cost other than the building?"

"The whole family's presumed dead," the fireman said. "I saw the bodies inside. I wish I could erase the memory from my mind. It was a thing of nightmares. They had a child."

CHAPTER SIX

I SHIVERED AT THE very idea, and now the flames appeared to be even more menacing than before.

"The whole family?" Emily asked. "You're sure."

"I know what I saw. There was the body of a mother and father, and I can only assume that the child would have been inside the home as well. It was horrific. I will never forget what I saw. Never."

I swallowed. It was too horrible for words.

A body on a board was wrapped in a white sheet. My chest clenched. I didn't know if I had ever seen such a horrible sight. Gratefully, I could not see the body, but the smallness of the form under the sheet worried me that it might be a child, like the fireman said.

"Have you been here long?" Emily asked the man.

"I have, miss. I have been here since the fire began and was the first inside. I will go back to fighting the fire in a moment. I just needed a bit of time to compose myself."

"It was very wise to take it. I believe it is a terrible thing that people don't spend more time contemplating what they see."

"I suppose," the fireman said. He looked as if he might cry. He turned away from us.

"How did the fire start?" Emily asked.

I was immediately wondering why Emily would ask a question like that. What did it matter how the family was killed? It was certainly not something that I wanted to think about for long.

"It is hard to tell while the fire is still burning, but I think it was something with the fireplace at the front of the house. The family had built a great fire in it for warmth during these frigid days. This cold weather seems to have snuck up on so many and they weren't properly prepared for the dark turn in the weather."

"You believe the fire started in the chimney?"

"Yes, but it leapt to the curtains in the front room. From there it grew out of control in a blink of an eye."

"How many children lived in the home?" I asked.

The volunteer fireman looked at me. "Just the one. That surprised me, though, since they are a Catholic family. A poor Irish-Catholic family, so we can only assume that they had many children as is their way."

I felt my back stiffen at his assumption. I had grown up poor as well and had only one brother. I wasn't Irish or Catholic, but I didn't feel it was right for the fireman to be saying this.

Emily folded her arms. "I think it would be best to confirm how many children were actually in the family and if there were even more before making such a statement about the family."

The man's face turned bright red. "I should return to help."

"Yes," Emily agreed.

When he was gone, Emily began to shiver; Carlo pressed his woolly body against her.

"Perhaps we should go back to the carriage," I said. "It will still be cold, but at least you will be out of the wind."

Emily shook her head. "I must know if a child was lost in the flames."

I felt sick at the very idea. I prayed that the fireman had been wrong. He seemed to know very little of the family. Perhaps there were no children.

Suddenly, Carlo lifted his broad nose in the air and sniffed. His whole body stiffened as if he caught a scent on the wind. I could smell nothing more than the acrid odor of fire.

Carlo sniffed the wind again, and then took off, straight for the flames.

"Carlo! Carlo!" Emily cried, and my mistress ran after him.

The dog did not stop and circled the house. Men fighting the flames with soot-covered faces yelled at him. They shouted at Emily as well when she ran by them.

It seemed that I had no choice but to follow. "Miss! Miss!" I called, but Emily didn't as much as turn her head.

Emily was out of sight around the side of the house before I ran more than a few feet. I had no choice but to go after her. I lifted my skirts high over my stout boots and ran. A cold draft encircled my legs and caused me to whimper from the chill.

I rounded the corner that was dark with night and smoke and ran smack into a wall or what I thought was a wall. It would have been a wall had it not had arms.

"Willa!" Matthew cried. "What are you doing here? There is a fire."

He told me that there was a fire as if it should be all that I needed to know to keep me away. In most cases that would be true but not when Emily and Carlo might be in some kind of danger.

"Emily," I said, speaking my mistress's given name aloud to anyone but her for the first time. Emily had given me permission to call her by her Christian name, but I remained careful that I didn't abuse that privilege in a public setting. There were many that would look down on the friendship of a first daughter of a prominent Amherst family with the second maid in the home. As a woman in domestic service, I always had to be on my guard and make sure that I didn't commit any breach in etiquette. Young women like me had been dismissed for much less.

Thankfully, Matthew seemed too shocked by my appearance at the fire to note my mistake.

He held me by the shoulders. "Where is she?"

"I—I don't know. Carlo ran off and she went after him. Then I went after her."

Matthew glanced at the raging fire that looked not any closer to being snuffed out, but it did appear that the men on the scene had been able to contain the flames to the single house. The home was lost and would be completely burned to the ground before the night was over.

It was a sight to see, to be sure, but it also caused me to wonder. I had had the misfortune to witness several house fires in my life, and I had never seen one that so engulfed a building.

A thought tickled the back of my mind and asked me why the fire would burn so hot and fast.

"I have to find Miss Dickinson and make sure she is all right," I said.

"I will go with you to make sure you don't get too close to the flames."

I frowned up at him, but he could not see my expression behind my scarf. However, I am sure that he could guess that it was there. "I am not a fool and would not run into the flames."

"You would if Miss Dickinson was there," he assured me.

I frowned, as I had no rebuttal to that as it was true.

Matthew and I went around the side of the building. There wasn't much behind it but a stand of trees that were in very serious risk of catching fire. If the flames jumped to the trees, there would be no stopping the fire short of another snowstorm. Thankfully, the wind was blowing in the opposite direction. Unfortunately, that direction happened to be toward the college. However, I reminded myself that the men fighting the fire were confident that the college would be spared.

I held on to the sides of my bonnet with the hope of keeping it in place against the cold wind.

The woods were dark. Emily and Carlo could have been anywhere. I prayed that Emily had found Carlo or he had found her. I worried about her alone in the dark wood in the middle of the night.

I cupped my mitten-covered hands around my mouth and called, "Miss Dickinson! Emily!"

There was no response.

Matthew looked at the woods. "We might have to get a

search party together to look for her. It is foolhardy to strike out on your own on a night like this that is not only freezing cold but has so much confusion and chaos from the house fire."

"I don't see it that way, Officer Thomas," Emily said from behind us.

Matthew and I both leapt in the air in surprise.

"Miss Dickinson," Matthew said. "I did not know that you were there."

She eyed him. "It's clear to me that you didn't, but I am glad to find the two of you. There is a matter that we all need to address."

"Where's Carlo?" I asked.

"I'll show you."

Matthew and I glanced at each other but allowed Emily to lead us into the woods. We walked no more than ten yards when she stopped and pointed in front of her. Ahead of us on the path, there was a large dark mass. At first, I thought it was a black bear and my heart skipped a beat, but then I realized it was Carlo curled into a ball.

"Is Carlo hurt?" I asked.

She shook her head.

Matthew approached the dog, and I was a few steps beside him. When I was within three feet of Carlo, I saw that he wasn't just wrapped into a ball, but he had wrapped his woolly body around a child.

I covered my mouth. It was a young girl. She couldn't have been more than eight years of age. There was soot on her cheeks, and she shivered as she clung on to Carlo's neck as if her life depended on it—and it just might, as she wasn't wearing a coat or even shoes on her feet.

Without a second of hesitation, Matthew removed his coat, wrapped it around the child like he was swaddling a baby, and picked her up. She didn't make a sound.

Carlo stood up, ready to do whatever was required to help the girl.

"We have to get her inside now." Matthew took off in the direction of the fire. Carlo, Emily, and I followed, but it was only Carlo who could keep up with him in the deep snow as our skirts weighed us down. We came around the side of the burning house just in time to see Matthew and the child disappear into a grand home across the street outside of Kelley Square. The house was a large block of a home with two chimneys that billowed hot air into the freezing sky.

"Come on!" Emily cried, and she took off at a run to the house.

"Watch where you're going!" called a man who was driving a horse and wagon down the road.

Emily didn't even stop to wave at the man.

I waited for the wagon to pass and then crossed the street. By that time, Emily was already inside the house.

CHAPTER SEVEN

I HESITATED AT THE foot of the front door. Dare I barge inside? It was clear to me that this was the home of a person of influence in Amherst, and as such the family living there would have servants. As a servant, I should go in through the back entrance, but in the snow and cold, I didn't want to walk around the large building as some of the snowdrifts had reached to the very tops of some of the windows.

I took a breath and recited in my head what I would say when the door was opening. "I am Miss Dickinson's maid. I saw that she came in here. Have you seen her?"

I knocked on the door reciting the lines that I had written for myself, but no one answered. Behind me, I could hear the shouts of men still fighting the fire. There was a great cry as the roof of the old house caved in.

I tried the doorknob, and much to my surprise, it opened easily. I cracked the door and stepped inside.

Inside the house, a staircase stood before me with a wrought-iron railing that went all the way up to and along the landing on the second floor. On the wall leading up those stairs were portraits of ladies and gentlemen, most wearing the fashions of decades ago. Looking at the portraits, I felt like the paintings were staring into my very soul. It was not a comfortable feeling.

"What are you doing here?" a stern voice asked.

I turned from the portraits to face a terribly thin housekeeper in a black waistcoat and skirts. Her black hair was tethered at the back of her head so tightly I could see that it pulled at the skin of her face.

"I asked you a question," she snapped. "You can't just come in here and drip on the carpets."

I looked down to see what she meant and saw that the snow that had clung to my skirts since my run from the woods was indeed melting and drenching the carpet at my feet.

I lifted the skirts a few inches from the ground and took care not to show my ankles because that would be crude and uncivilized of me, and I had a feeling this woman would not stand for it.

"I am sorry, ma'am, but my mistress, Miss Emily Dickinson, just came into this house, and I wanted to see if she was all right. She was following a police officer with a child."

"Yes, Miss Dickinson is here. She and the officer are in one of the bedrooms with the girl. They are not alone," she said as if I would dare think anything unseemly is going on. "Mrs. Weston is with them and two of the maids. A doctor has been called."

"This is Mrs. Weston's home?" I asked.

She glared at me. "Of course it is. Where did you think you were? That is all you need to know on the matter."

"Can I go to them?" I dared to ask.

She scowled at me.

"As Miss Dickinson's maid, it is my duty to make sure she has everything that she requires. I am sure her father, the treasurer of the college, would agree with me."

"Very well, but you can't stay long, and take care."

I followed her. I had thought Margaret O'Brien was a harsh domestic, but she was a pussycat when compared to this woman. I had yet to learn her name.

"I am Willa Noble," I said to her back.

She looked over her shoulder as if she wondered why I would have the audacity to speak to her again.

She scowled, but her impeccable manners took over. "Mrs. Brubaker, the Westons' housekeeper." Then she turned back around and continued walking.

We came upon a corridor, and I saw two young maids standing in the hallway peering into a door. "Penny, Louisa! Don't the two of you have better things to do than snoop?"

They jumped and scurried down the hall.

Mrs. Brubaker stopped just short of the door. "I trust that you can find your way out."

I didn't trust that that was true at all. There had been so many twists and turns before we came upon this room that I was thoroughly confused. Furthermore, I had been so worried about Emily and the girl that I had not been paying attention to where we had been going.

Before I could give the housekeeper an answer, she went down the hallway in the same direction as the maids.

After the housekeeper disappeared from my sight, I peered in the room. Emily sat by a large four-post bed and held the little girl's small pale hand. A doctor removed a glass thermometer from the child's mouth.

Mrs. Weston stood by the burning fireplace next to Matthew. Matthew held his police hat in his hands.

She was incredibly lovely even at this time of night and with her hair falling from her pins. She had curly, coal black hair and light skin. Her blue eyes shone brightly in the firelight. She was petite. I had always thought that Emily was small in stature, but Mrs. Weston was like a tiny doll that someone had blown the breath of life into. Her small size was even more noticeable standing next to Matthew, who was a tall man with broad shoulders.

"We cannot keep her here," Mrs. Weston said. "My husband has much to do in his research for the college. The weight of caring for the home falls on my shoulders and my shoulders alone because of it. We cannot take on a charge."

In a low voice, Matthew said, "She is an orphan now. She has lost her parents and her home. She needs somewhere safe to go. There is no orphanage in Amherst. She will have to be taken away, perhaps as far as Boston."

"I don't know what to tell you," Mrs. Weston replied. "My heart breaks for her, of course, but I know what I cannot handle in this home. That has to be the end of the conversation."

"She will go home with us," Emily said with confidence. "We will take her in when others will not."

She didn't even attempt to hide her pointed comment at the professor's wife.

The doctor stepped back from the bed. "She has some mild frostbite and the beginnings of a cold, but all in all, she is well. It is quite a miracle as we don't know how long she was out in the cold."

The little girl was awake but did not say a word.

"She will start speaking when she recovers from the shock," the doctor said with more confidence than seemed warranted.

"Is she safe to move?" Mrs. Weston asked.

The doctor looked over his shoulder. "Yes."

"Then, if you are going to take her, you should," Mrs. Weston said, directing her statement to Emily. "I have been told that the fire across the way is finally well controlled. The firemen believe there is no chance our home will come to harm. It is time for the house to settle for the night. My husband has run off to ensure that his lab is safe, and he will be returning soon. He will need peace and quiet after a night like this."

Emily stood. "Officer Thomas, can you carry the girl for me?"

Matthew stepped forward and picked up the child, who was wrapped in a blanket as well as his coat. He carried her to the door and stopped short when he found me standing there. "Willa—I mean Miss Noble; I did not know that you were here."

I gave him a small smile. "It took me a bit of time to discover where you all went." I peeked into the room again. "Where is Carlo?"

I knew he wasn't hiding in the room. There were very few

places to conceal him, and he would never be able to squeeze under there.

"He's in the laundry," Emily said, joining us at the door. She glanced over her shoulder at Mrs. Weston. "Not everyone is as welcoming to animals as they should be."

The professor's wife opened and closed her mouth as if she was going to say something in return but stopped herself. It was for the best. I didn't believe she was much of a match for Emily's sharp wit, and it would only upset Mrs. Weston more to know how Emily truly felt about her.

"Miss Dickinson, are you all right?"

"I am well." Her cheeks were pink from the cold and exertion. "I am glad to see you, but I expected that you would be here, Willa. I always expect it."

Before I could reply, Matthew, carrying the girl, came out of the room.

"What is her name?" I asked.

"Norah Rose Doolan," Emily said.

"Doolan? Was that not the family Miss Susan said she agreed to take on for Mrs. Turnkey?"

Emily nodded. "Yes, I believe you are right. I knew the name sounded familiar to me, but in all the chaos I didn't make the connection. This must mean the Boyles are close by too."

"Yes," I said. "Miss Susan said they were neighbors."

"I do hope their home wasn't harmed in the fire. The houses are so close together here. We will have to come back in the morning and see. Right now, we need to take Norah Rose home so that she might rest."

"But what will your father say?" I asked. The question came from my mouth before I had the chance to stop it.

"Father always bends to my will in the end." She followed Matthew down the hallway.

Before going after them, I took one more look into the bedroom where Norah Rose had been cared for. The doctor packed up his medical bag without a word, and Mrs. Weston stared into the fire. A single tear rolled down her cheek.

CHAPTER EIGHT

It took some time to find Jeremiah and the carriage as he'd moved it from where he'd left us during the confusion of the fire.

I spotted it first. "There. Jeremiah is there."

Matthew, still holding Norah Rose tightly to his chest, nodded and hurried over to the carriage.

We found Mr. Dickinson and Jeremiah standing outside of the carriage. Jeremiah directed Terror to march in place to keep him limber and as warm as possible. He had also put a horse blanket over the animal. I didn't know if the stomping in place or the blanket was doing much good at all for him to fight off the cold. The sooner he returned to the cozy barn at the homestead the better. The sooner we all went home the better in my mind.

"There you are, Emily," Mr. Dickinson said. "How can you run off under these circumstances? I could not find you and was preparing to leave for home."

Emily folded her arms. "You would have gone home without me?"

"I'd have sent Jeremiah back to look for you. I knew you would be safe as long as Carlo was with you. I can't wait here any longer. And who are you?" Mr. Dickinson asked Matthew even though he had met Matthew on several occasions before.

"Officer Thomas, sir," Matthew said.

"And what are you holding in your arms?"

"It's a child, sir."

"A child? What are you doing with a child?"

"We are taking her home to care for her," Emily spoke up. "She is a victim of the fire and needs safety. We can provide that."

Mr. Dickinson scowled at the bundle in Matthew's arms. Norah Rose had burrowed into the blanket for warmth, so Mr. Dickinson could see nary a hair on her head.

"Your mother's nerves will not stand to have a child in the house." Mr. Dickinson clasped his black leather gloves in front of himself as if as far as he was concerned, the conversation was over.

"Very well. I will take her to Susan. My sister will do the right thing even when my parents will not."

"Watch your tongue," Mr. Dickinson said. "As a family we do more for charity than any other in Amherst."

"Is giving money enough?" Emily asked. "We have a chance to save a life that is right in front of us, and you would turn your back? Officer Thomas, put Norah Rose in the carriage."

Matthew glanced at Mr. Dickinson as if asking permission. The patriarch of the family gave a slight nod. Emily had been right; her father would bend to her will.

Emily and Mr. Dickinson climbed into the carriage after

that. Matthew closed the door after them while Jeremiah removed Terror's horse blanket.

Matthew and I walked to the front of the carriage where we couldn't be seen by the passengers inside.

"What will happen to the girl?" I asked.

"We will look for relatives to take her in."

"And if none are found?"

Matthew winced.

"Willa, let's go. Mr. Dickinson will get cranky if I don't start the carriage moving soon," Jeremiah said from the driver's seat.

"Yes." I turned to climb up to the seat, and I felt Matthew's hand on my elbow as I made my ascent.

He squeezed my arm and removed his hand. I was barely in the seat when Jeremiah flicked the reins, and the carriage jerked forward.

The fire was all but out now, but the acrid smell remained. I watched the burnt house disappear from sight. A man and woman had died in that place. Not just any man and woman but Norah Rose's father and mother. It was all so terrible that I vowed then and there that I would do whatever I could to help Norah Rose in the days to come, even find out how and why her parents had died.

Back at the homestead, Margaret met us at the door with hot tea.

She was shocked when Jeremiah carried the little girl in the house. Perhaps even more shocked when I walked through the front door after the family. "What is happening? What is this?"

"Not what, who," Emily said. "This is Norah Rose. She will be staying with us."

Margaret opened and closed her mouth. "Where will she be staying, miss?"

"I think Austin's old room will be just fine for her."

Mr. Dickinson removed his overcoat, hat, and gloves and handed them all to Margaret. Emily removed her outer garments and handed them to me. I jumped back into service and was at full attention for whatever needs the family had that night.

"She is staying one night, and then she will be moved elsewhere." Mr. Dickinson's voice was stern.

"Father," Emily said. "You are as cold as the temperature outside."

He glowered at her, and it was clear to everyone in the room that Mr. Dickinson had made up his mind on the matter.

For once, Emily backed down. "I will take her to Susan in the morning. Thanks be, I have a sister with a compassionate heart."

Mr. Dickinson climbed up the stairs without another word.

After Mr. Dickinson was gone, Jeremiah, who was still holding Norah Rose in his arms, asked, "Should I take her upstairs, miss?"

"No," Margaret said, aghast. "You will not be stomping on my clean carpets with those dirty boots. Hand the child to Willa. Willa, I assume as a sturdy girl, you can carry this slip of a child."

I nodded and I took no offense to Margaret saying that I was sturdy because it was true. I was taller than most men in Amherst and had broad shoulders. My size, although not fashionable, helped me with my work. I could carry more than other female servants and I had a longer reach when cleaning.

Jeremiah set Norah Rose in my arms.

"Be careful with her," he whispered. "Her heart is beating wildly through the coat and blanket."

That's when I realized that we still had Matthew's coat. I hated the thought of him out in the cold without it. As much as I wanted to rush out of the house and give it to him, Norah Rose had to be my first priority, and I knew that he would have wanted me to put Norah Rose first.

"I will," I whispered back.

"Thank you, Jeremiah," Emily said. "We will make sure the child is well cared for. Now, go to your cabin and see if you can get a bit of rest."

Jeremiah nodded and walked toward the back of the house to exit through the laundry servants' entrance.

Margaret shook her head. "I will have to spend the better part of tomorrow trying to get his boot prints out of the carpet. When will stablemen learn they are not welcome in the house?"

"These are special circumstances, Margaret," Emily said, and I was grateful that she came to Jeremiah's defense. Had it been I who said that to the first maid, it would not have been as well received.

Even so, Margaret sniffed. "I'm heading back to bed. Willa and I have much work to do in the morning." She gave me a pointed look as if to say I was expected to complete all of my duties, no matter how tired I might be. I wouldn't have anticipated anything less.

Carrying the child, I followed Emily up the stairs. While I went, the coat fell off her face. Her features were small and delicate, and she had the most striking green eyes I had ever seen. They were the color of a cat's eyes, I thought, and there was terror in those eyes. It was the terror of having to navigate the world completely alone. It was a fear and reality that I knew all too well.

CHAPTER NINE

It is difficult to work in domestic service and not feel the weight of muscle aches and mental fatigue. I was always tired. Some days, my biggest daydream was taking a nap in the middle of the day like Carlo or one of Miss Lavinia's cats. That was all I would need to be content. However, naps were never an option for a maid even in illness. The fire still had to be started, the meals prepared, and the beds made. The work was never ever done. Without the maid, the house was at a standstill.

The morning after the fire, I felt like I required a year's worth of sleep to recover from the events of the night before. After Emily and I settled Norah Rose into bed, I had sat quietly with the child to reassure her she was safe. In all this time, she spoke not a word.

I never made it to my room that night and I awoke at five like I always did. The child was sleeping, and I slipped out of the room. I hoped that when she awoke and saw I wasn't there, she wouldn't be afraid, but either way, I had to go about my duties.

After running up to my own room to change my clothes because they smelled of smoke, I headed to the kitchen, where I tied a fresh apron around my waist. I was happy to find that I beat Margaret to the stove. It gave me time to start the ovens and she would be none the wiser that I hadn't slept in my own bed.

By the time Margaret came into the kitchen, the fire was roaring and the porridge was on. I was quite pleased with myself, but I was far too wise to say that to her.

After taking a sip of the coffee that I had brewed on the stovetop, Margaret asked, "How is the girl?"

"Terrified. I believe she's in shock. She has not said a word, but she's more than old enough to speak."

"Do you believe she's dumb?" she asked in her blunt way.

"I—I don't know. I pray that's not the case."

"Hmmm, well, let us start the fires about the house and set the dining table. It promises to be an eventful day at the Dickinson home."

I agreed that it did.

I went to start the fires in the parlors. I took great care to clean both fireplaces before I ignited the flames. After what happened at the Doolan home, I was terrified of fire. I sat on the cloth that I used to protect the carpets and stared at the flames. Was this what Norah Rose's mother saw before she died? Was she just trying to keep her family warm in this wretched weather?

As I thought that, I realized that I didn't know her parents' first names. That felt wrong. They deserved to be named and remembered as the whole people they'd been, not just as Norah Rose's parents.

I stood, folded the cloth, and pulled back the curtains on the front window that faced the street. Snow swirled in the air, but it was not actively snowing. The wind was high, and the fallen snow blew through the air in a stream of miniature cyclones. The chill permeated the glass. I closed the curtains again, as it was the only barrier we had from the cold.

"Willa, there you are," Emily said as she came into the first parlor. She wore a gray wool dress with a black lace shawl over her shoulders. "I'm glad I found you. It's time to take the child to Susan."

I blinked at her. "Now, miss, it's not even half past seven in the morning. She had a restless night. She may still be asleep."

"It is best if she's moved before my father comes down to breakfast. I don't want to anger him on the subject. He was very firm last night that he didn't like the idea of Norah Rose in our home. Even I know where the line is with my father, and I don't want him to forbid Austin from allowing Norah Rose to stay at the Evergreens. Austin can be weak of mind at times, and he has never been able to stand up to Father."

"I certainly don't want her to be removed from the family's care until Officer Thomas can find her relatives. Do you want me to take the child to the Evergreens?" I asked.

"We will both go. Susan can be prickly around you, as you well know, and she might not be very receptive if I'm not there."

I knew that to be true.

I glanced in the direction of the dining room. "Your sister, mother, and father will be down to breakfast at any moment. I should help Margaret with the service."

"I have already spoken to Margaret, and she has agreed to serve the rest of the family breakfast."

I wondered what terrible task Margaret would assign me that afternoon for making her serve breakfast alone. I had a feeling that I would be scouring the ovens, a job I hated the very most.

"Shall I give Norah Rose breakfast before we leave? She must be hungry."

Emily frowned. "I'm afraid not. Susan will feed her. Go collect her and I will tell my father where we will be."

She left the parlor with a swish of her skirts.

As quickly as possible, I tucked away my cleaning supplies for the fireplaces and was grateful that the fires were already warming the parlors. By the time the family entered after breakfast, the rooms would be tolerable.

I went upstairs and knocked on the bedroom door where Norah Rose was staying. There was no answer, and I went inside. My heart caught in my throat. The bed was empty. Had she left the room? My worry was suspended almost as quickly as it came as I spotted little Norah Rose in the corner of the room, wrapped in Matthew's coat. She had her head buried in her knees.

I walked over to the child and knelt in front of her. "Norah Rose? It's Willa. I'm going to take you to Miss Susan's house. You will like Miss Susan very much."

She lifted her small head, and I saw that there were tears in her eyes. "Why can't I stay here with you? I would like to stay with you. You stayed with me last night. I had my eyes squeezed shut, but I knew you were there."

I stifled a gasp of relief that she could speak but felt pain for all that she had endured and would still endure in the coming days. "I would like you to stay here, I would, but I am just a maid. I don't have any say in any of it."

She wrapped Matthew's coat more tightly around her body. "Because you are poor like me."

I felt a pang in my heart. It's difficult for the poor to make choices. For her to know that so well at such a young age was heartbreaking. Norah Rose would grow up fast like I had and like so many other girls in Amherst had who came from families without a single penny to spare.

I patted her knee. "I will visit as often as I can. Miss Susan lives right next door. It's a very short walk between houses, and I even work in her house from time to time."

She nodded. "Do you know when my mother is coming to fetch me?"

I bit my lip. I was fairly confident that one of the burnt bodies in the fire had been her mother. Matthew had said as much. However, since I wasn't certain, I didn't want to tell her that.

"I will find out what became of her," I said, trying to give the child the most honest answer that I could without telling a lie. She didn't deserve lies even in the name of comfort.

I helped Norah Rose get dressed. Her nightdress was torn and soiled from being outside in the storm, but there were no children in the Dickinson family, so I didn't have anything else to put on her. Perhaps Miss Susan would have some clothes for her.

We met Emily at the front door. She smiled at Norah Rose and said, "I measure every grief I meet."

Norah Rose stared up at her with those bright green eyes as if she didn't know what to make of Emily. I imagine that I had much the same expression when I met my mistress for the very first time.

"I have told Father what we are doing, and we will stay until Norah Rose is settled." She examined the child. "Can you speak?"

Norah Rose glanced at me and squeezed my hand a little tighter.

"Miss Dickinson is a friend. You can tell her."

Norah Rose nodded. "Yes."

Emily smiled. "I knew that you could. The moment that I saw you, I knew you were a bright little thing."

Norah Rose pressed her small body into my side.

I wrapped Norah Rose in Matthew's coat, and we went out the door. The wind was howling, and the child leaned close to me and put her small hand in mine. Emily glanced down at our joined hands and a peculiar look came over her face. It was as if she had come to some sort of decision. What that decision was, I did not know.

Horace Church had shoveled a path between the homestead and the Evergreens under the canopy of trees that divided the homes from each other, but the wind had made a mess of his work and large drifts had blown onto the path.

Some of the drifts were as tall as Norah Rose. I picked her up and carried her the rest of the way. When we knocked on the Evergreens' door, I felt a rush of relief that Katie, the housemaid, answered.

"Miss Dickinson, what are you doing out on a day like this?" she asked in her thick Irish accent. "Even walking a few yards in this wind and snow, you could have lost your way and froze to death."

"This is true," Emily replied. "But we have important matters to discuss with Mrs. Austin Dickinson. Where can I find my sister?"

"She is in the parlor reading, miss." Katie stepped back to allow us inside.

Emily nodded and led Norah Rose and me into the parlor. Katie's eyes went wide when I walked by her holding Norah Rose's hand.

"Emily!" Miss Susan said just as my mistress stepped into the room while Norah Rose and I waited just outside. "You are a fool even to walk across the yard in this weather, and you haven't brought Carlo with you. I would have felt much better if you had him with you to ensure that you would not lose your way."

"I will wait until the wind dies down before I go back," Emily said.

"Then, I believe you will be waiting quite a long time. Austin says that the newspapers claim this weather could go on until March. Heaven knows if we can survive so long. We will all need to thaw out in the spring."

"I dream of spring every day," Emily said. "I miss the bees, the birds, and the flowers."

"I believe that we all do. Even those who say that they love winter. No one can love a winter like this."

Norah Rose and I waited in the entryway.

"Willa, please come in."

"You brought the maid with you? I do not—" She stopped short when she saw Norah Rose and me walk into the parlor.

"What is this?" Miss Susan asked.

Emily sat on the settee across from her sister-in-law. "I'm sure that you heard of the fire last night."

"Yes, of course, Austin went out in the night to help fight it. It is why I am sitting here in the parlor reading and not eating breakfast with my dear husband like I normally would. He returned well after four in the morning and went straight to bed. He has not stirred since."

"Did he tell you anything about it?" Emily asked.

"Nothing more than the fire was out, and the college was safe. Those were his main concerns. He was too tired to say more and even telling me that seemed like a struggle for him."

Emily nodded. "This is Norah Rose. Carlo and I found her in the woods behind the house fire. She has nowhere to go, and I'd like you to take her in."

Miss Susan stared at Emily, but she didn't appear to be completely surprised by the request. I knew that Miss Susan was close to Emily and had taken part in Emily's peculiar requests in the past, but taking on a child was the biggest favor that I had ever heard her ask.

"Emily, you cannot be serious."

"I am deadly serious, and it is only for a few days. Officer Thomas from the police is looking for her relatives. You only need to keep her until the relatives are found."

"Until the relatives are found? Where are her mother and father?"

"It is believed that they died in the fire. Their last name was Doolan."

"Doolan?" Susan asked in surprise. "Was that not the family I agreed to care for during this chilly weather?"

"It was," Emily said.

Miss Susan blinked at Emily. "And they are dead?"

"All but little Norah Rose," Emily said.

I bristled at the matter-of-fact way that Emily revealed Mr. and Mrs. Doolan had passed. I squeezed Norah Rose's hand. They spoke as if the child weren't in the room, and I knew that the child could hear and understand every word they said. It took all my good manners not to interrupt them and ask them not to speak of this in front of Norah Rose.

Something I had learned over my years in service of the wealthy: servants and children were almost invisible. No regard for their presence was taken into account when the adults in the family were speaking.

"You had planned to help the family anyway," Emily continued. "This will be a great act of charity if you take her in."

Miss Susan arched her brow. "I take it your father did not want her in your home."

"You know he worries over anything that might set off Mother's nerves."

"Oh yes, and he does not like complications, so I am the one who should take in the orphan."

"It is the Christian thing to do." Emily folded her hands on her lap.

Miss Susan shook her head. "Do not appeal to my Christian charity, Emily, when you have not attended services in years and years."

"My apologies, Susan. I only wish to help this unfortunate child and believed you would want the same."

Miss Susan nodded. "I suppose I can care for her for a short time. Austin is so busy at the college and at the family law practice that he has no time for me. He doesn't try to make time either," she said bitterly. "I would love to host a house party for a welcome distraction, but with this weather it seems ill-advised. The child will keep me occupied for the time being."

"I knew you would make the right choice, Sister," Emily said.

"And what does Willa have to do with all of this?" Miss Susan asked.

"She was with me when I found the child. Willa is always one to help me."

"Yes, I know you believe that," Miss Susan said in a measured voice. She eyed me and then said, "Come here, child," to Norah Rose.

Norah Rose did not move and was pressed so close to me that it almost felt like we were one person.

"I said come here," Miss Susan repeated, but her voice was not harsh, just commanding. "If you are going to live in my house you will have to follow my rules, and that includes coming to me when you are called."

I nudged Norah Rose to encourage her to step forward. "Miss Susan is kind."

Norah Rose stepped forward, glanced at me one more time over her shoulder, before shuffling over to Miss Susan.

Miss Susan examined her like she would a piece of muslin she was deciding whether or not she should buy.

"She is a very pretty little thing." She stepped back. "But she smells like smoke and something worse. The first order of business will be a bath. Where are the rest of her things so that she has a change of clothes after the bath? What she has on now surely should be tossed into the rubbish."

"She is wearing all of her possessions on her back. Everything else was lost in the fire."

"This won't do at all. I don't have children's clothes here."

"Not to worry. While you give Norah Rose a bath, Willa and I will go downtown and buy some clothing for her."

"In this weather?" Susan asked.

"No matter the weather, it must be done. The child needs clothing. She is far too small to wear one of our dresses."

"And will your father pay for it?" Miss Susan asked skeptically.

"I have a clothing allowance. He never asks what I buy, and if I stay within my means, what difference does it make?"

"Very well," Miss Susan said. "But if he hears of this, please warn me because I don't want to be anywhere close by when he finds out." She took Norah Rose by the hand. "Let's get you cleaned up. We can put you in one of my dressing gowns until they return."

Norah Rose looked at me as if she was begging me to stay. I gave her a reassuring smile, but my chest constricted at the child's expression. How many times had I looked like that when I was young? I'd had a loving mother, but she had been sick. There were times, more than I wanted to admit, when I just wanted someone to swoop in and save me. No one ever did, and then when I was an adult, it was too late for me to want to be rescued any longer. Matthew would have rescued me years ago. He wanted to rescue me now, but I wouldn't allow it, as I had learned how to care for myself.

Miss Susan and Norah Rose left the room, and I saw Matthew's coat over the arm of a chair. I picked it up and folded it over my arm. Perhaps we would run into him when we were about town. I knew he needed it, but I also knew he would never ask Norah Rose to give it up.

Emily was at the door. "Willa, are you coming?"

I glanced back at the parlor door through which Miss Susan and Norah Rose had disappeared.

"Yes, miss," I replied as I held Matthew's coat and kept it close to my chest.

Emily glanced at the coat but said nothing, for which I was grateful.

Carlo was waiting for us outside of the Evergreens.

Emily patted his head. "Have you been waiting for us all this time, you faithful boy?"

He looked up at her with sheer adoration.

"You can come with us to the dress shop."

Carlo wagged his tail, and I fell into step beside Emily.

"Should I tell Jeremiah that you need the carriage for the trip to the dress shop?" I asked.

"No, of course not, the shop is not far, and I intend to walk. This weather will not deter me from doing something that I enjoy as much as walking." She paused. "And before you ask, do not fret over Margaret. I will address her concerning your whereabouts when we return. Do remember, dear Willa, it is always better to ask forgiveness than permission."

I didn't think either scenario would help with Margaret in regard to me, but I didn't say anything. The truth was, I wanted to go with Emily to the dress store and help her pick out clothes for little Norah Rose. I had a feeling that some of the practical items a child would need would be missing if I wasn't present.

CHAPTER TEN

Mrs. Feely's Clothier was just on the other end of Main Street. We stopped by the homestead long enough for Emily to tell her sister where we were headed and then made the walk there in silence. I think the frozen world around us kept us from speaking. Everything was eerily quiet as if the trees, buildings, and lampposts had all been suspended in time, frozen into place. There were no delivery boys running this way and that. There were no college men laughing on the street corners on recess between classes. All was still. It was as if we were the only living things in all the town.

I had been to the clothing shop many times before with Emily. She liked nice things, and Mrs. Feely had the nicest in all of Amherst. The prices were high compared to the other dress shops, but Emily insisted the quality was worth the price.

It was still early in the morning before the shop was set to open on a normal day, and this was most certainly not a normal day.

Before Emily could knock on the shop door, it opened. A petite plump woman stood on the other side of it. She had satiny brown hair bound at the top of her head with a set of knitting needles, and a measuring tape hung about her shoulders.

"Good morning, Miss Dickinson," the shop owner said. "What brings you into town on this horrible day? I didn't expect anyone to come out with this weather and so early in the morning too. I wouldn't have even opened the shop myself if I and my husband didn't live above it."

"A little snow isn't going to keep me from shopping." Emily held the door open. "I have Carlo with me. Can he come in? Normally, I would have him wait outside, but it is awfully cold out there, even for a dog as furry as he."

The shopkeeper eyed the giant dog. "If he stays by the door, I will permit it. I don't usually allow animals in my shop, but I'm not so cruel that I would turn him out in this weather."

Sometimes I wondered if Carlo understood what we were saying because as soon as Mrs. Feely gave permission, he plopped down by the door and crossed his paws as nice as you please.

Mrs. Feely blinked at the dog. "Does he know what we are saying?"

Emily smiled. "Of course. He's a Dickinson."

Mrs. Feely's forehead creased, as if that wasn't exactly the answer that she had been looking for. The shopkeeper shook her head. "Miss Dickinson, you say the strangest things."

"I am glad to hear it. It's better to speak in a peculiar way than to simply contribute to the mundane."

Mrs. Feely narrowed her eyes as if she was trying to determine whether or not Emily had delivered a thinly veiled insult. I didn't think it was a pointed comment at the shopkeeper. Emily found most conversation mundane. It was not Mrs. Feely's fault if she was in that number. Very few people weren't.

"What can I help you with today, Miss Dickinson? You have my undivided attention for once, as no other woman in the village will be as foolhardy as you to venture out today."

It seemed that Mrs. Feely was going to issue her own verbal dart, and thankfully, Emily didn't take offense to being called foolhardy.

"I would like to buy some children's clothes for an eight-year-old girl. I would say she was slight for her age." Emily glanced at me. "Do you agree, Willa?"

I nodded. I had thought when I first saw Norah Rose that she was underweight. I was certain Miss Susan's Irish cook would fatten her up in no time with her hearty winter stews and roasts. The cook's favorite activity was to feed people, and since she had only Miss Susan and Austin to cook for most of the time, she would be thrilled for another mouth to feed.

"A child?" Mrs. Feely asked aghast. "Who in your family has a child? Don't tell me your young cousins are coming to visit in these conditions. No one should go more than a mile in any direction until the weather clears."

"It is not for my cousins, but for Norah Rose Doolan, a young girl who is in dire need of help. My family is caring for her temporarily and we have nothing at all for her to wear. That is why I need your help."

Mrs. Feely covered her mouth and looked as if she might cry. "Norah Rose is with you? She survived the fire? Heaven be blessed. That is the best news I have heard. I had been told that no one survived. It was bad enough to lose Eve. I still can't believe it."

"Eve?" Emily asked.

"I thought you knew. She was the mother of the house. Eve Doolan was a sweet young woman, and I never thought Hugh was good enough for her. I told her that more than once, but she wouldn't listen to me. She was in love with him, there was no doubt of that. I just knew it would end badly for her, but I didn't imagine it would be anything like this."

"You know the family?" I asked.

Mrs. Feely shot a look at me as if she disapproved that I dare speak up. I thought she wasn't going to answer my question, so I was surprised when she said, "Yes, I know the family. Hugh worked at the college."

"He was a teacher?" Emily asked.

"Oh no." Mrs. Feely laughed. "He didn't have the money for the education to do that. He was a janitor of sorts, from what I understand. He helped with the buildings. He must not have made much because they were quite poor, and Eve helped me with seamstress work to make ends meet. She was very talented with the needle, and I would have given her more work if I'd had the money. As it was, I gave her all the work that I could."

"When was the last time that you saw Eve?" Emily asked.

Mrs. Feely frowned as if she regretted admitting that she knew Eve well. "It would have been the day before last. I sent her home with ten dresses that needed mending." She shook her head. "I suppose they were lost in the fire. Mrs. Stearns will be so upset."

"The college president's wife?" Emily asked.

Mrs. Feely nodded. "She is a very short woman and so all of her dresses have to be hemmed, with the cuffs shortened. She has an impossibly small waist as well, even without a corset, so everything had to be taken in. Her store-bought dresses that she orders from Boston have to be almost completely dismantled and reassembled for her. It is tedious work and not something that I have the patience or time for with all of my other duties here in the shop. Eve never minded it."

"So, Mrs. Stearns knew Eve," Emily said.

"Yes, many times Eve would deliver the dresses directly to the president's home and would double-check the fitting on the president's wife before she left."

Emily placed a hand to her chin as if she was considering this, and her thoughtful look had me wondering what she might be thinking. Why would Emily find it odd that the wife of the college president had a dedicated seamstress?

Mrs. Feely paled slightly as if she realized that she said something that she should not have. "I'm sure Mrs. Stearns is overwhelmed by everything that was happening. I heard the faculty members were terrified that the fire would spread to the campus. It would have had to tear through Kelley Square first, but I didn't hear of anyone being afraid of that. However, I'm certain the residents were."

Emily pressed her lips together.

I studied Emily's face and tried my very best to decipher what she was thinking, but as always, I was at a loss. Emily could hide her thoughts very well. Perhaps it was a skill she honed as a child by attending prestigious schools, which I assumed had some of the strictest rules that could be enforced on a young girl. She didn't speak of it much, but she had said once that her mind was the safest place in which to run. She never told me what she was running from, and out of respect I had never asked.

I was the opposite. Everything I felt or thought was written on my face. I knew well of this flaw, as it did not serve me at all in a life of service, so I had grown proficient in looking away and not making eye contact with a person I was displeased with. Thankfully, servants weren't thought of often, so I went unnoticed most of my life. At least that had been the case before I began working for the Dickinsons. Emily saw me, and I was almost certain she saw everyone else who stepped into her line of view. That could not be said for most young women of her stature.

Mrs. Feely placed her hands over her heart. "I am so glad that Norah Rose was spared. I would take her in if I could, but there is no space for a child in the rooms over the shop that I share with Mr. Feely."

"Did Eve Doolan have any other special clients like Mrs. Stearns?" Emily asked.

"She sewed for many of the fine ladies in town. I have even had her work on your sister's, your mother's, and your dresses, though you might not have known it. She did most of her work for the professors' wives on campus, but I would say Mrs. Stearns and Mrs. Weston were the ones whose dresses she worked on most often," Mrs. Feely said.

"Oh, isn't she the new professor's wife in town?"

"Yes, she has been here since October, I believe. Her husband was hired by the college just about that time." She frowned. "She said my selection of dresses and other garments was 'provincial' and orders all of her clothes from Boston and New York. She orders her clothing from elsewhere but had no qualms about having Eve work day and night to have her garments fit her like a glove." She shook her head. "She is just the kind of wife I cannot stand." She slapped a hand over her mouth. "Dear me. Please ignore that I said that. I'm so embarrassed. That was so unprofessional of me."

"You don't need to be professional in any way in front of Willa and me." Emily leaned close. "I, for one, would love to hear why she is the kind of wife that you cannot stand."

Mrs. Feely twisted the end of her measuring tape around her index finger.

Emily placed a hand to her heart. "If for the only reason that I do not behave that way; as a lady of Amherst it is expected that I will be married one day, and knowing how to behave as a wife would be vital to my success."

I raised my brow. Now, I knew that Emily was spinning a yarn for the dress-shop owner. She had made it very clear to me and anyone who asked her that she had no interest in marriage whatsoever. It would be too great of a sacrifice for her to give up her writing for a husband, home, and family.

Mrs. Feely cleared her throat. "Yes, well, being a good wife is vital to your success someday." She let out a deep sigh. "If you must know, she is one of the wives I dislike because she is much younger than her husband. This is not her fault, of course. Many men like young brides. They believe it is a badge of vitality or some such nonsense. She is the type of young bride who feels entitled and spends her husband's money with abandon even though she is not loyal to him."

"Not loyal how?" Emily asked.

Mrs. Feely's cheeks turned bright red. "Oh, you know."

Emily shook her head. "I don't know. What do you mean?"

Mrs. Feely opened and closed her mouth, as if she couldn't bring herself to say the words.

"She means she flirts or worse with men who are not her husband," I said.

Mrs. Feely's face was now as red as a tomato in July. She nodded and gave me a small smile of thanks. It seemed that I won her over by saving her from saying what she meant.

"Hmm." Emily tapped her index finger on the tip of her chin. "Any man in particular?"

Mrs. Feely averted her eyes. "I would not know, miss."

Emily looked like she was going to question the shop owner further, but it was clear to me that Mrs. Feely was extremely uncomfortable with the topic at hand. Furthermore, I needed to return to the homestead before Margaret complained to Mrs. Dickinson about my absence.

"Shouldn't we buy the clothes for Norah Rose? She must be out of the bath by now and will be very uncomfortable in Miss Susan's dressing gown."

"Yes, yes, Willa, you are right as usual in these matters." Emily walked around the shop. "She truly has nothing to wear. The nightdress that we found her in will have to be tossed into the trash." She stepped in front of a display of fur hats, gloves, and muffs. She selected a white child-size muff from the display. "We will start with this."

My eyes went wide. The muff would not be the first thing I would have selected for a poor young girl who lost everything. I guessed that it cost several months' worth of my wages. I would never buy something that elaborate.

Mrs. Feely smoothed her hands over her skirt. "Are you sure that's what you want to give her? It's not very practical for a girl in her place. One trip to the garden and it will be soiled."

Emily added a fur muff onto the counter. "I am not here to be practical. I brought Willa for that. She will know the child's needs much more than I would. This gift will lead to daydreams," Emily said. "Daydreams are important. There are times when they are all that we have. Now is the time that the child will need to cling to her daydreams with the tightest of grasps."

Mrs. Feely's brow furrowed. "Does she have money for it? It's quite expensive, and I'm sorry but I can't take promissory notes at this time. As you must know, this weather has been hard on all the shops in Amherst and mine has not been spared. Ladies do not care about the latest fashions when they are simply trying to keep their children warm."

"Just put it all on my allowance."

Mrs. Feely's eyes lit up at the prospect. "If you insist."

I could almost see the dollar signs dancing in front of her eyes.

While Emily was occupied with that, I looked at more practical items to buy for Norah Rose, quickly going around the shop and gathering the modest items she would need from undergarments to a nightgown, to two dresses: one blue-and-white gingham and one brown. Finally, I found her a pair of sturdy black shoes, but I had to guess the size of her foot. I tilted to the larger size, thinking that she would grow into them, and until that time, we could tuck muslin in the toes to make the shoes fit.

I set all these items on the counter. I chose all the most

modest offerings I could find. Even so, when Mrs. Feely told Emily the total, I suppressed a gasp. Emily, however, barely batted an eye.

Mrs. Feely cleared her throat. "Are you sure that you want to put this on your allowance? It is only January, and you will spend half of what your father has permitted you to spend for the whole year."

"That's no concern to me. I am not a child. I am no longer growing, and where do I have to go, but from my room to the dining room to the garden on most days? I do not need a new frock for that. I have all I need. I spend more time in the mind than I do in a corporal place."

Mrs. Feely nodded and wrote up a receipt. After she handed it to Emily, she began wrapping all the purchases in brown paper. She would not question Emily again.

CHAPTER ELEVEN

EMILY AND I left the clothier with Carlo in tow. I carried the brown paper–wrapped packages and could not wait to see Norah Rose's eyes when she opened them. I hoped that they would make her feel more at home with the Dickinsons for however short or long she was there. But a new dress or an expensive white fur muff would never take the place of her parents.

"That was very generous of you, Emily," I said. "I know that Norah Rose will be happy with all of these gifts."

"I am glad. I have never bought anything for a child. So, I was very happy for you to be here and assist." Emily increased her pace to keep up with Carlo. It seemed even the woolly dog wasn't fond of this severe cold snap.

I kept pace with her. "I don't have any children in my life, either, but I do know what I needed when I was young. I believe that helped me make selections."

She nodded. "I do think it is odd that Mrs. Weston did not

mention that she knew Eve Doolan. If she was her seamstress, they would have had a close relationship. There are not many people that a woman will share her measurements with no matter how tiny her waist."

"Do you think she initially gave the impression that she didn't know Eve?"

Emily nodded and tightened the ribbon of her bonnet. The wind picked up, and any tiny bit of exposed skin was under a very real threat of frostbite. I pulled my scarf over my nose. Even under all the many layers I had on, I could feel the chill seep into my skin and deep into my muscles until they ached.

"We should head straight back to the Evergreens and not stay long before making our way to the homestead. It feels like the snow is going to kick up again," I said.

A ray of bright sunshine broke through the clouds and all around us the snow shone and sparkled. It was close to blinding, but I couldn't look away. It seemed to me that Emily felt that same way. She stared at the brightest spot on the snow-covered church steeple. "There's a certain slant of light on winter afternoons," she murmured.

I didn't ask her what she meant; I had long given up trying to decipher what she meant when she spoke with that peculiar look in her eyes.

I carried the packages from the clothier and still had Matthew's coat hung over my arm. It helped keep my hands warm. If Emily thought it was odd that I carried Matthew's coat all the way into town and back, she did not mention it.

We reached Main Street just as the snow began to fall in earnest. The flakes were large and clung to our clothes and eyelashes. Carlo's brown back was dusted in white, giving him the uncanny appearance of a giant skunk.

The large dog did not seem to be bothered by the giant flakes and tried to catch them with his long pink tongue.

While romping in the sea of white before us, Carlo froze and then took off down the street. When he went more than twenty feet away, he was out of our sight because the snow was so thick.

"Carlo!" Emily called, and she ran after him.

Again, I found myself following in turn. I hoped that the great dog would not find another lost child.

In the street, dark shapes came into view. I noted Emily first and then there was a man, whom it appeared Carlo was attacking. I ran faster, sliding on the slippery road in front of me. Just as quickly as my concern stirred it fell away. Carlo wasn't attacking the man; he was licking his face.

The large dog set his forepaws on Matthew's broad shoulders and licked his face up one side and down the other.

Matthew was laughing, but he wiped at his wet cheeks with his gloved hands. "The last thing in the world that I need is dog slobber frozen to my face. Miss Dickinson, can you please call off your beast?"

Emily whistled and Carlo dropped his large paws to the icy ground. He looked at his mistress as if to ask what he possibly had done wrong. He was simply greeting an old friend. Was he not?

It was in that moment that I made out the fence around the homestead. We stood on the street, but the snow was so thick, I couldn't see the grand yellow house rise in front of us.

Matthew wiped a handkerchief over his face. "I am glad I saw you, despite Carlo's friendly assault."

"I am glad that we ran into you too. I was hoping that we would," I said.

Matthew's eyes lit up. "You were?"

I felt a blush rise on my cheeks, and I was grateful that my scarf hid my face from sight. "Yes, I have your coat that you allowed Norah Rose to have last night." I held the coat out to him. "You must be very cold without it."

Matthew wore a much lighter coat over his uniform. That would not be nearly warm enough in these frigid temperatures.

He accepted the coat and put it on. "Thank you for returning it."

I could be wrong, but there was a slight blush on Matthew's face as well.

Emily looked from Matthew to me and back again with a frown on her face.

"Why were you looking for us, Officer Thomas?" Emily asked.

Matthew blinked as if he was bringing himself out of some sort of trance. "I would like to have a conversation with Norah Rose. Has she spoken at all?"

Emily glanced at me. "To Willa, but no one else."

Matthew nodded and glanced at me and didn't appear to be surprised by this.

"Willa has a calming presence. The child gravitates toward it," he said. "I cannot blame her for that." This time he looked me full in the eyes.

Another blush crept up my cheeks and, yet again, I was more than grateful that my scarf hid the majority of my face.

"I'm happy to have bumped into you so we can talk," Matthew said when he looked away. "But I must ask what you are doing out in this terrible weather?"

"We just went to the clothier to buy Norah Rose a few things as we don't know how long she will be with us," Emily said. "She came to us with nothing. We must do right by the child."

"That was very kind of you," Matthew said. "I can't tell you how long Norah Rose will be with your family. This case has grown more complicated."

"Case?" Emily arched her brow, which was lined with snowflakes. "You would only say that if some sort of crime had been committed."

He nodded. "A crime *has* been committed." He paused. "The fire wasn't an accident at all."

"How can that be?" I asked. My voice was muffled by my scarf, and I repeated my question.

Matthew frowned. "Someone set the home on fire."

"Are you sure it wasn't the fireplace as was first believed?" Emily asked. "The family must have had a fire going all the time in this cold just like we have at the homestead."

"Yes, it made sense to think that at first, as it appeared that the Doolan family likely hadn't had a chimney sweep through the home in a very long time. They would not have been able to afford a professional chimney sweep. As a result, the creosote deposits inside the chimney may have caught on fire. At that point, there would have been no stopping the flames."

"So, it was an accident not a murder," Emily said. She could not hide the relief in her voice, and I felt much the same way.

"I didn't say that."

"If there is a fire in the fireplace, how can it possibly be anything other than an accident?"

"We can't determine if it started in the fireplace. The home is too far gone."

Emily wrapped her cloak more tightly around her body. "Then, how do you know that it wasn't an accident? House fires happen all the time and especially in the winter when it is freezing out."

He frowned. "The doors of the house were blocked from the outside with heavy rocks, piled one on top of the other. The police didn't know about it at first because by the time we arrived, firemen and other volunteers had moved the stones, attempting to remove the occupants. Unfortunately, they were too late."

I gasped. "If that is true, how did Norah Rose escape?"

"Perhaps out a window," Matthew said.

Emily frowned. "Why didn't they all go out the window, then?"

Matthew didn't have an answer for that.

"There is a lot in the death of Mr. and Mrs. Doolan that doesn't add up," Emily said.

Matthew nodded. "I was hoping that Norah Rose could provide some answers about how she made her way out of the house and why her parents didn't leave. That is why I must speak to her."

I bit the inside of my lip. I could understand Matthew's need to speak to the girl, but at the same time, she was in a fragile state. "Let us see how she is before you come. She's very frightened. Perhaps you can drop by tomorrow. She is going to be staying at the Evergreens."

He nodded. "I would like to speak to her now, but I can understand your wish to protect her." He brushed snow from the sleeve of his coat. "I'll be there tomorrow afternoon."

Emily nodded. "Very well. We will let Susan know. Willa and I will both be there when you speak to Norah Rose."

"Police usually conduct interviews alone."

"Norah Rose Doolan is the Dickinsons' ward for the time being. As a result, we will be there. She is just a child and will need someone to hold her hand."

"Of course," Matthew said. "It was very kind of your family to take the child on."

"The Dickinsons are not first and foremost known for their compassion, but I can assure you it runs deep in the family."

Matthew nodded and glanced at me, his gaze lingering a moment longer, before he said, "I will be off, then."

He disappeared into the falling snow.

CHAPTER TWELVE

EMILY, CARLO, AND I hurried to the Evergreens, but before we reached the house, Horace stopped us. He was shoveling the drive so that the horse and carriage could leave the barn. Ice crystals hung from his beard. "Willa, I would get myself back into the homestead kitchen if I were you. Margaret is fit to be tied that she is working alone this morning. I would not be surprised if she gave all the servants cold soup because of her disdain."

I grimaced. It would not be the first time that Margaret had done so to the servants. That time, too, I had been blamed for her foul mood because Emily had dragged me from the homestead for one of her rambles through the woods. Margaret did not appreciate that.

I looked down at the packages for Norah Rose in my arms.

"Return to the homestead, Willa. Do not worry. Susan is a mother at heart and will do very well caring for the child," Emily said. "It would be better if you return to your duties now so that you can join me when Matthew returns tomorrow. That is when Norah Rose will really have need of you. I will also need you later when I call on the Boyle family."

My eyes widened. I had forgotten about the Boyles and Emily's promise to Mrs. Turnkey of the Ladies' Society of Amherst that she would look after them during this cold spell. But I knew that Emily probably now had a secondary motive to call on all of them. They were neighbors to Eve and Hugh Doolan.

Even knowing all this I hesitated. There was something about the young child that pulled me toward her. I wanted to protect her. I wanted her to know that someone cared for her and she wasn't alone. Unfortunately, I had other duties, and as we did not know how long Norah Rose would be living with the family, I did not want Margaret to resent her or me any more than she already did.

"Horace can carry the packages," Emily said.

I handed Horace everything that was in my arms and headed to the homestead. I was grateful to see that Horace had dug a path in the deep snow from the front of the house to the back.

When I stepped into the laundry, I could hear Margaret singing Irish ballads to herself in the kitchen. This was a habit that she had when she thought no one was listening.

She had a very nice voice, but I knew if I told her that she would know that I'd overheard, and she would be embarrassed. I removed my cloak, scarf, and bonnet, and changed from my boots to my house shoes. I then opened and closed the back door to the laundry hard to warn Margaret I was there. If I walked in on her singing, she would know that I knew her secret, and that was the last thing in the world that I wanted.

As soon as the door slammed shut, the singing stopped. I waited a few beats before I went into the kitchen.

"Good morning, Margaret."

She eyed me. "Good morning for you, I take it, as Miss Dickinson grabbed you and took you off on one of her rambles. This is a luxury I know nothing about."

"Miss Dickinson needed help with Norah Rose, the little girl who lost her parents in the fire last night."

"Yes, I heard, but you were gone a very long time. How long does it take to settle a child? All she needs is food, water, and a place to lay her head."

I wasn't a mother—and neither was Margaret, for that matter—but I believed that children needed a great deal more than those essentials to thrive.

"Things took longer than we expected them to." I wasn't going to tell her that Emily and I went clothing shopping for Norah Rose, and if all went well, she would never know about it.

Margaret's face softened. "She is a poor little sprite. She has a very difficult road in front of her."

I nodded. "What will happen to her if they don't find any family to take her?"

"She will be sent to an orphanage or maybe even on a train out west to a family that needs a child to help with their work on the frontier."

I shivered at the very idea of it. I didn't know how, but I wasn't going to allow either of those terrible fates to meet this little girl, I simply wouldn't.

"Now, get to work. All the chamber pots need to be thoroughly cleaned."

On my list of duties about the homestead, the chamber pots were the lowest of the low.

I made it through my list of tasks by luncheon, and it was a good thing, too, as Margaret came flying into the kitchen while I was stirring the soup.

"We have to make another quiche."

I stared at her.

"A quiche," she said as if she found me dull. "Mrs. Dickinson just told me that the college president, his wife, and the Westons will be here again for luncheon. Don't these people have a cook of their own? Why does it fall on my shoulders to feed them?"

She began hurrying around the kitchen and removed a ham from the larder to fry on the stove.

I set the soup to simmer and went about to gather the rest of the ingredients for the quiche.

Margaret was in such a state that she sent me to prepare the dining room for our guests. I was setting the additional places at the table when there was a knock on the front door.

I looked down at my apron to make certain that it was free of stains. There was a small soot mark from the oven on the edge of the apron, but I could easily cover it with my hand.

I opened the door to find the Westons, both wrapped in heavy wool and fur, standing at the door.

"Professor and Mrs. Weston, please do come in." I stepped back and waited for them to remove their outer garments.

Before too long my arms grew heavy under the weight of cloaks, coats, hat, scarves, and bonnet.

I curtsied as I held all the items. "You are welcome to wait in the front parlor through the door there. I will tell the Dickinsons you've arrived. Would you like a warm drink while you wait for them? We have tea, cider, and coffee."

"Some tea would be nice," Mrs. Weston said. "Something light. I never drink coffee before a large meal. It wreaks havoc on the digestion."

"Bourbon," Dr. Weston said.

"Dr. Weston," his wife reprimanded.

"After the night and day that I have had, I need it, Verona. And I don't want to hear another word about it. Everything I have worked for is on the brink of collapse. You don't want that to happen as much as I don't. It would bring an end to your allowance."

My cheeks turned red at Dr. Weston's talk of finances right in front of me, but I took note that what he said seemed to match up with what Mrs. Feely said at the dress shop. Mrs. Verona Weston liked to spend money on herself.

His wife scowled but said nothing more. I curtsied again and carried their garments from the room. It was funny that I felt the need to curtsy to the Westons. I never did to any of the Dickinsons, and I hadn't even when I served dignitaries in Washington when I had accompanied Emily there two years ago. Something about the couple told me that they demanded respect. The question that I kept coming back to was whether that respect was earned or simply given with their titles.

I carried the garments to the second floor. There were too many items to stow in a closet, so I placed them in the spare bedroom. The empty bedroom had been that of Mr. Austin

Dickinson. It was also the room where Norah Rose had slept the night before. I stepped inside and found everything as tidy as a pin. Nothing was out of place, but at the same time an uneasy feeling washed over me. Like fear. It permeated the room.

I wasn't one to believe in ghosts or auras or any of that, but in that moment, I felt like someone was there.

As quickly as I could, I set the garments on the bed. Even in my haste, I took care not to bend or wrinkle them. The very last thing in the world I needed was Mrs. Weston telling the Dickinsons that I'd mistreated her bonnet.

I set the bonnet on top of Mrs. Weston's cloak and the bed moved as if jumping up from the floor. I gasped and took a step back as the bed moved a second time. I was just about to fly from the room when Carlo's broad head peeked out from under the bed.

"Carlo! You scared me almost to death."

The large dog shimmied out from under the bed. It was truly a miracle he had been able to fit underneath there. A moment later, Baby Z, Miss Lavinia's black cat, shot out from under the bed and out of the room.

Carlo lunged as if he was going to chase him, but I grabbed him by the collar and stopped him.

"Leave the cat alone," I said. "If you leave him alone, he will leave you alone."

Carlo sat back on his haunches and looked up at me as if to say that he didn't believe me. I didn't blame him. Baby Z loved to torment the dog.

With Carlo looking up at me, I saw a piece of metal sticking out of his mouth. I held out my hand. "Give it to me."

He kept his jaws clamped tight.

"Give." I held out my hand again.

He bowed his head and gave a soft growl.

"If you eat whatever that is, you will get sick, and Emily will be beside herself with worry. Give."

This time, he dropped the metal object into my hand.

I grimaced, as the object was covered with dog slobber. I was surprised to see it was a small key, half the size of a house key. The key's teeth were sharp and jagged, reminding me of shark's teeth I had seen drawn in one of Mr. Dickinson's books. I had been known to read a chapter or two from his library when I was in his study dusting. I was grateful that Margaret hated dusting, so she always gave me that task.

The head of the key had a hole to be attached to a key chain and there was a rose engraved in the key's head. I flipped the key over, and the other side of the head was blank.

I could have been wrong, but it looked to me as if the rose and number had been engraved after the key was made.

I held the key flat in my palm. "Where did you find this?"

Carlo cocked his head at me.

I was dying to peek under the bed to see what else might be hidden under there. That was assuming that the key had been purposely hidden and not carelessly dropped. However, there was no time for that. Both Mr. and Mrs. Dickinson prided themselves on throwing impeccable dinner parties, and I knew that Mrs. Dickinson in particular would want to impress the college president's wife, even though they had been at the homestead just the night before.

I needed to make my way to the kitchen as quickly as I

could. I tucked the key into the pocket of my white apron and patted Carlo on the head. "Good boy."

He licked my hand. I would have to wash it before I served the evening meal. That was for certain.

I hurried down the hallway to Mrs. Dickinson's room to tell her guests had arrived.

The door was open, and I peered into the room, and Mrs. Dickinson was at her dressing table, tucking a lace scarf into the collar of her dress. She scowled at herself as she did the task, and her face was drawn and pale.

The last two years that I had worked for the Dickinson family, Mrs. Dickinson was always thought to be unwell, but in all that time, no one had said what she suffered from. It seemed to be tiredness or headaches or agitation. I knew from my own experience caring for my mother, who had died young, that all of those claims were likely symptoms of what was actually hurting her body. However, the doctors either had not found it or weren't looking in the right places for what caused Mrs. Dickinson's troubles.

I had my own feelings about doctors. I saw so many of them talk down to my mother when she was in the middle of her illness. I wished they had properly answered her questions about the prognosis. That way, we might have prepared for the inevitable end a little differently.

I knocked on the doorframe, and the bedraggled expression on her face smoothed over. Her wrinkles seemed to disappear before my very eyes. The mask that she wore was back in place.

"Yes?"

"I'm sorry to interrupt you, Mrs. Dickinson, but the Westons are here. I imagine the president and his wife will also be here shortly."

She nodded. "Do not apologize. It is your job to tell me when guests arrive." Her face was now clear, and she wore her usual placid expression. I thought the face I saw before was her true one.

"Mrs. Dickinson, are you all right?" To ask such a question was a step out of my role of the second maid. Even Margaret would be hard-pressed to get away with asking such a personal question, but I could not stop myself.

Mrs. Dickinson looked so small and utterly alone sitting at her dressing table. I tried to remember one instance when I saw her and Mr. Dickinson even reading in the same room together. They didn't eat meals most of the time together unless they were entertaining like they were today. Mrs. Dickinson preferred to have meals alone in her room.

In many ways, Emily reminded me of her mother, and I didn't want that fate for my friend. I didn't want her to hide and appear only when it was absolutely necessary. But considering how she took after her mother, it was possible.

"I will be down promptly. You may go," she murmured.

I had been dismissed. I wasn't hurt by this. It had been the longest conversation I'd ever had with Emily's mother.

I backed out of the room. As I did, I almost stepped on one of Miss Lavinia's cats. As to be expected, it was Baby Z again. The small black cat looked up at me and then pawed at my apron.

As he did, it reminded me of the key in my pocket. I

shook my finger at him and whispered, "No, you can't have it back."

He turned and waltzed down the hallway with his tail held high. I could see why Carlo had so many disputes with this particular feline. Even so, I loved Baby Z's spice.

CHAPTER THIRTEEN

I WALKED INTO THE front parlor with Dr. and Mrs. Weston's drinks on a silver tray. While I had been upstairs, the president and his wife had also arrived. To my surprise, there was a third woman in the room whom I didn't know.

She was slight and had dark hair parted severely in the middle and cut short so it swung loose by her ears. However, I had never seen a woman in men's trousers, and I had certainly never seen a woman in trousers coming to luncheon at the Dickinsons' home. Along with the trousers, she wore a man's jacket and a skirt that fell just to her calves over the trousers. I had never seen an ensemble like it.

The unknown woman cleared her throat. "I will have tea with a bit of lemon if you have it. My throat is raw from speaking."

"It's no wonder, Lucy," Mrs. Stearns said. "You have been speaking for days with your lectures. I don't know how you do it."

"I don't know how I can't do it. This forced stopover in Amherst has been difficult. Olive, you are a dear for allowing me to stay with you, but I would much rather get back on the road and spread the message of women's plight in society."

Dr. Weston crinkled his nose at the comment. Whatever Lucy's message, Dr. Weston was not fond of it.

Margaret stepped into the room, carrying another tray of warm drinks, presumably for the college president, his wife, and this newcomer I did not know.

I handed Mrs. Weston her tea first and then gave Dr. Weston his short glass of bourbon.

"Miss Stone, I don't believe that you have ever met Mrs. Dickinson," Mrs. Weston said. "I do hope she is feeling well enough to attend luncheon this afternoon."

"I have not met any of the Dickinsons. And I have asked you time and time again to call me Lucy. I do not care for titles."

"I can imagine that is true, as you don't carry your husband's name," Mrs. Weston said with a sniff. "It must be troublesome when you are addressed, as people do not know if they should refer to you as Miss or Mrs."

Lucy raised her brow. "It is only troublesome to those stuck in a time where such distinction matters. My name is my identity and must not be lost."

Mrs. Weston's glare at the other woman was returned with such ferocity that a bit of her pretty mask began to fall. I held my breath and waited to hear what she would say in reply because I knew it would be cutting. Why the two women had such a palpable disdain for each other, I didn't know, but it was clear to me the dislike ran deep into them both.

Before Mrs. Weston could reply with a biting remark, Miss Lavinia and Emily stepped into the parlor.

"We beat our father here?" Miss Lavinia asked in surprise. "I was certain that he would be here first."

President Stearns stood up. "That is my fault. I asked him about some accounts for the college, and he went in search of the numbers for me."

His wife stood beside him and placed a hand on his arm. "Truly, William, you should stop fretting over the college budget for one afternoon. After being up so late last night worried over the fire, too, I'm quite afraid your anxious nature will make you ill."

"Olive, it is my primary concern, especially in the midst of these trying times," President Stearns said.

Mrs. Stearns dropped her hand from her husband's arm and frowned.

"I'm sure Father will join us shortly," Miss Lavinia said in an artificially cheerful voice. She wanted to break the tension in the room. I didn't know if most of that tension was coming from the Stearnses or from Lucy and Mrs. Weston. In any case, the room felt heavy under the weight of so many unspoken words.

Mrs. Weston stood holding her cup of tea. "If the men have pressing business to discuss when it comes to the college, we should let them. We are all in shock over the events of last night."

"Very true," the college president said. "I am thankful that it wasn't worse, and all the buildings were saved."

"All the buildings?" Emily asked. "You don't count the Doolan home in that number?"

He examined Emily through the lenses of his glasses. "I

was referring to the college buildings. As the college president, it is my duty to preserve and protect the college and those who reside in it."

"But didn't Hugh Doolan work at the college? I believe he was a janitor," Emily said with a single, arched eyebrow.

President Stearns paled slightly. "Yes, he was a janitor."

"If he was a janitor, he would know our groundskeeper, Horace Church. Horace works at the college as well."

"Yes." He gave a solemn nod. "I know Horace well. Hugh Doolan had not worked for the college long. Only a few months, from what I understand. I don't know much about him. He and his family lived in Kelley Square. I don't believe that I ever interacted with him. It is not common for the college president to speak to a janitor."

Emily turned to Dr. Weston. "But you surely spoke to him, Dr. Weston. Is that not true? Your home was right across the street from his. In fact, when we were at the fire last night, we took shelter from the cold in your home." She smiled at Mrs. Weston. "Verona was kind enough to welcome my maid and myself in along with little Norah Rose."

Mrs. Weston pressed her pink lips together into a thin line, making her lips appear as white as the piles of snow outside of the window. "It was the charitable thing to do."

From across the table, Dr. Weston watched his wife with a frown on his face. Was he upset with her for giving us shelter from the cold? For becoming involved in the fire in any way?

Emily cleared her throat, and I was well aware she was far from done with her questioning of the couple. In many ways, Emily was like Carlo with a bone when she got an idea into her head.

"Where were you last night, Dr. Weston? I would have thought you would be at your home to make sure it was secure and safe since it was so close to the fire."

"I was in my lab."

"Oh, you have a lab? What is it you teach?" Emily asked.

"Botany."

"Truly?" Her eyes shone. "I have a passion for botany. When I was at Mount Holyoke, I was the star pupil on the subject. I also have an extensive herbarium. I would love to show it to you sometime."

Dr. Weston visibly relaxed as the conversation turned from the Doolans to plants. It was clear plants brought him comfort just as they did to Emily.

"Anytime you come to campus, I would be happy to give you a tour. It is refreshing to meet a woman interested in botany, not just gardening, but in the science of plants. It is my passion."

"I'm sure your wife shares that passion."

He barked a laugh. "No, she does not. Verona and I have very little in common."

Emily raised her brow. "If that is the case, I'm surprised that you agreed to the match."

"We fell in love," he said with a frown on his face.

"How can a person fall in love with another person if they have nothing in common? What is there to talk about? How can you maintain even a friendship, let alone a marriage?"

Miss Lavinia grabbed her sister's arm and nodded at the professor. "I'm so sorry to interrupt, Dr. Weston, I just need to speak to my sister about the seating chart for luncheon."

"What do I care for the seating chart?" Emily asked.

Miss Lavinia forced a laugh and yanked Emily into the foyer.

"Emily," Miss Lavinia snapped. "Please. Why are you interrogating a man you don't even know about his marriage? It's unseemly."

"I was merely having a philosophical conversation with a scholar, Vinnie. There is no reason for you to snap in such a way."

Just above a whisper, Miss Lavinia said, "Truly, Emily, there are times when your incessant questions are embarrassing."

"I'd rather be embarrassed than uneducated."

"You are never embarrassed," Miss Lavinia scoffed. "It is the rest of us who are. Think of us for once before you open your mouth."

As I was watching the exchange, Margaret appeared down the hallway and waved at me. That was my cue to return to work.

I hurried into the dining room and made sure that everything was set for the meal. As we had not previously planned to have guests that day, Margaret had scrambled to make another quiche, but thankfully she always made enough soup for a small army. For dessert, we would be serving leftover pound cake that Emily had made yesterday morning. I precut the slices and set them on small dessert plates, arranging them on the sideboard so that the guests would not know that it was a reused dessert. Then I added some lemon drizzle on top with a dollop of cream.

Just as I was double-checking the place settings and noting that we were one short due to the surprise of Lucy Stone's arrival, Mr. Dickinson and the rest of the party came into the dining room.

My heart was in my throat as they took their seats. I would have to sneak in another place setting while they were all at the table. This would not only be humiliating for me but for the family as a whole. It was a disaster. I chastised myself for letting this happen. Had I not been in the parlor so long listening to the conversations, I would have noticed the issue earlier and corrected it before anyone was the wiser.

Mr. Dickinson stood behind his chair as he waited for all the ladies to be seated. "You will have to excuse my wife," Mr. Dickinson said. "Like all of us, she was up late last night when the church bells rang alerting us of the fire. She is quite overcome and won't be able to join us for luncheon. I am very happy that most of you were able to converse with her last night." He sat down. The other gentlemen in the room did as well.

At the sideboard, I let out a sigh of relief. Mrs. Dickinson's absence allowed the number of place settings to be just right. I was saved.

Mrs. Weston and Mrs. Stearns sat closest to where I stood. Mrs. Weston leaned in close to Mrs. Stearns. "How very rude that the lady of the house is not here to host the meal! Are we to believe that Miss Dickinson will take over in her stead?"

"Verona, please. I know that you are new to Amherst, but you should have heard by now that Elizabeth Dickinson is victim to spells."

"I don't believe in such nonsense. A woman should be made of stronger stuff. How is she to run a household from her bed?" Mrs. Weston asked.

"As you can see, the Dickinson household is very well run," Mrs. Stearns whispered back.

"That's your opinion on the matter. A luncheon like this would be considered a mere snack in New York."

"You aren't in New York any longer. You're in Amherst."

"Oh, I know," Mrs. Weston said bitterly.

"It would serve you well to remember that," Mrs. Stearns said.

"Every day I am here, I cannot forget," Mrs. Weston said.

The party chatted as I set bowls of Margaret's root vegetable soup in front of them. It was different from the soup that they had been served the night before, but not by much. I believed that there were more parsnips and carrots, and Margaret threw in a little extra thyme. I was certain that Mrs. Weston would not be impressed, and the "country" soup was like nothing she had ever eaten in New York.

CHAPTER FOURTEEN

ONCE EVERYONE WAS served, I took my place in the corner of the room, glancing toward the doorway every so often in case Margaret needed help in the kitchen with the quiches.

"Mrs. Stearns, you must be terribly upset over Eve Doolan's death," Emily said.

The president's wife looked at her. "Yes, I am. I am upset anytime a young life has been cut short."

"But since she was your seamstress, there is a personal loss for you, too, no? I know myself how attached I grow to my servants." Emily glanced at me.

I didn't show any reaction because I knew either Mr. Dickinson or Miss Lavinia would pounce on it.

Mrs. Stearns set her spoon on the edge of her dish. She had taken no more than two spoonfuls of the soup. I hoped Margaret wouldn't be too offended by that.

"How did you know about that?" Mrs. Stearns asked, and

then blushed as she realized that she had asked the question so loudly she received the attention of the entire table. She lowered her voice. "It's no secret, of course, it just seems odd that you would know who mends and fits my clothing."

"Oh, it's not odd at all. Don't all the ladies in Amherst use Mrs. Feely's Clothier downtown?" Emily asked.

Mrs. Stearns visibly relaxed when Emily explained.

It made me wonder if there was a reason that the college president's wife wouldn't want anyone to know who her seamstress was.

"Yes, yes." She chuckled. "It's silly of me. Better than anyone, I know what a small place Amherst is. I have been a very good customer to Mrs. Feely for years, and she was kind enough to send Eve to my home for my fittings. It saved me a great deal of time from going down to her shop."

"I'm sure it did," Emily said. "When was the last time that you saw Eve?"

Mrs. Stearns raised her brow. "The last time I saw Eve?"

Emily nodded and leaned closer to the older woman. "Yes, was it at your house?"

"I imagine it was at my home. I only ever saw her in my home when she was measuring me for fabric or mending a garment."

"How was she? What did you talk about?"

"She said that she was hoping to start a seamstress business of her own out from under the umbrella of Mrs. Feely's shop. She wanted to pick and choose her clients. She said that she had a group of ladies with whom she worked, who had influence in Amherst to spread the word about her new business. I told her that I would help any way I could and encouraged her to do it. I told her that she was far too talented to work under Mrs. Feely's thumb. She needed to spread her wings."

Emily glanced at me again as if to check that I was still listening. I was, to every word. As the soup course came to an end, I went around the table and collected bowls. I wanted to stay in the dining room and listen to Emily's conversation with Mrs. Stearns about Eve Doolan, but duty called.

In the kitchen, Margaret had the quiche ready to serve. Each plate had a generous portion of quiche and a small apple salad with raisins and poached pears.

Margaret clicked her tongue when I came back into the kitchen after delivering the plates of quiche to the table.

"This is the very best I can do on such short notice. Why don't they have these functions at the Evergreens? I would like to know. That house was built for entertaining and there is nothing more that Miss Susan likes than playing hostess. They have that Irish cook too. Miss Susan sent her to Boston to take lessons, and I am over here scrambling to make enough fruit salad so that everyone won't leave hungry."

"You've done a wonderful job, Margaret."

She grunted in reply. "Tell me what they are talking about out there. I know that you were listening."

I didn't even try to deny the fact that I had been listening to the luncheon conversation, and I knew very well that Margaret would have been, too, if she had been in the dining room. Any servant would have. Listening was a main part of our occupation and our entertainment.

"For the most part they are speaking about the fire."

"I would have expected as much."

"Mrs. Stearns knew the mother who died. She was her seamstress."

Margaret nodded. "Yes, I knew Eve too. I would see her and her daughter in the town square sometimes."

"You know Norah Rose?" I asked. This was shocking news to me because Margaret had not mentioned it before, not even when Norah Rose was staying right here at the homestead.

"I knew her mother only enough to say hello, and I did not know the child's name. Norah Rose was in such a state when she arrived that I had not realized the connection until she moved to the Evergreens."

"What was Eve like? Even though you didn't know her well, you must have had some sort of impression of her."

I said this because Margaret had an opinion about everyone, and she wasn't afraid to share. I had gotten an earful from her about almost every guest who had ever walked through the doors into the homestead. If she didn't have something to say about someone, that was the most noticeable.

"She was very sweet, kind, and refined."

"Refined?" It was an odd word choice to say of someone in our class. Usually, when I thought of that word, it was in relation to someone with money. Eve and her family had lived in Kelley Square; money that would have led to any kind of refinement wasn't something that Eve Doolan had a lot of.

"Yes, refined. I had heard that she came from a well-to-do family in Dublin and went to all the finest schools. Perhaps it was at one of those schools that she learned to sew so well. It is a skill that must be properly taught to be at the level of her workmanship."

"How did she end up here?"

"What do you think? When do young women make the worst choices? When do they give up the good in their lives for something new?"

I shook my head and it felt like she was speaking in riddles.

"It is when they fall in love. She fell in love with Hugh Doolan, and that ruined her life."

Ruined her life? That seemed like a sharp judgment. Eve chose to leave Ireland for Hugh. In her mind at least, she must have felt like she was making the best decision for herself. However, to me, the most interesting part of the conversation was the fact that Eve had family, family that might be willing to take in her little girl.

"If she has a wealthy family in Dublin, then they would be Norah Rose's family too. Perhaps they will take her in."

Margaret shook her head. "I doubt it. An Irish father scorned is not quick to forgive."

I couldn't believe that. Of course Eve's family—whoever they were and wherever they were—would want to take care of the child. She was their flesh and blood. She was a piece of their daughter. How could they turn their back on that?

Without warning, my thoughts turned to my own father. He had walked away from Henry and me. He'd turned his back on us, and that was the end of that. We never would have survived had it not been for our mother.

I shook my head. I had been thinking of my father more often over the last several days and that had to do with the proximity to Kelley Square in this case. The last time I'd seen him had been in Kelley Square. He hadn't known that I'd spied on him. He was walking away with another woman. I'd been so young that the memory was more an impression than a real recollection. There were no faces when I brought the memory back into the forefront of my mind, just the knowledge that it had been my father and he was not with my mother.

Margaret flipped her tea towel in my direction. "Now, get out to the dining room. Heaven knows that they will all be in want of something by this time."

Margaret was right about the luncheon, of course. They were done with the quiche. I quickly cleared the dishes away and set the doctored pound cake in front of them. If the family noticed that it was the same cake they'd had for breakfast that morning, they didn't say so. I was quite relieved that they remained quiet on the subject.

It seemed it did not matter in the end that the cake was a day old. Every last crumb was gone at the end of the meal and there were several compliments about it too. I could not wait to tell Margaret. She would be relieved, if not pleased.

The men from the party excused themselves to Mr. Dickinson's office while the women went to the front parlor. The pocket doors between the front parlor and the family parlor, where the piano resided, remained closed. This was a signal to me that Miss Lavinia and Emily weren't perfectly comfortable with their guests to let them see such a personal space.

I went around the room asking the ladies if they would like anything to drink.

Lucy waved me away. "Heavens no, I feel like a stuffed turkey after that meal. Is that how the family eats every day? It's a wonder that any one of you can walk. I am far more used to my meal of bread, jam, and coffee while I am on the road. Any more than that just seems overindulgent."

Mrs. Weston eyed her. "It's interesting you say that since you seemed to have no trouble at all packing away that piece of cake."

Lucy smiled at her. "I was being polite."

Mrs. Weston snorted and then covered her mouth, looking around to see if anyone had noticed the indelicate noise she'd made.

Emily, who was like a dog with a bone when she wanted information, perched on the edge of an ottoman by the fire. "Mrs. Weston?"

Mrs. Weston wrinkled her brow and looked at my mistress. "Yes, Miss Dickinson."

"Call me Emily, please. We are peers. Like Lucy, I don't feel right with such formality."

Mrs. Weston nodded. "And please call me Verona."

"I was told that Eve worked for you as a seamstress as well. I don't believe you mentioned that you knew her the night of the fire."

"And where did you hear that?" Mrs. Weston asked.

"Just as I told Mrs. Stearns, we all use the same dress shop. In fact, I was there this very morning."

"You went out in this weather for a new dress? Fashion must be at the forefront of your mind." Mrs. Weston patted her silky hair as if to make sure it was still in place. Not a single strand would dare move; I was certain of that.

"It's not," Emily said. "Far from it, in fact, but I do not let a little snow here and there stop me from going about my day."

Across the room, just inches from the closed pocket door, Miss Lavinia stood biting her lip while she watched her sister. I knew it was taking everything in her not to interrupt. I felt the same way. I also had many duties and tasks to return now that the luncheon was over, but I just could not tear myself away. I wanted to see how this conversation played out.

Mrs. Weston stared at Emily with a new respect in her eyes. It was almost as if she recognized that she had met her match. She cleared her throat. "Mrs. Feely is a gossip. At times I believe all the shopkeepers in Amherst are. It keeps them occupied on slow days. My only wish is that they wouldn't gossip about the men of the college as much. Our husbands have great reputations to uphold."

"And what about your reputation?" Emily asked.

She eyed her. "I am merely an extension of my husband. It is one of the very first things a woman learns when she marries. You will see that for yourself soon enough."

Lucy sniffed. "I am married, and that is not a lesson I subscribe to."

Mrs. Weston narrowed her eyes at the other woman. "Honestly, I do not know why you are here."

"Verona, please," Mrs. Stearns said. "Lucy is my guest."

Lucy smiled. "I am. Olive was nice enough to give me a place to stay when I was out on my lecture tour and caught in this horrid weather."

Emily's eyes lit up. "Your lecture? What do you speak on?"

"Don't get her started, Miss Dickinson. None of us will have any peace when she gets going," Mrs. Weston said.

CHAPTER FIFTEEN

LUCY FROWNED AT Mrs. Weston and said, "I speak on women's rights and equality." She then glanced at Mrs. Weston. "Not everyone is open to listening to that, but there will be a time when they have no choice, so in actuality, Verona, I speak for you as a woman even though you have no appreciation of it."

"That is quite a bold statement," Mrs. Weston said from where she sat near the fire. "It seems everyone these days claims some sort of right. It can be quite exhausting. I believe it is better for society if everyone knows and accepts their place. Everything would go much more smoothly in this world if each and every person accepted their station given by birth. Was it not God's choice where you landed? Are you not questioning God's wisdom by trying to move into a different grouping of society?"

"Perfectly answered by someone born with a silver spoon in her mouth," Lucy said.

Mrs. Stearns leaned forward on the settee where she sat next to Lucy. "It does not surprise me that the two of you do not see eye to eye, but please do not quarrel when we are guests in the Dickinson home."

"I don't mind the quarreling," Emily said. "It's quite enlightening. How do you two know each other?"

Mrs. Stearns smiled. "Lucy is my friend, and I am quite enjoying her visit even though it was unplanned. She had been traveling through the commonwealth and came to take shelter from the storm."

Lucy nodded. "I can't thank you enough for your hospitality, Olive. I hope not to make a nuisance of myself. Since the trains have stopped, I'm trapped here for the foreseeable future."

"You could never make a nuisance of yourself, Lucy. I love you like my very own sister." Mrs. Stearns squeezed her friend's hand.

Across the room, Mrs. Weston scowled at the two women as if she didn't like what she was seeing one little bit.

There was a knock on the front door and before I went to open it, Austin and Miss Susan came into the house. They both had furrowed brows and seemed to be upset about something. Miss Susan was able to put on a happy face as soon as she saw the other women. However, Austin's mood did not improve in the least.

They handed me their outer garments.

Austin preceded his wife into the room, and Miss Susan scowled at his back as if she could not believe his bad manners. She wore a navy blue dress paired with a gray lace shawl. She pulled up short. "Oh, I was not aware you had guests again."

It was not unexpected that Miss Susan was surprised. The homestead did not entertain often, and it certainly didn't entertain essentially the same party two meals in a row.

"This is a surprise," Austin agreed.

Mrs. Weston stood. "Is it a good surprise, Mr. Dickinson?"

His face grew red. Miss Lavinia frowned and Miss Susan's face showed utter disgust. However, Emily appeared to be mostly confused, as if she couldn't quite understand why Austin reacted in such a way.

I, too, didn't know.

"You are happy to see me, Austin?" Mrs. Weston asked with a smile.

Austin pulled on the collar of his shirt. "Yes, I am happy to see you and Dr. Weston. He is in my father's study, I gather."

He nodded at the other ladies and left the room.

"You will have to forgive my husband," Miss Susan said. "We haven't been married a year and still some social norms come as a surprise to him."

"I'm sure that you will get him there, Susan," Mrs. Weston said. "I have always had the impression since knowing you that you are able to convince most people to fall in line."

Susan frowned and cleared her throat.

"Emily, you will be happy to know that the child is doing just fine. She's a resilient little thing considering everything that she has been through," Miss Susan said.

"The child is still with you?" Mrs. Weston asked.

"She is. We hope it is a short stay as the police are looking for her relatives," Miss Susan said.

Mrs. Stearns touched a handkerchief to the corner of her

eye. "Every time I think of that little child, tears come to my eyes. It is so good of you, Susan, to take her in."

Miss Susan sat up a little straighter. "It was the Christian thing to do."

Emily made a face at this comment.

"What will become of her?" Lucy asked.

"If she has any family they are likely back in Ireland and as poor as church mice," Mrs. Weston said. "They won't want another mouth to feed."

I held my tongue from saying what Margaret had relayed to me in the kitchen, but I wondered if their opinion of Eve would change if they knew that she possibly came from money.

"The orphanage might be the only answer," Miss Lavinia said.

It was a great concern to me. When I was a child with no father and an ill mother, the fear of one day ending up in the orphanage was very real. And that was the place Henry and I would have been sent if we were lucky. There were worse places.

I believed it was by sheer force of will that our mother lived long enough so I was grown enough to care for Henry and myself. She saved us from that terrifying fate until her last dying breath.

"It happens to so many children, and I am sure that the numbers will go up this winter with the cold. It seems like every day I hear of someone dying in a fire," Mrs. Stearns said. "As always, my husband's focus is on the college, as it should be. We need to preserve it and most importantly, make sure that all the students and faculty are safe during this trying time."

"Hugh Doolan wasn't safe," Emily said. "He worked at the college and was the man who died in the fire alongside his wife."

"Emily," Miss Susan said.

She looked at her sister-in-law. "Shouldn't this be a concern to the college as a whole that a member of their staff died?"

"The death of Hugh and Eve Doolan is a sad tragedy, but it has nothing to do with the college. I am certain of that," Mrs. Stearns said.

I was far less certain, and I knew Emily would agree with me on that.

CHAPTER SIXTEEN

I WASN'T ABLE TO slip away to the Evergreens until well after dark, when all of my tasks around the house were complete. The tasks were increased tenfold after the luncheon because all of the good linen had to be set to soak overnight and the good china to be washed and dried before being packed up in tidy cloth-lined wooden crates, only to be seen again when another person of importance dined at the homestead.

I found something that Margaret and I finally agreed on, and it was that we both hoped the Dickinsons didn't entertain any more guests for a long while. We both needed to recover.

Margaret was decidedly quiet as we went about our work. She usually liked to grill me about all the goings-on in the dining room, as she was back and forth between the dining room and the kitchen because she did the lion's share of cooking for the family. She wanted to know who was there, what they said, and most important of all, had they liked her food.

On the last part I always told her that they had, whether or not it was true. One white lie to spare her feelings here and there never hurt, and besides, Mr. Dickinson liked her cooking, and his opinion was the only one that mattered as far as her position in the home went.

However, on that evening, she kept her head down and concentrated on her work. Whenever I asked her a question, she didn't so much as grunt. That was just fine with me. I was determined to finish all I had to do with the hope that I could see Norah Rose before she went to bed.

Finally, I set the last saucer in the crate and closed the lid. I carried the heavy box to the pantry, where I set it on the floor next to the others like it. Not for the first time, I wondered why Mrs. Dickinson didn't display her china. It was so very lovely, as it was bone-white with a floral pattern in blue and gold. Instead, it was kept tucked away where it would be safe until bidden to come out and impress strangers. Much like Mrs. Dickinson herself, I realized.

I stepped back into the kitchen as Margaret wiped her hands on a towel. "You worked hard and fast today, Willa. I like this newfound spirit."

"I will do my very best to keep it up, but I must admit that I was motivated because I wish to go to the Evergreens tonight and check on Norah Rose."

The lightness on Margaret's face disappeared. "You should not be tangled up in that mess. And I don't believe that Miss Dickinson should have brought the girl anywhere close to the family."

"What was Miss Dickinson to do? Norah Rose had nowhere to go. It's only temporary until her family can be found."

"They won't find any family for her here, and her family in Ireland won't want her. You can quote me on that." She hung her apron on the hook by the door.

"Why do you say that? Do you know something?" I asked.

But she had already gone out the door. I was speaking to an empty room.

As I bundled up in my cloak, mittens, scarf, and bonnet to cross the lawn between the homestead and the Evergreens, I wondered about Margaret's reaction. Typically, she was indifferent or amused by the situations that the Dickinsons found themselves in.

I opened the back door to find that the path that Horace Church had shoveled for the staff was gone. In its place were large drifts of snow, some almost waist height. I nearly turned back.

The logical side of my mind told me that it would be better to go in the morning when it was light out and after Horace had cut a path, but I couldn't make myself wait. I had an indescribable pull toward Norah Rose. I had to know that she was safe and comfortable, and after that I could rest.

The drifts were the very worst up against the house where the snow was stopped from making its way across the yard and piled upward. Using a broom, I broke through the drift the best that I could. When I came out of the other side of it, I was covered head to toe in snow, but it was not stopping me.

Thankfully, it was so cold that the snow was light and powdery. If it had been heavy wet snow I would have been trapped. I stuck the broom in a snowbank and promised myself I would remember to take it inside when I returned.

Thankfully, the snow on the path between the two homes

wasn't as deep, as the tree line blocked it from blowing too far into the interior of the yard.

As I made my way to the Evergreens, I couldn't see the gardens where I had spent so much of my time the spring and summer before. It was times like this that I had to remind myself that spring would indeed come again, as far away as it felt.

I hurried to the back door of the Evergreens and was relieved to find it unlocked. I blew in with the snow. Katie, the maid, jumped up from where she was sitting at a table soaking her hands in a pot of hot water. Steam rose from the metal pot. "Willa Noble, you gave me a start. You shouldn't barge in on people like that."

"I'm very sorry, Katie," I said. "I was just trying to make it in the house with as little snow as possible."

"That seems hard to do. All we have around here nowadays is snow, snow, snow. It makes me want to move south to a warmer place. I heard from a cousin that Georgia is always hot. Not that there is much domestic work there for an Irish girl like me. They force enslaved people to do our jobs below the Mason-Dixon Line. That's what I heard at least. Why pay me a living wage if they have free labor?"

"They should pay their workers. It would be more equal for all of us," I said, thinking of the Black men and women I had met when I visited Washington with the Dickinsons, and thinking of Jeremiah, who would be enslaved if he didn't live here in Amherst with us.

She laughed. "Who says that as if anyone other than the poor care about such things? That's not been the case in my experience. I can tell you that. I'm soaking my hands because the rich don't care about us. Do you know Mrs. Dickinson had me shovel the front steps? That's not my job, but I had to do it, nonetheless. Even with my mittens on, my fingers turned ice-cold."

That explained the pot of steaming water.

"I believe Horace is the one who usually does that," I said. "He was at the college today. They had extra work for him because they plan to resume classes soon despite the weather. The worst of the snow is supposed to be over. It is just the cold that we will continue to contend with."

"Yes, I heard that. Still, I don't think that it's my place to shovel. I have enough to do already when the day maids can't come to work due to the cold." She shook her head in disgust.

"Do some of the maids come from Kelley Square?"

"They all do. My family is there too."

"Did you know the Doolans?"

She sighed. "It is terrible, isn't it? Just terrible. The whole community is up in arms about it. It shouldn't have happened. Hugh was a janitor. He should have known better than most that the chimney needed upkeep, but it's like they say, the cobbler's children go barefoot, yes?"

"The chimney is blamed for the fire."

"Isn't it always when it is running all day and night these last several weeks?" she asked.

"Did you know the Doolans well? Were they friends?" I asked.

She shook her head. "I didn't know them well. I could pick them out in a crowd and chat on the street with them. They went to mass when the priest visited from a neighboring town, as there is not a Catholic church in Amherst. My family goes to mass, too, when we can. My mother has been beside herself since she heard the news, and then when she learned that their daughter was staying here where I worked, she was fit to be tied. She has sent me no less than three notes to warn me to be careful because of what happened to the Doolans. She cautioned me not to get attached to the child too. What does the little girl have to do with all of this? She's the one I feel for the most."

"What was the warning?" I asked.

She licked her lips. "There is a rumor that the Doolans were *murdered*."

I didn't tell her that it appeared that that wasn't just a rumor, but the truth.

"She told me if they were murdered, then they must have been up to something dangerous, and I need to stay away from the girl if that's true because she might be the next target." She shook her head. "Why would anyone want to hurt an eight-year-old girl? Even if her parents were up to something, she would know nothing about it."

I agreed with her, but then I remembered that Matthew had said just about the same thing that Katie's mother did. Matthew making that comment certainly gave it a little more weight.

"People in Amherst know Norah Rose is here?" I asked.

"Oh yes. Everyone in the community does at least. If they know, so do their employers. Gossip goes both ways in society."

"What community do you mean?" I asked as I removed my bonnet and scarf. How I longed for warm summer days when I didn't have to disrobe every time I came inside.

"The Irish workers, everyone in Kelley Square, of course."

This was the longest conversation that I had ever had with Katie, but it seemed when her hands were forced to be still in a bowl of hot water, she was willing to talk. The other times that I had come to the Evergreens she was always a flurry of activity. Mrs. Austin Dickinson wanted her home to be as spotless as the homestead and held her servants to the highest standard. She liked things to be just so, but I also believed she wanted to prove to her mother-in-law that she was just as good of a home manager as Mrs. Edward Dickinson, if not better.

Katie wiggled her fingers in the water as if to check that they still worked. "My mother is full of superstitions that she brought with her from Ireland," she continued. "I bet her warning has something to do with that. I have learned to ignore her as I've gotten older."

As she had gotten older? Katie was nineteen if she was a day.

"If your mother went to church with them, I just wonder if she knew something more."

Katie shrugged. "My mother gave me good advice in her way. She told me to stay out of it, and that's just what I plan to do." She looked up at me. "That's some advice for you to take, too, Willa. We all know that you are too close to Miss Dickinson. That won't serve you well in the long run. We can never truly be their friends. I hope you learn that before you get burned."

"Burned" was an odd choice of words considering we had just been speaking about the unfortunate Doolans.

Katie cleared her throat. "Miss Dickinson is in the parlor with Mrs. Dickinson and Norah Rose. I assume that's why you are here."

I knew she had to be talking about Mrs. Austin Dickinson.

There was no way Emily's mother would have dared come outside in this weather, especially after dark.

I nodded and left the kitchen in the direction of the parlor. Hearing that Emily was already at the Evergreens didn't come to me as a surprise.

Hushed voices greeted me as I reached the open door. "If the police can find no one else to take her, we have no choice other than to contact the orphanage in Boston. I hate to do it, but that is the way it must be. We cannot keep her."

"I can't care for a child," Emily said as if the very idea was terrifying. "I have no aspirations to be a mother, but you and Austin can care for her. You want children, don't you?"

"Do you think your father wouldn't have a word or two to say about that? He wants Austin to have a son and carry on the Dickinson name. A daughter outside of the bloodline will not be an acceptable replacement in his eyes."

"You and Austin are married. You are making your own life. You should be able to make your own family as you see fit."

"Your brother would have to spend time with me to accomplish that." Her voice was bitter.

Emily's cheeks turned pink. "Yes, I know."

"He has been far too busy with the law firm. He is determined to prove to your father that he is capable of taking it over someday. When he is not at work, he's trying to prove himself to your father in other ways, helping at the college, volunteering at the church. The list goes on and on. I have always been told that as a married woman, you compete against your husband's mother. That has not been the case when it comes to Austin. It has been against his father from the very beginning."

Norah Rose sat on the floor on the opposite side of the parlor, stacking blocks over and over and then knocking them down. She was likely too old to be playing with such toys, but it might have been all that Miss Susan had on hand. As she'd said, she and Austin had not started a family of their own yet.

Emily looked up and saw me standing in the door. "Willa, there you are. I was wondering when you would arrive. We're glad that you are here."

Miss Susan sipped her tea and didn't appear to be nearly as pleased as Emily was.

CHAPTER SEVENTEEN

"I WANTED TO STOP by to see how Norah Rose was faring before I went to bed. I hope that is all right." I directed the last bit of my statement to Miss Susan.

Miss Susan gave the slightest of nods. Emily, on the other hand, smiled brightly. "We are glad that you are here. You seem to be the only one that Norah Rose has any interest in speaking to. She has said no more than five words to Susan and me combined."

I glanced at Norah Rose and saw that she was no longer fiddling with the blocks, but instead she was watching me so intently I wondered if my hair might have stood on end when I removed my bonnet.

"Why don't you try to talk to her?" Emily suggested.

With Emily and Miss Susan watching me, I sat down on the cold floor across from Norah Rose. I picked up one of the blocks and turned it over in my hand. The letter C was inscribed on one side of the block and on the opposite side there was a carving of a cat. I wondered if these blocks had been Miss Lavinia's when she had been small because she would certainly have approved of the cat block.

"Have you enjoyed playing with these?" I asked.

She looked me in the eye. "I'm eight. I am too old for blocks." Her voice was crisp and clear.

I let out a breath that I hadn't even known I had been holding. I'd feared that she wouldn't speak to me again, that I had been away from her too long and she'd gone back into the shell she had created to protect herself.

"Norah Rose, I'm Willa. I brought you to this house this morning."

"I remember." She stacked the blocks again, but this time she didn't knock them over. "Why did you bring me here? Why couldn't I stay with you like yesterday? I felt better when you were near. You have the same quiet sweetness of my mam."

I swallowed and felt a pang in my heart. After I lost my own mother, all that I had ever wanted was the calm, steady presence she had provided me with until the day she had passed. Even in her last hours, she had been focused on Henry and me and how we were feeling. It sounded to me that Eve Doolan had been much the same to her daughter. The only difference was she did not have the time like my mother did to prepare her child for this lonely separation between earth and heaven. Their separation was abrupt, like a tree severed in half by lightning.

"Miss Susan's house is a better place for you," I said. "She has the time and space to care for you properly."

"Then, why can't you stay here?"

"I am a maid in the house next door. I do not make the choice as to where I sleep."

She frowned but did not argue with me on that point.

"Do you understand what happened to your parents?" I asked.

Tears came to her eyes, and I felt my eyes watering as well.

"They are dead. I know this."

"Do you have any other family in town?"

She shook her head.

It was both what I expected and what I feared she might say. Miss Susan was perhaps right that Norah Rose was destined for the orphanage. However, I reminded myself that there might be a relative or family friend in Ireland, or even in another part of Massachusetts who might be willing to take her. She might not have known everyone in her parents' lives. I vowed not to give up hope that someone would be found to raise her.

"What do you remember about yesterday?" I asked.

Behind me I could feel Emily's and Miss Susan's eyes boring into my back. They were hanging on to every word. At least Miss Susan was, because when I looked over my shoulder at Emily, I saw that she had that faraway look in her eye. I was sure that she planned to include what Norah Rose had said in her next poem. The look on her face could mean only that she was searching for the right words.

"There was a fire," Norah Rose answered.

I nodded encouragingly.

"My father said we had to get out. We tried, but the doors wouldn't open. He broke a window and set me outside. He told me to hide in the trees and he would be there with my mother straight away. He never came."

What had happened when Hugh Doolan had gone back for

Eve? Had the smoke grown too thick, and he lost his way? Was that possible? The home had been so small with only one floor.

"What is the next thing you remember?" I asked.

Norah Rose glanced at Emily. "Her dog licked my cheek."

I sat back on my heels. I didn't know what else to ask her. I knew everything that had happened to Norah Rose after the moment that Carlo found her.

"My, Willa," Miss Susan said. "Norah Rose certainly was able to tell you more than anyone else. What a terrible accident."

"It wasn't an accident," Norah Rose said, looking directly at Miss Susan for the first time. "My parents were murdered."

The room fell silent, save for the crackling of the flames in the fireplace. Having fire so close to us was disconcerting considering my conversation with Norah Rose, but the winter weather required fires at all hours of the day or night.

"Don't be ridiculous," Miss Susan said. "It was a mere accident."

"It was not," Norah Rose snapped with more emotion than she'd expressed the entire time we had known her. "My parents were killed. My father said it was going to happen, and he was right."

Miss Susan and I gasped at her pronouncement, but Emily didn't appear moved or surprised. She nodded like she expected Norah Rose to say this all along.

"When did he say this?" Emily asked.

Norah Rose appeared to withdraw into herself when Emily asked the question. The anger and frustration that animated her face just moments ago disappeared behind a protective wall.

It pained me to see her slip away.

Emily nodded when the girl didn't answer her, as if she understood that at times a person needed to pull away to protect herself. Miss Susan, on the other hand, was not so understanding.

"Are you going to answer the question?" she demanded.

"Susan, please, the child has had a very long day, and Officer Thomas will be here tomorrow to speak to her. Let her rest. The days to come will be difficult."

I gave a sigh of relief at Emily's words. It was true that Norah Rose needed to rest. The more she was pushed, the less she would trust us. We needed her to trust us if we wanted to find out what happened to her parents.

One thing was certain though. I believed her. I believed that her parents had been murdered, and I feared because of it, this orphaned child in our care was in grave danger.

CHAPTER EIGHTEEN

THE NEXT MORNING after the breakfast dishes were washed, dried, and tucked away, Emily came looking for me in the laundry. She looked smart in a navy gingham dress and had seemed to spend extra time on her dark red locks. They were tucked into an elaborate knot on the back of her head. "Willa, are you ready to go?"

I looked up from clothes that I was sorting for washing. "Go, miss?"

"Yes, we have to visit the Boyles. I am sorry that we didn't have the chance to do it yesterday after the luncheon, but I had a poem stirring in my brain and I had to tame it before my mind would rest."

I had forgotten about our promise to visit the Boyles.

"I should check with Margaret," I said.

Emily waved her hand as if Margaret should not be a concern. "I have told her. I also informed her that Father will be at the office all day, Mother has taken to her bed, and Vinnie can fend for herself when it comes to meals or anything else she requires. Margaret won't have to worry about a thing."

I pressed my lips together because I knew that wasn't true. If the family had no need for her, Margaret would move on to other tasks that we typically didn't have time for, such as polishing the silver or dusting Mr. Dickinson's books. In a home this large and of so much import to the town of Amherst there was always a long list of duties to be done.

If Emily thought that we just cared for the family she was so very wrong.

I knew Margaret would be angry at me for leaving yet again, and I wondered how much longer we could go on like this, where it appeared that I could come and go as I pleased. Or I could come and go at Emily's whims. There had to be a breaking point when Margaret would no longer tolerate it.

Even so, I wanted to go to Kelley Square just as much as Emily did. I had to find someone who knew more about Norah Rose's family so that we might contact them. If I could find that information before Matthew returned to the Evergreens to speak to Norah Rose, perhaps he could write to the family in Dublin.

It pained me to think of Norah Rose traveling that far, and to a country where she had never been and knew little about. Would she travel alone? How would she get there? There were so many questions dancing in my head over this possibility, but I pushed them away the best that I could. There was no reason to leap too far ahead of myself.

I gathered up my cloak and bonnet.

"Why is there a broom out in the snow?" Emily asked.

"That's my fault. I'm glad we came upon it before Horace did. He would give me an earful about it."

"I don't know that we will see much of Horace for the next few days. Father said at breakfast that he will be at the college helping the other custodian until they hire a replacement."

I nodded. I had expected as much. He might not do it happily, but Horace could always be counted on to lend a hand wherever there might be a need.

The sky was high, and the air was cold, but the sun shone down on our heads. It felt like a kiss. Even though it was so cold, just having sunshine to guide us on our walk felt like a gift.

Carlo ran ahead of us as always and barged through any and every snowdrift that he could see. He was enjoying the sunny morning as well.

I wished that it was just a normal morning stroll like I would take with Emily in the summer when we would go into the woods and collect plants for her garden or inspiration for her poems. This walk was much different. We headed away from the woods toward the narrow lanes and alleys of Kelley Square.

Even though the fire was two days ago, when we were within a few hundred yards of Kelley Square, the scent of fire still hung in the air.

The Doolans' home had been just inside the square, so it was one of the first buildings when walking from the homestead and the train station. I had passed it hundreds of times throughout my life, and never noticed. I never thought about the people who lived there. I hadn't thought of Kelley Square much at all after my mother moved us away from the community.

However, walking through the sunshine into the square, memories came back of playing tag with my brother and the other children in the neighborhood, the smell of corned beef being fried in a skillet, and an old man playing a fiddle while sitting on an overturned bucket by his front door. It had not been all bad living there. It was good to remember that.

I was a bit out of breath as we walked to the front of the Boyle house. As we did, I pulled up short as I saw the rubble of Norah Rose's home across the street. It was the first time that I saw the wreckage in the daylight. The remains were even more shocking in the light of day. The only piece of the structure that remained upright was the chimney, and even that looked as if a light breeze would topple it to the ground.

A cast-iron frying pan sat in the rubble, and seeing it made my heart hurt. Other things were even more difficult to see. The remains of a picture frame and of a lamp—articles of everyday life that were gone. Whatever drawing or artwork had been in the frame was gone. I feared it might have been a daguerreotype of Norah Rose's parents. If that was true, it had been incinerated with the rest of their lives.

There was a thin layer of snow over the burnt building now, which somehow made it seem even sadder.

I had hoped that there might be something I could salvage from the burnt home to take back to Norah Rose, but there appeared to be nothing that wasn't blackened beyond recognition or frozen to the ground.

"It looks much worse this morning," Emily said.

I nodded.

"Truly, it is a miracle that Norah Rose survived. We must not forget that. She was spared for a reason."

I nodded. Ahead of us, I spotted Mrs. Turnkey walking up the street and carrying a market bag.

"Heavens me! I am glad to see you here, Miss Dickinson," Mrs. Turnkey said. "I was not surprised when you didn't come yesterday. I do make some allowance for what has occurred. The ladies are working harder than ever to raise funds and awareness so that accidents like this don't happen again." She eyed Emily. "Even so, we cannot take time off from the cause due to tragedy."

"Hello, Mrs. Turnkey," Emily said. "We are here to call on the Boyles."

She pointed at the heavy basket in my hands that had everything from canned beans and beets, to flour, molasses, and apples. I had taken everything from the pantry that Margaret had been willing to spare. It took some negotiations. Without the trains running, it would be very difficult to get these items restocked in the pantry anytime soon, so I had taken only duplicate items for the most part.

"I see. I suppose late is better than never, and I have to say that many of the ladies about town who volunteered to minister to a family in Kelley Square did not show up yesterday either. I was here, of course. I won't let a little soot and smoke keep me from helping others. It is my calling as a Christian woman and good citizen of Amherst." She straightened her shoulders. Mrs. Turnkey's fox wrap lay across her shoulders like the dead animal that it was. I tried not to look at it too closely.

Every time I saw it, I thought of the sweet little fox who lost his life for her sense of fashion. I knew that some viewed foxes as a nuisance, but I never saw them that way. I loved their smiles and mischief. Maybe it was because they reminded me of Henry, who many had also viewed as a nuisance when he was alive.

Mrs. Turnkey glanced at the burnt home. "Is it true that little Norah Rose Doolan is staying with your family?"

Emily nodded. "She is staying with my brother, Austin, and his wife."

She furrowed her brow to the point that her dark eyebrows looked like a caterpillar across her face.

Mrs. Turnkey frowned. "There are very many families in Kelley Square. Shouldn't she be with her people?"

"Her people?" Emily asked.

"The Irish."

"I was told that she doesn't have any other family in Amherst, and I have been told that everyone in Kelley Square is aware of whom she is staying with. You know how rumors travel around town. I would think if any of the square's residents had a close relationship with the Doolans they would have come forward by now to call on her. Or at least inquired about her well-being. No one has."

Mrs. Turnkey sniffed. "This is very unfortunate news. I hate to say it, but the girl is destined for the orphanage in Boston. As I work with so many charities that the Ladies' Society of Amherst raises funds for, I can reach out to them and see if they have any openings. During this cold snap, I am sure if they are not full, they are close to it. When a family is starving, the children are the first to be sent on their way."

I shivered at her words and how she talked about families

abandoning their children in such a matter-of-fact way. I could not understand it. I didn't know if I would ever be a mother, but if I were, I would guard that child with every fiber of my being.

"That's awful," Emily said, clearly having the same line of thinking that I did. "Families should be together."

Mrs. Turnkey shook her head. "It's not that simple. You would know this if you interacted with the impoverished more. It is my belief that privileged women have a calling from God to help the less fortunate."

"I don't know that I want to know more sad tales like this." Emily tightened her scarf around her throat. "Knowing nothing is protective."

"It's protective, but that does not serve anything on the road to progress. You could join the Ladies' Society of Amherst. It is our mission to bring awareness to such failures in society."

Emily folded her arms. "I am a solitary creature, Mrs. Turnkey. I am happy to help here and there, but I cannot commit to joining a group of any kind."

"That is a shame, as we have a thrilling meeting scheduled in two nights' time. We have put our meetings off for far too long due to the weather. We can't let these conditions stop us so easily. The Ladies' Society is essential for not just helping those less fortunate but also in the business of building up women. However, I do not mind that the meeting was postponed, as we now have the opportunity to hear Lucy Stone speak. I'm sure you've heard of her. She is a leader in equality for women of all groups and communities. It could be a rousing discussion."

"I had not heard of her until yesterday." Emily cocked her head. "But I have met her. She came to our home as Mrs. Stearns's guest for luncheon yesterday. She seems like a fascinating woman, but I didn't have much opportunity to ask her about her lectures. As you can imagine, the main topic of discussion at the meal was the fire."

Mrs. Turnkey nodded. "I would assume that would be the conversation over every meal in Amherst over the last day. Whether you join groups or not, you should come and hear for yourself what she has to say. I believe that it will stir something deep in the heart of every woman in attendance. Bring your sister and brother's wife with you as well. I would invite your mother, but I don't believe she should come out in the cold considering her poor health."

"This is very true," Emily said. "Thank you for the invitation. I think we will come. You have made me quite curious about what she may have to say."

Mrs. Turnkey smiled. "Very good, and when you come to the lecture, you might be surprised what you learn about the Ladies' Society. It might be something that will change your mind altogether."

We had been standing on the side of the road by the sad remains of the Doolan home for a long while, long enough to gain the attention of the neighbors. The front door of the Boyles' home opened, and my stomach turned as I saw Danny Boyle in a checkered coat, top hat, and pipe hanging from his mouth, poised in the doorway. I had not seen him in a very long time, but I knew him straightaway.

"I see the Boyles are ready for your visit. I have a few more calls to make in the square myself," Mrs. Turnkey said. "I will be off on my way." She nodded at Danny. "Mr. Boyle."

She hurried away. It seemed to me that she wanted to avoid Danny Boyle just as much as I did.

Danny chewed on the end of his pipe, and when Mrs. Turnkey was gone, he looked at Emily and me, but instead of addressing Emily, he spoke to me. "Well, if it isn't burly Willa Noble in the flesh."

As he said that, I realized Danny Boyle had not changed one single bit.

CHAPTER NINETEEN

Danny Boyle gnawed on the end of his pipe. "What brings you back to the square? I had heard that you were working for rich folks in Amherst." He glanced at Emily. "Is she the rich folks?" He laughed at his own joke.

"Burly? Did you call her burly?" Emily asked. "Is that any way to speak to someone who is bringing you alms?"

He removed his pipe from his mouth and dumped the ashes at our feet. I had to jump back to keep them from landing on my shoes. "The description fits her. Willa has always been as big as a man, even when she was a child. My father told me she would be the type that could give you a litter of babies."

I felt sick to my stomach and my face was red with humiliation. I had dreaded coming to the Boyles' because I knew it was likely I would see Danny. I had thought at best he would not recognize me and at worst he would make a snide comment. I didn't know that he would behave as horribly as this.

Emily glared at him. "You are speaking to a Dickinson right now, so I would watch your tongue if I were you. My father has a great deal of influence in Amherst."

He turned his gaze to her. "Oh, I know. And your brother does, too, when he is not flirting with women who are not his wife."

Emily jerked back as if she had been slapped across the face. "How dare you say such a thing."

"I dare to say whatever I wish. You do not own me. The rich may think that they own the poor, but it is the poor's choice to hold themselves back from retaliation. Have you not heard of the French Revolution?"

Emily glared at him.

"Are you surprised that I know of such moments in history, then? That is a judgment on your part, is it not?"

"I am not surprised. I am relieved to see the public school system has served you well."

He barked a laugh.

I touched her arm as if to tell her it was time for us to go, but Emily Dickinson never gave up so easily.

She shook off my hand. "We are not here to debate society or history. We have brought this basket of food for your family on behalf of the Ladies' Society of Amherst."

"My family has no need of your charity. Just because I am Irish does not make me a beggar."

"We are not saying you or anyone else in Kelley Square is a beggar. We are just offering gifts to help you through the cold, dark winter."

"We have no need of them," he repeated.

He stepped back into the doorway of his house and was about to close the door when Emily called, "What did you see the night that the Doolan house burned?"

"Why do you think I saw anything at all?"

"You are the closest neighbor. You would have had the best view of the fire."

"I would if I had been home. I wasn't home."

"Where were you?" Emily asked.

"That is not a question you have a right to ask, as it is none of your business."

"It is the police's business. Have you already spoken to the police?" Emily asked.

"I have no use for the police. They are against the Irish and would blame us for every wrong that befalls this town. I will not take the blame for the fire as well."

"Was your wife home the night of the fire?" Emily asked. She was determined not to give up until Danny gave her something that would help our investigation.

"She was home. She is always home because that is where I tell her to be. If she was not in the place I told her to be, that would cause a great deal of trouble for her."

Emily made a face. "If that is true, can we talk to her?"

Danny stared at Emily with an incredulous look on his face. "No. You can't talk to her. She saw nothing. She saw nothing because I told her to see nothing. She would not be looking out the window at the fire when she was caring for my children."

"What is her name?" I asked. It was the first question that I managed to get out of my mouth since seeing Danny for the first time.

"Moira. Not that it is of any import. She's my wife, and that is all you need to know. I will not let my family be bothered by a woman who has no family at all." He looked me straight in the eye. "How awful that Henry was trampled to death by a horse. It seems fitting."

"Watch your mouth," I snapped.

"Or what? You will run to your daddy for help?"

Confusion washed over me. Why would he say that?

My answer came a second later when he continued, "Truly, I thought you were knocking on doors to ask after your father."

"What do you mean? Danny, I'm not in the mood for your riddles."

"Your father. He is here back in Kelley Square, but I would have thought that you knew that. You are his daughter after all. Would he not come to your door first if you were of any import to him?"

Emily's head swiveled in my direction.

"I know that you are a liar, Danny, but don't tell such hateful stories! It is too low, even for you."

He shrugged. "It's not a lie. Damien Noble is here in Amherst, and he is looking for you."

With that, he slammed the door in our faces.

Emily and I both jumped back, startled.

"Willa, are you all right?" Emily asked as we walked back to the pile of rubble that had been the Doolans' home.

I shook my head. "I—I need to breathe."

"Willa?" Emily asked in concern.

"I just need one minute. One minute." I hurried away from her, down an alley behind the Boyles' house.

I felt a sob gathering in my gut, moving up to my chest and

then to my throat. I pushed it down so it would not come out of my mouth. What was my father doing in Amherst? Was he really in Amherst looking for me as Danny said? I didn't trust Danny or believe him, but still my mind raced.

"Miss, miss, do you need help?" a high-pitched voice asked.

I looked up to find a thin, petite woman. Her cheeks were drawn, and she had a baby on her hip with a toddler clinging to her skirt, which was stained with jam and heaven knew what else. Even though she was young, maybe even younger than my twenty-two years, there were silver threads in her dark hair as if her locks could no longer hold on to the color because of hardship.

I took a few gulps of air before I answered her. I didn't want to start crying because if I did, I knew that I might never stop. Henry wouldn't want that. He would want me to be strong. He would expect me to be strong.

I didn't even know why Danny's words affected me in such a way. Perhaps it was being back in the square and the heightened emotions that came with it. Surely, Danny was lying about my father. He had been a cruel boy and grown into a cruel man.

I was glad that I had taken a minute away. Emily was kind to me and a friend, but it was hard to explain to her what I had been through when considering her sheltered life. I knew her life wasn't perfect—no life was—but some lives were more difficult. I knew that too.

I glanced around as I gathered myself in the alleyway. The snow had not been shoveled away back here, but there was a clear path left by dozens of feet walking behind the house to another row of houses. There were no gardens or yards to speak of, just rows and rows of homes, some of which I knew could house two or three different families inside them.

I thought of the Dickinsons' vast property and how open and spacious it was, how the gardens on summer mornings shone with dew. I was blessed to have landed there, and I would never take it for granted.

"Miss?" the young woman asked again. Over the arm not holding the baby, she carried a basket much like the one I held, but not nearly as full.

"I'm sorry. I just had a little attack of the hysterics. I am fine now."

She studied me. Her complexion was bright red from being exposed to the cold for far longer than was safe.

She then nodded and began walking toward the Boyle home.

"Are you Mrs. Boyle?" I called after her.

She nodded. Her eyes were blank, and I felt like I might be sick. I had hoped when I'd learned that Danny had married and now had children, that he would be a changed man. That perhaps he was caring and affectionate to his family, that he worked hard to provide them with everything that they needed. It appeared that was not the case.

"Yes," she said. "I am Moira Boyle." She said her name in a dull tone that lacked feeling and a confidence in who she was.

I held out the basket. "I'm Willa Noble. I'm a maid to the Dickinson family here in Amherst. We are working with the Ladies' Society of Amherst to provide for families in need during this terrible winter weather. The Dickinsons would like to help you and your children."

She licked her lips when she looked at the basket. There

was no question that she was hungry. Her children must have been hungry, too, but she would be even more so because as their mother she would give them all she had before taking care of herself. That was the plight and gift of mothers.

"I will have to ask my husband if I can take it. He does not wish us to take charity even when money is tight. He says that it looks poorly on him as the man of the house. I don't think he will like it." Her face fell.

"I know that he won't like it," I said. "I just offered the basket to him, and he rejected it."

She looked over her shoulder. "Then I can't accept it. I can't take the risk."

I held it out to her. "Could you take it without telling him?"

Usually, I didn't condone lying to one's spouse, but in the case of Danny Boyle, I would make an exception.

She hesitated.

"There are canned beans, beets, flour, molasses, and apples. There is butter and honey in there too."

She shuddered. "I will take it, but it's for the children."

"Of course," I agreed. "You are making the right choice for your children."

She nodded as if she was trying to convince herself. I walked over to her, and she took the basket from my hands. I wanted to offer to carry it for her, but I knew that if Danny saw us together, she would be in a great deal of trouble.

"Thank you," she whispered. Her Irish accent was thick. It was much different from Danny's, who barely had an accent at all. "You have been very kind."

"You're most welcome. If you ever need anything, anything

at all, again, I'm Willa. I work for the Dickinsons. You can find me there."

She nodded, but I would be shocked if she ever came to the back door of the Dickinson home asking for help.

I tucked the cuff of my mitten into the sleeve of my coat. "We had planned to bring you the basket yesterday but were sidetracked due to the fire."

Tears were in her eyes. "You will have to excuse me. I'm just so broken up over Eve and Hugh. They were the kindest people. Eve always made a little extra of her cakes and cookies and brought them over for the children. She only did so when Danny wasn't here, of course. She was my friend." She shook her head. "I feel awful about little Norah Rose. She is such a darling child. Even though she was so young herself, she watched my children many a time when I needed to complete tasks around the home. I would never have been able to get them done without her help. I don't know what I am going to do now." Tears rolled down her cheeks. "But my heart is broken for her most of all. I know what it feels like to be utterly alone. I wish there was something that I could do, but I can't bring her into this." She lowered her voice. "You can understand that, can't you? My children and I are barely getting by. I am afraid what Danny would say if I even suggested it."

The very last place I would want to put Norah Rose was in Danny Boyle's home.

"Do you have other children too?" I asked.

"I just have these two, and I am doing my very best for there to be no more." She didn't meet my eyes when she said that.

I bit my lip, not wanting to ask her how she was managing that because I feared that I would find the answer disturbing.

"Since you are a friend of the Doolans, I feel like I can tell you that Norah Rose is safe. She is staying with the Dickinsons."

Her shoulders sagged as if she was greatly relieved.

"For Norah Rose's sake, my mistress, Miss Emily Dickinson, and I are trying to find out what caused the fire."

Her eyes were wide. "Why would you do that?"

"To know if it was an accident or not. If it wasn't, the person behind their deaths needs to be held responsible."

She began to shake. "I don't believe that is wise. It is too dangerous."

"Because someone set the fire?" I asked. "Is that why you are so afraid? What do you know?"

She shook her head. That was one question she would not answer. "I need to get my children inside. It's far too cold for them out here."

I knew she was right, but I had one more question. "Can you tell me what you saw the night of the fire? Was anyone around?"

She looked me in the eye. "Nothing. I saw nothing. Take that as the truth."

Just because she wanted me to take something as truth didn't mean that it was truth.

CHAPTER TWENTY

I STEPPED OUT OF the alley and found Emily in the middle of the burnt house. Carlo pawed at the scorched rubble, and Emily looked everything over as if she were Dupin in Edgar Allan Poe's *The Murders in the Rue Morgue*. It made me wonder if Emily discovered her interest in solving crimes from those stories.

However, the most worrisome part was the state of her cloak and boots. Both were covered with soot, as was Carlo's fur. I could just imagine what Margaret would have to say about that when we arrived home.

Although it was difficult to tell the layout of the house because it had been burned to the very ground, I knew where the front and back doors were, based on the piles of blackened rocks that were at the front and back of the house. Those were the rocks that had kept the family trapped inside the home and sentenced Eve and Hugh to their deaths. I shuddered.

"Emily, you will ruin your boots," I said. "And Carlo's paws are filthy."

"Shoes can be replaced, and paws can be washed," came her answer.

Truly spoken by the person who would clean neither.

"Willa, come in here. I have something to show you."

I hesitated at first. My boots and cloak were not so easily replaced. However, curiosity won out. I wanted to see what Emily had found just as much as she wanted to show me.

Tentatively, I made my way into the remains of the house. I took care to lift my skirts and the edges of my cloak high. I felt a cold draft as a result, but it was better than the alternative of ruining my garments.

I considered each step I took and found Emily in what must have once been the bedroom because I could just make out the shape of a bed emblazoned on the soot-covered ground.

Emily, who didn't care a bit about getting her clothes dirty, squatted in front of an old steamer truck.

She had it open. Inside, the fabrics were blackened but not completely destroyed. She held up a small frame for me to see.

It was a daguerreotype of a young woman. She couldn't have been more than sixteen in the picture. Her hair was piled on the top of her head in soft curls. She wore a high lace collar and a string of pearls hung from her neck. She was beautiful. Even in the black-and-white image, I could see the resemblance to Norah Rose straightaway.

I flipped it over and on the brown backing of the frame was writing in pencil that read, *To Hugh with love from your Eve.*

"It's Norah Rose's mother," I whispered.

Emily nodded.

"What else is in the trunk?" I asked.

"Clothing," Emily said. "But from what I can tell all of it is ruined."

I nodded. "If nothing else, this portrait was worth our trip to Kelley Square today. I know Norah Rose will always cherish it."

"I don't understand how she could have such a picture if she was poor. Do you have a daguerreotype of your mother?"

Her question pained me because the only way I was able to remember what my mother had looked like was by foggy recollections in the back of my mind that became more faded with the passage of each year. There were many times when I wondered if the same curse would befall my memories of Henry. I could not lose the image of them and be able to go on.

"I do not," I said, and left it at that. I wrapped the picture in my scarf and tucked it inside of my cloak. "Eve Doolan didn't start out as poor. I haven't had the time to tell you what I learned from Margaret yesterday."

Emily's eyes sparkled with interest. "Do tell."

"I will on the way home. Officer Thomas will be there soon to talk to Norah Rose, and we should be there."

She agreed, and then she looked at my hands. "What happened to your market basket?"

"I will tell you that on the way home as well."

I was grateful on the walk back to the Dickinsons' property that Emily let me tell her the stories I was willing to share. She didn't pry into how I knew Danny or his comment about my father being back in Amherst. I knew that the latter had to be a lie. My father would never come back to Amherst. He'd made that clear when he left. To be honest, I didn't even know if he was dead or alive. As horrible as it was to say this about my own father, I didn't think I cared either way.

By the time we walked the short distance from the street to the Evergreens, I was frozen to the quick. It wasn't snowing, but the temperature had dropped very low. I guessed the air temperature was lucky to be holding at ten degrees.

Emily walked briskly down the path, and I was grateful for that. I could not wait to get in out of the cold.

She walked around the house to the grand front door, and I could do nothing but follow. It didn't appear that Horace had shoveled a path to the back door to the Evergreens as he had for the homestead.

Emily went straight into the house and into the parlor. She removed her bonnet as she entered the room and handed it back to me. I caught it just before it hit the floor and then I helped her out of her cloak.

Miss Susan and Austin were in such an intense conversation by the fire that they didn't notice Emily's grand entrance.

"We can't keep the girl indefinitely," Austin said. "She needs to be with her own people."

"Her own people?" Miss Susan asked. "What do you mean by that?"

"She's Catholic. We can't have a Catholic in the family."

"That is your reason? Her religion? She is far too young to know what she believes on such matters. If she was in our family, she would not be Catholic."

"She would still be Irish," Austin said.

"And what does that matter? Is your father afraid that she will be the only child we have and an Irish girl would inherit it all? You are both attorneys; you could write up documents to ensure that wouldn't happen."

"Susan, please, I know that you want children, but we want children of our own, not that of a stranger."

While the younger Dickinsons quarreled, I spotted Matthew sitting on a dining room chair across from Norah Rose.

"Susan, Austin," Emily said. "Why are the two of you constantly at odds?"

"We aren't at odds," Miss Susan and Austin said at the same time, and then they glared at each other.

"Of course you aren't," Emily said.

"Emily!" Miss Susan said. "Do not take one more step into this parlor. Your boots are covered in soot. What on earth have you been up to? Did you take a roll in a fireplace?"

"Not at all. Willa and I were looking at the scene of the crime."

At Emily's words, Matthew made eye contact with me, and he didn't appear to be happy with what he heard.

I removed my bonnet and cloak.

Miss Susan nodded to me. "And I suppose it was also your idea to take Willa on such a venture. The two of you are like conjoined twins. Is it too much to ask that just my sister comes to visit, not my sister *and* her maid?"

"Oh, Sister," Emily said. "You know the child only has interest in speaking to Willa. She has to be here."

Matthew stood, and Norah Rose—who was curled into a

ball in the corner of a settee—buried her face into her knees. It was a position I knew well, as I had sat like that many times as a child and even a few times as an adult when I was alone in my room.

Matthew's expression softened when he looked down at the child. He stared at her with such tenderness and care that my heart ached. He would be a wonderful father—one like I'd never had—someday. I knew also that he yearned to have children. Why he was waiting for me to make up my mind was beyond me. There were any number of young women in Amherst who would have married him in a heartbeat.

"Miss Dickinson, Miss Noble, I am glad you are here. Norah Rose said that she will only speak to you, Miss Noble."

I swallowed. I'd expected to hear no less. For whatever reason, Norah Rose and I had a bond that I couldn't explain. Because of it, I had to make sure that she was safe and would go to a loving family after this ordeal. However, after overhearing Miss Susan and Austin's conversation, I guessed that there had been no luck at finding any friends or relatives to take her in yet.

"You spoke to her yesterday?" Matthew asked.

I nodded and lowered my voice. "Both Emily and I did. She said that her parents were murdered."

"By whom?" he asked.

"The only other thing she would say about the matter was that her father predicted that this would happen."

"Hugh Doolan knew that he was in danger." He glanced over his shoulder. "I'm afraid that she might be right. Both doors leaving the house were blocked by rocks."

"That is difficult for me to believe," Austin said. "This is quite ridiculous to think that it was anything other than a terrible accident."

"I don't agree, Mr. Dickinson. The fire appears to have started in a bedroom. From what we know about the layout of similar houses on that street, it was likely the parents' bedroom," Matthew said.

"How did it start?" Miss Susan asked.

"We are trying to find that out. With the home in the condition that it is, it's difficult to determine."

"Then, how can you tell that's where the fire started?"

"Everything in that room was charred beyond recognition, including the bed where it appears Mrs. Doolan had been sleeping when the fire began."

I covered my mouth as the horrible image came to mind. My gaze traveled across the room so that I could reassure myself that Norah Rose had not overheard. She was still curled up in that tight ball with her head buried in her knees. I prayed that meant she couldn't hear anything at all.

Based on Matthew's description of where the fire started, we must have found the steamer trunk in another room in the house, perhaps the living room. If it had been in her parents' room, it would have been destroyed as well. I wanted to give Norah Rose the daguerreotype, but I had to wait until the time was right. Also, I feared that Matthew might want to take it to the police station to examine it. The image needed to be in Norah Rose's hands, not in the hands of the police.

"Why don't you have a superior with you?" Austin wanted to know. "If this is a murder, shouldn't there be someone higher up in the police department to take this case?"

Matthew pulled on his collar. "You are right, and I will be

honest with you that I'm not here in my official capacity. The police chief has decided not to pursue the case."

"But why?" I asked.

All four of the other adults in the room looked at me like they just remembered that I was there. It was not an unusual feeling for a maid to be overlooked.

Matthew cleared his throat. "I can't say."

Emily cocked her head as if she didn't believe him, and I had to agree with her. He couldn't say or he wouldn't say. I believed it was the latter of the two.

Austin shook his head. "Our family cannot be involved in something that the police department didn't sanction."

"Austin, really, he only wants to help the child," Miss Susan said.

He glared at her. "My father spent most of his life rebuilding our family's reputation after my grandfather swindled it away. I won't be the one to destroy it again."

"Your reputation is all that you think about. What about the young man who wanted to go out west to make his own way in the world out from under his father's thumb?"

He narrowed his eyes. "You and my father effectively killed him."

Emily, Matthew, and I stood frozen in the middle of the room. This was not a conversation between a married couple that we wanted to hear.

Austin blinked as if he'd just realized we were still in the room.

"I want nothing to do with this." He scowled at Miss Susan. "I will not kick the child out of my home. I'm not so cruel as that. But if a family member does not come forward in the next fortnight, we will have to find another place for her to go. She is not my child to raise." He left the room.

Miss Susan hurried after him and we heard them arguing in the hall as they went. Their voices grew farther and farther away.

CHAPTER TWENTY-ONE

EMILY CLEARED HER throat. "You will have to forgive my sister and brother. They have not been married long and are still adjusting. Austin very much wants to make a name for himself in law, and Susan wants to run the home well. There are many outside pressures."

She didn't say that most of the outside pressures came from Emily's own father. After hearing Miss Susan and Austin's argument, she didn't have to.

"I do wish we could find family to care for her. That would be the best," Matthew said.

"She does have living family in Dublin." I went on to tell him what Margaret had told me about Eve's well-to-do family in Ireland.

Matthew nodded. "That is promising. With that to go on, I should be able to find them. I will reach out to the police in Dublin. I will write them, but seeing how they are on the other side of the Atlantic, it might take weeks before we hear back."

That's what I was afraid of. We didn't have weeks, according to Austin.

"I will work on my brother, then," Emily said. "He will agree to wait until we hear from her Dubliner family before turning her out of the house. He is a kind man at his core."

"I think we have no other choice."

Across the parlor, Norah Rose made a small sound and lifted her head. "Do I have to leave? I have nowhere to go."

I sat on the settee next to her. "No, no, you don't have to leave. Officer Thomas is looking for your family. Do you have any other family in Amherst?"

She shook her head. "It was always just the three of us. My father brought my mother here before I was born. I don't remember, but that is the story I was told."

"What about family friends? Who were your parents close to?"

She shook her head. "I don't know. They were always working."

"I will write to the Catholic priest tomorrow. That is where your family went to church?" Matthew asked as he sat back down on the dining room chair.

Norah Rose nodded, and her cheeks turned red. "We didn't go often. My parents had to work even on Sundays, and it was too far away for me to walk to Sunday school alone. Many nights my father would read the Bible to us. I think God was happy with that."

I squeezed her hand. "He was very happy indeed."

"Perhaps the priest there will give us someone else to turn to if our first plan fails." He cleared his throat. "Norah Rose, did your mother ever talk about her family back in Ireland?"

"Not often. When she did, she cried. They were angry at her for marrying my dad."

That didn't bode well for convincing the Dubliner family to take the child on.

Norah Rose cast her eyes down at our interwoven hands.

A few feet away, Emily perched on a footstool by the fire. Carlo lay on her feet like he often did in the winter to keep his petite mistress warm. Emily appeared deep in thought.

"Norah Rose, can you tell us more about that night?" Matthew asked. "How did you get out of the house?"

A tear fell into her lap, and I squeezed her hand.

"Officer Thomas wants to help," I told her gently. "He is a good man and my friend. I trust him, so you can trust him."

I felt Matthew watching me as I said this.

She took a breath. "I was asleep on the floor by the fireplace. Our house was small, so I always slept there. My mother was in the bedroom sleeping. Father must have been up because the next thing I knew, he shook me awake. He said that the house was on fire, and I had to get out. He threw a chair through the window. It made a terrible sound." She covered her ears as if she could hear it still.

"I asked why we couldn't go through the door. He said because it was blocked. I told him I wasn't leaving without him and Mama." She closed her eyes tight. "He picked me up and put me out the window. He told me that he would get Mama and for me to wait in the woods. They would be there soon. He promised."

"He saved your life."

She looked at me with tears in her eyes. "He should have

saved Mama first. She was closer to the fire. He chose me before her," she whispered.

I held her hand. "It was the choice your mother would have wanted him to make. You should know that."

"How do you know?" More tears gathered in her eyes.

"It's the choice any mother would want the father of her child to make. I am certain of it. It is the choice I would want my husband to make."

She seemed to take this in. I didn't know if she truly believed me, but my words did appear to comfort her.

Matthew leaned back in his chair and folded his arms in thought. I still had more questions for Norah Rose, but I didn't know how much longer she could tolerate them. She was just a child. I didn't want to push her too far and break the trust that we had forged.

Emily didn't have the same concerns. "You told Willa that your father knew he was in danger. Why did you say that?"

Norah Rose blinked a few times as if she was surprised to know that someone else was in the parlor with us.

"He told my mother he was scared. He said that 'they will not let it be when they find out, I know,'" Norah Rose said.

"What was he talking about and who is 'they'?"

"I don't know." She lowered her head as if she realized she had disappointed us in some way. She had not.

I wrapped my arm around her shoulders. "You have been very brave," I whispered into her ear.

At that moment, Miss Susan came back into the room. She looked to Matthew. "Was there anything else that you required, Officer Thomas? My husband is quite eager for you to leave."

Matthew stood up. "I understand."

Katie stood in the doorway with Matthew's coat.

"He is quite firm on the fortnight, so I want you to take heed of that," Miss Susan said. "As he is the head of this household, my opinions on the matter do not carry as much weight as his."

"I understand, Mrs. Dickinson. You have been more than kind to take in Norah Rose from the start."

Miss Susan glanced at Emily. "As usual, my sister gave me very little choice in the matter. The Dickinson children make up their own minds, no matter the cost." Miss Susan then turned her attention to Norah Rose. "While you are staying here, Norah Rose, we will continue your education. It's the least that I can do while you are here."

Katie handed Matthew his coat.

"Katie," Miss Susan said, "go help Norah Rose wash her face and then take her to the library. I will be there shortly to practice reading together."

I hugged Norah Rose before she stood up, and whispered in her ear, "I won't let anyone hurt you. I promise."

She looked at me and there was more hope in her green eyes than I could bear.

Katie took Norah Rose's hand, and they left the room.

I gathered up Emily's and my cloaks and bonnets where I had haphazardly left them on the bench by the front door. I was surprised that Miss Susan hadn't made a point to mention how careless I had been, but then I supposed she had other things on her mind.

"We will go out with you, Officer Thomas," Emily said, stepping into the hall.

Matthew eyed her as if he knew that there was something more than just being kind in her motive to walk him outside.

Bundled in our winter garb again, Miss Susan closed the door behind us. Emily and I walked Matthew to the street. The air was just as cold as I remembered, and in many ways, it felt worse after being in Susan Dickinson's cozy parlor. I buried my mitten-covered hands into my cloak, but my fingers were already burning from the cold.

"Thank you for walking me out," Matthew said.

"We did because we need to speak to you privately," Emily said.

Matthew sighed. "I expected as much."

"Why did the police chief decide not to investigate Hugh and Eve Doolan's deaths?"

Matthew pulled on his collar. "If you must know, the college has a lot of pull with the police department. As Mr. Doolan was an employee, we would have to investigate on campus. The police chief believes that would cause friction."

"Did the college president ask him not to investigate?" Emily asked.

"I don't know the extent of their conversation or even if he discussed it with any of the college officials, but I do know the police department is very careful not to upset the college."

Emily frowned and I found myself frowning as well.

"I promise you that I don't plan to give up," Matthew said. "I want to do this for Norah Rose. She deserves to know the truth."

Emily nodded. "And I fear she might be in danger. What if the person behind this believes she saw something? They will want to remove her too."

I shuddered at the very thought, but it was one that I also had.

Matthew swallowed. "I have thought of this too. She cannot leave your brother's home alone ever. Not until I catch her parents' killer."

Emily and I nodded, taking his word of warning to heart.

He said his goodbyes and crossed the frozen street.

There wasn't a single wagon or carriage on Main Street. Not even the paperboy ventured out.

Emily patted Carlo's head. "I suppose this all means that our next stop has been determined."

"Home?" I asked hopefully.

"Home?" Emily repeated as she straightened the bow on her bonnet. "Of course not. It's the college. We have a murder to solve."

CHAPTER TWENTY-TWO

EMILY WAS ALREADY crossing the street on her way to the college. I ran to catch up with her and Carlo.

"Emily," I said, somewhat out of breath. "Are you certain this is wise? You heard what Matthew said about the police chief and the college."

"Yes, I did, which is the exact reason we have to find out what is happening on campus. You don't want Matthew to stick his neck out on this, do you? If the police chief finds out that Matthew is going out on his own, asking questions at the college when he was specifically told not to, he could lose his position in the department. I don't believe that is what you want." She arched her eyebrow at me.

"Of course it's not." I tied the ribbons of my bonnet under my chin.

"Then, I say we beat Matthew to it. We are doing this for him. Do not forget that, Willa."

I glanced at the homestead, which was fringed in snow.

"Do not worry about what Margaret will say. I will set her straight."

That was just what I was worried about. I didn't know how much longer Margaret would put up with my absence from the homestead before she broke down and said something to Mrs. Dickinson, or even worse Mr. Dickinson, about it. Even so, there was no way I could let Emily go to the campus without me.

With a sigh, I followed Emily and Carlo across the street. It wasn't that I didn't want to know what happened to Norah Rose's parents. I very much did want to know, but I was torn. It was not fair of me to leave Margaret behind to do all the work at the homestead. Emily didn't know how much friction this would cause between us. But if Norah Rose was in as much danger as we feared, I had no other choice. The child had to come first.

When I caught up with Emily, she glanced over her shoulder and seemed pleased that I was following her. As if I had another option. I didn't want Margaret to be mad at me, but having Emily upset with me was even worse.

"I think we should start at the maintenance shed. Hugh was a janitor. Those are the men who are likely to know him the very best."

Normally, when walking through the campus, Emily and I would cut across the Dickinsons' field of grain that separated the campus from the Dickinsons' land. However, on that day it was impassable as there were at least four feet of snow over the field. There wasn't as much as a deer track through the blanket of white.

Instead, we walked down Main Street to the main entrance of the college. I realized in all my time working for the Dickinsons and the countless times that I had been on campus or cut through campus on an errand, I had never walked through this entrance.

Normally, during the school year, the grounds were a flurry of activity, but not now. I had overheard Mr. Dickinson say that classes were canceled for days due to the extreme cold, but they planned to reopen soon. As Mr. Dickinson said, "The students would just learn how to cope with the frigid temperatures."

I could see why classes were canceled. It was cold everywhere in Amherst, but it seemed worse on campus, and the gaps between buildings created narrow passageways for the glacial wind and intensified the force of the gusts.

I lifted my scarf over my face and hunched forward, trying to protect myself the very best that I could.

I caught up with Emily. "Do you know where the maintenance shed is?"

She turned her head so I could see her face inside her bonnet. "I know this campus better than most of the faculty. Follow me and watch for ice."

It was a good thing that she reminded me because I looked down to where I was about to step on ice. I skirted around it, into the snow.

An old barn came into view. It was weathered and worn and it seemed it had seen many storms so much worse than the blizzard that Amherst had just experienced.

There was a great yell of frustration as Emily, Carlo, and I came around the side of the barn.

A large black form hit the hydrant again and let out a string of foul words I had not heard uttered since my brother, Henry, stopped working at the warehouse years ago.

The man threw the giant wrench at the hydrant. The wrench bounced off the hydrant and hit the man in the shoulder.

He fell to the snow and held his shoulder. The swearing at that point only increased in ferocity.

"I truly don't know what most of those words mean," Emily said.

I knew what they meant, and I had no intention of telling her. "Not one of those words is worth repeating," I said.

Emily cocked her head as if she wasn't so sure about that. "The love of language should include all language." She walked over to the man and offered her hand. "You are lucky that wrench didn't hit you in the face."

He rubbed his shoulder. "Maybe it would have put me out of my misery if it had."

He had a thick Irish accent much stronger than Margaret O'Brien's. Margaret's accent seemed to come out only when she was upset or barking orders at me. Both of which happened relatively often, now that I thought about it.

He put his hands on his hips. "Now, the blasted thing is lost in the snow. I won't see it until spring, and by that time it will be rusted through. It seems to me that nothing is going right."

"What else went awry?" Emily asked.

He glanced at her. "It's none of your business, miss. And speaking of business, you have no reason to be here right now. Go home and sit by the fire and knit or do whatever you spoiled young ladies do while men work."

Emily glowered at him. "I'm Emily Dickinson, daughter of Edward Dickinson, the college treasurer." She let that last statement hang in the air. "I believe that you owe me a little more respect than that."

He tightened the scarf at his neck. "I didn't know that, miss. Of course, I have great respect for Mr. Dickinson."

Emily cocked her head. "Is that because he is in charge of the college budget and therefore determines your salary?"

"That would be one reason," he muttered.

Emily chuckled at his response and some of the tension in the air between them fell away.

"I always appreciate a man who is honest," Emily said. "In fact, I find it to be the most respectful attribute of a person."

"Then, you will like me. I am honest to a fault, and it's gotten me in a bit of hot water from time to time with my colleen."

"Is trouble with your colleen what is bothering you so much?"

He nodded. "There is always trouble there. If I let that rule my day, I would never be pleased. She is a spiteful woman. I wish I didn't care for her so, but the heart and the head don't always match up, you see."

"I would have thought you would say it was the death of Hugh Doolan that has upset you so. You worked with Hugh, didn't you?"

The man paled. "I knew Hugh, yes. And I'm sorry he's dead, but I wouldn't know anything about that either."

"What's your name?" Emily asked.

He frowned. "Why should I tell you?"

"Because I told you my name."

He pointed at me. "That may be true, but I don't know her name."

"That's my maid, Willa," Emily said.

There was a small pang in my chest, not because Emily said anything inaccurate about me, but how casually she said it. I was just Willa the maid. I knew she didn't feel that way, but I also knew she was so accustomed to having servants, plus introducing them like an equal was not common practice in her world. In fact, it wasn't a common practice in mine either.

"I'm still not telling you my name."

Emily shrugged. "Very well, I will just ask my father to find out who you are. The college can't have that many janitors, and one is recently dead, so it wouldn't take long for him to narrow it down."

"Jimmy O'Malley is my name, and I know nothing at all about what happened to Hugh. You can leave it at that."

"We heard," Emily said, and nodded to include me in the conversation, "that he was worried that he was in some kind of danger."

"Did you hear what I just said? I know nothing about it."

As he spoke, he looked away into the high, bright blue sky. If there weren't so much snow around, one would have thought it was the middle of the summer from how clear that sky was.

"So, you know nothing of Hugh at all. You worked together every day and never had a conversation."

"I don't, and I have nothing more to say to you. I have to return to work." He marched away.

Emily watched him go as she petted Carlo on the head. "He knows something."

"He may, but it is clear that he doesn't want to tell us."

"We will just have to make him."

Before I could ask Emily how she thought she was going to accomplish that, she, too, walked away.

CHAPTER TWENTY-THREE

I CAUGHT UP WITH Emily and Carlo. "What do we do now?"

"We knock on every door on campus if we have to until we find one person who knew Hugh and is willing to talk about him." She said this in a matter-of-fact way, like it was no trouble at all.

I grimaced. It would take us all day, if not all week, to knock on every single door. At any rate, it would take long enough for Margaret to be irate that I was away from the homestead for so long.

I was debating how to tell Emily that it wasn't a good idea when she snapped her fingers. "How could I be so naive? It is clear where we should go next."

"Where is that?" I asked with more than a little trepidation.

"Follow me."

I fell into step behind Emily and Carlo, feeling ill at ease that I didn't have any idea where we were going.

In the freezing temperature, Emily and I had not seen a single person walking through campus since Jimmy O'Malley stormed off. However, we were near the library when a woman appeared in the snow. She wore stout boots, wool pantaloons, a man's winter coat, and a knit cap.

She pumped her arms so vigorously while she walked that I was afraid she might knock herself in the face.

She came to a halt in front of us but kept pumping her arms when her feet came to a stop.

"Lucy," Emily said. "What are you doing out in this weather?"

"I'm out getting my exercise. It's important that a person stays active even in the foulest weather. I walk three miles every day, even when I am on the road, and I won't let a little snow stop me from doing that. It helps me keep my energy up for the rigors of travel."

I looked around campus. Snowdrifts covered the lower windows of half the buildings. I would not call this 'a little snow,' and I didn't believe anyone else would either.

Lucy continued to pump her arms and began stamping her feet. If I hadn't known that she was doing this on purpose, I would have thought she was having some kind of fit.

"And I could ask the same of you," Lucy said as she marched. "This cold air could give a woman of your constitution a fever. If you chose to wear men's clothing as I have, you would be much more comfortable and warmer. Skirts are an instrument of torture for women. Why shouldn't my legs move as freely as a man's? I have two of them just as he does. There are no differences in our appendages."

"I can assure you that my constitution is quite fine, and

even I am aware I put my father through enough already. He does not need to see me in men's trousers as well. The poor man would have a stroke."

"I have only ever found men and insecure women to have an issue with it. My husband is not threatened in the least."

"You must have a very special husband," Emily said.

Lucy nodded, and for the first time since we had met her, her face softened. "I do. If marriage is something you fear, dear Emily, rest assured there are good men out there who will allow you to be the person you want to be. All you must do is be willing to look."

Emily wrinkled her nose as if she didn't believe this for a second, but something deep in my heart stirred as Matthew came to mind. He would let me be the person who I wanted to be. I knew this. Why was I fighting so hard against it? It was an answer I did not have, and standing in the cold with Emily and Lucy was not the time to allow myself to examine my feelings on the matter.

Lucy glanced at me. "Are you and your maid also out on a walk, then?"

"You could say that," Emily replied. "As we are out and we are walking."

"Well, as I am almost done with my three miles, I was returning to the president's home for tea. You should join us. Olive will be happy to see you. She does need some cheering."

"We would love to," Emily said with a smile. "In fact, that was just the place we were heading. I wanted to make a call on Mrs. Stearns. She has been so kind to come to our home multiple times, I wanted to thank her for doing that."

Lucy nodded. "She will be happy to see you. It will be a

nice distraction. She is much more upset about the fire at the Doolans' home than she appeared to be earlier. She keeps fretting over the little girl. Honestly, if she had her way, she would take on the child herself, but President Stearns will not hear of it. Their own children are grown. I cannot blame him for not wanting to start over."

I felt a pang in my chest when I heard that. The Stearnses were a prestigious couple in Amherst. Norah Rose would do well to be their ward. They could give her a good life and more than that, a very good education. Maybe she would even attend Amherst College someday, assuming a woman ever could. Even as I thought this, I felt the pain in my chest.

Lucy made an abrupt turn and began marching down the snowy sidewalk.

"I think she wants us to follow her," Emily whispered.

"Then, we had better hurry up," I said. "I have never seen a woman walk so fast."

Emily chuckled. "It must be the trousers."

We made it to the president's house in half the time that it would normally take Emily and me to walk there.

Lucy stuck her hands on her hips. "Every time I think of the fire, I shudder over how horrible it is. It's unbelievable to me that someone could do that to a family."

"Do that to a family?" Emily asked. "You don't believe it was an accident?"

Lucy removed her stocking hat and smoothed her dark hair. "I don't believe anyone thinks it was an accident, do you?"

She ran up the steps to the Stearnses' front door, leaving Emily and me to wonder what the out-of-town lecturer might know about the people of Amherst.

Emily and I shared a look and then followed Lucy into the house.

As I walked through the front door, again, I was uncomfortable not being in my place. I knew that it was no matter to Emily, but she wasn't the one who would be judged for acting above her station.

Mrs. Brubaker, the Westons' housekeeper, held the door open for us and raised her brow at me when I followed Emily inside.

Emily cocked her head, and I knew she recognized Mrs. Brubaker from the Westons' home too. She opened her mouth as if she was going to say something on the subject but was stopped by the arrival of Mrs. Stearns.

Mrs. Stearns came elegantly down the wide staircase. "Miss Dickinson, how lovely to see you. I wasn't expecting you, but I do have an extra place set at the table. The pastor's wife from First Congregational had to cancel her plans to come. The church is in the midst of a crisis right now, but I am sure you know all about that."

Emily removed her cloak and handed it to me. I stood by and waited until she removed her bonnet as well.

"I did not know there was any kind of crisis happening at the church."

"Oh." Mrs. Stearns covered her mouth. When she lowered her hand, she said, "Maybe I shouldn't have said anything, then, but surely as the head of a founding family your father knows. Also, I was there this morning taking over some linen and saw your sister-in-law, Susan, there. She said that Lavinia was coming over too."

Emily frowned. "I don't know anything about this. Why are they at the church?"

Mrs. Stearns rested her left hand on her waist. "It's the cold, of course. The church is opening its doors to those who are struggling to stay warm during this wretched weather. The church council made the decision last evening."

"I wish my family had told me. Although I have very little concern for the church, this is a very admirable act, and I would be willing to help, just like Vinnie and Susan."

"There is plenty to do, and I am sure the church would be grateful for an extra set of hands. They don't even know how many people will be arriving this afternoon, but I think it could be close to one hundred when the word gets out." She patted Emily's shoulder. "We can talk about it more over tea. I know Lucy and Verona will be interested in hearing about it too."

"Verona Weston is here?" Emily asked.

"Oh yes, I'm sure you saw her housekeeper, Mrs. Brubaker, at the door. My own housekeeper had to leave suddenly because her mother has taken ill. Verona offered Mrs. Brubaker until I can find a replacement, which I can assure you has been a challenge with the cold. No one dares even to leave their homes. It's quite frustrating. Do people not want to work? That is what I would like to know."

"I was wondering why it was Mrs. Weston's housekeeper who opened the door."

"Verona is a godsend to me. She has become a very dear friend of mine and anytime I have a tea, I invite her. You are much closer to her age than I am. I believe you two will be fast friends too."

Emily wrinkled her brow at that idea.

Mrs. Stearns glanced back at me and cleared her throat. "I see that you have brought your dog and maid."

I tried my very best not to take offense that I was mentioned *after* Carlo. The large brown dog looked up at me as if he were apologizing for Mrs. Stearns's rudeness.

"I don't let animals in the parlor. Your maid can take the dog back to the laundry behind the kitchen. Mrs. Brubaker will show her the way."

The housekeeper scowled at Carlo and me. I wasn't sure which of us she was more annoyed at seeing. "Follow me."

Carlo whimpered and hung back until I followed the housekeeper first.

CHAPTER TWENTY-FOUR

THE PRESIDENT'S HOUSE wasn't that much bigger than the homestead. The kitchen and laundry were through a door below the grand staircase. I may not have even seen the door as I walked by, as it was painted matte black. I believed that had to be on purpose.

Mrs. Brubaker opened the door to allow Carlo and me to traipse inside.

"Oh my, that is a mighty fine dog," the cook said in a heavy Irish accent. "I had a dog like that back on the Green Island. I had to leave him behind when I came to America. It nearly broke my heart in two. I always wondered what happened to the poor soul. I left him with a fisherman at the docks. He promised to take good care of him, but you never know with fishermen if they are telling the truth or spinning a tale of yarn."

"Addy," Mrs. Brubaker said stiffly. "Miss Dickinson's maid and dog are to remain here with you."

After Mrs. Brubaker left the kitchen, Addy waved her hand. "Don't fret about her. She got off the boat with a stick—"

I interrupted her before she said too much. "Mrs. Stearns said Mrs. Brubaker is here because your housekeeper's mother fell ill."

"Yes, and I personally cannot wait until Nelly gets back. Mrs. Brubaker is far too stern for my taste. I told Mrs. Stearns that she would change the atmosphere in the house, and I was right. I have known Mrs. Brubaker for many years. We even came to America on the same boat. As fate would have it, we both landed here in Amherst for our final destination. The Lord works in mysterious ways. I would have guessed that Mrs. Brubaker would have been destined for New York or Boston, but no, she ended up here in little Amherst." She shook her head as if she couldn't quite believe it.

Carlo's tongue hung out of his mouth and he dripped drool on the floor.

"Would it be possible to get a bowl of water and a snack for Carlo?" I asked.

"Of course, of course. Those ladies can wait until the dog is well cared for. The only animal that lives in this place is Mrs. Stearns's princess of a cat. She believes herself to be the Queen of Sheba."

"My mistress doesn't care for cats, either, but I do love them myself."

She shook her head. "They are tricky and are apt to keep too many secrets. I like straightforward animals like dogs. All they think about is how they can please their masters. They aren't plotting to overturn the government like many cats do."

I have never found cats to be tricky, but I wasn't going to

argue with her about it when she was being so kind to both Carlo and me. I did suppress a smile that she mentioned cats overthrowing the government. I had met several in my day who might have been thinking those very thoughts.

She opened the ice chest and pulled out a block of cheese. "How would a nice piece of cheddar sound, Mr. Pup?"

Carlo's plume of a tail began to wag vigorously. He loved cheese, and it wasn't something that Margaret would give him as she said it took far too much work to make to be wasted on animals.

Addy cut a large piece off the block and then cut it into fourths. She set the cheese on a metal dish and filled a matching metal bowl with water. She set both at Carlo's feet, and he dove into the cheese. The four pieces were gone before I could even blink.

Addy clicked her tongue. "My land, you were hungry. But I'm afraid that's all that you are getting. If Mrs. Brubaker knew that I gave you some of President Stearns's fine aged cheddar she would throw me out on my ear."

Carlo gave a great sigh and then began drinking his water. He lapped at the bowl with so much enthusiasm that it washed over the sides and onto Addy's clean floor. I winced as I remembered what Margaret said whenever that happened at the homestead. Addy didn't even notice.

"Do you need any help with the food for the tea?" I asked.

"Isn't that sweet of you, but everything is done, and the maids have already taken it upstairs to the parlor. I can sit and rest a spell while they are eating. Why don't you have a seat, too, and remove your cloak? You will warm up fast in here with the oven going. Sometimes I walk outside just to cool off.

The summer is close to unbearable. I don't mind this cold weather one bit."

I removed my cloak. "You might be the only one who doesn't mind it," I said.

She rested her hands on her stomach. "You speak clear and fine like an American. I take it that you are not Irish. Most of the servants around here are Irish."

"I'm not Irish. At least not as far as I know."

"You should ask your family. It's good to know your heritage. I can say that I am proud of mine. Not everyone likes the Irish, but I have to tell you they are the best kind of people that you can meet." She laughed. "In my humble opinion, of course."

"I don't have any family to ask." I did my best to keep any emotions out of those words.

"Oh, you poor lass. Let me make us some tea. We have time for a cup, I think, before Mrs. Brubaker comes in here on her high horse about something or other." She filled the kettle with water and set it on the burner. She then sat back down at the table. "Oh, it's so nice to be off my feet. When I was young, like you, I could go all day long. Now, I have to take breaks from time to time. I never do when Mrs. Brubaker is bustling around the kitchen. She would not approve. She has ten years on me but moves like a teenager. I don't know where she gets all that energy. She makes me tired." She patted her belly. "It could be because she never takes a second serving of pudding, and I always do." She removed her shoe and began rubbing her foot. There was a hole in the bottom of her stocking.

The kettle whistled.

"Would you be a dear and make the tea? Everything is on

the counter. Working for the Dickinsons, you can make a decent cup of tea."

"I'd be happy to." I jumped out of my seat and went about making the tea. I put the loose leaves in the plain white teapot, allowed it to steep. When enough time had passed, I poured the tea over a small strainer into two teacups, one for Addy and one for me. It smelled heavenly, and just by being so close to it, I felt warmer. It was a welcome feeling as I still was frozen through after our walk outside. I gave Addy her cup first.

"Oh, that's very good," she said with closed eyes. "What would make it even better would be a spot of milk in it and two lumps of brown sugar. However, if Mrs. Brubaker appears, I did not use any of the brown sugar. The woman has all but rationed us and everything that we have since she arrived. She claims it's because of the bad turn in the weather. If you ask her, the trains will never run again, and we will all have to hunt for our dinner and live off of the land."

I added milk and brown sugar to her cup.

She stirred her tea and took a sip. "Oh my," she said. "You are very good at making tea. That is just how I like it."

I sat with black tea in front of me. I was loath to drink it because it was warming my hands, which were wrapped around the cup so well. My hands needed the warmth much more than my stomach did.

"Is it true that the Dickinsons have Norah Rose staying with them?" she asked.

"Yes," I said. I saw no reason to lie about it since it appeared that everyone already knew, and Addy had been so kind to me since the moment that I met her.

"I am glad. She needs to be safe and secure. She was a sweet child. I can't believe what she has gone through. No one should have to bear that, and certainly not such a young child."

I agreed. "Did you know Hugh and Eve Doolan?"

"Oh yes! I lived just down the road from them. I would see Hugh every morning when I walked to the president's house."

"You don't live here at the house?"

She shook her head. "I don't. I'm married and have a family of my own. I arrive at five each morning and leave after dinner at seven. They are long days, but my oldest is a great help with the younger ones at home. The only live-in servant is the housekeeper, but as you know, Nelly is away now caring for her mother. I hope that she returns soon because I have the inkling that Mrs. Brubaker is going to petition Mrs. Stearns for her position. It would be a great feather in her cap to be the housekeeper of the college president's house and not just a mere professor. Dr. Weston doesn't even have tenure. I know that hurts Mrs. Brubaker's ego to work for an underling professor."

"Would you speak to Hugh in the mornings?" I asked, hoping that I could steer the conversation back in the direction of the Doolans and what she might have known about the young couple.

"Nothing more than a wave and a greeting of hello. It is early, as you know, and I'm not an early bird. If I had my way, I wouldn't speak to a single soul until after seven in the morning. I might be bright and cheery now, but it's midday. The maids know to stay out of my way until I finish my second cup of tea." She cleared her throat. "I knew Eve better, of course, since she was here in the house often."

"What was she like?" I found myself fascinated with Norah

Rose's mother, a woman who was willing to give up her comfortable life for love.

"She was the sweetest woman you ever could meet, and she had the most beautiful voice. She was classically trained, you see, back in Dublin."

This came as a surprise. Private voice lessons would have to be expensive.

Addy seemed to understand my confusion. "She came from a well-to-do family back in the Old Country. She trained to be a professional singer and left everything behind to marry Hugh. She was very modest about her accomplishments, but I also have family in Dublin, who know how successful her family is. They are in the jewelry business and have establishments all over the city."

My hands tingled as she said this. "Do you know her family name?"

"Yes, it's Reilly. I believe her father is Sam Reilly."

"Thank you. That's so helpful. The police want to write Norah Rose's family back in Ireland to see if they will take the child." I took a small sip of my tea.

Addy wrinkled her nose. "I would not put much hope in that. By Eve's own telling, her family completely cut her off when she ran away with Hugh. She was sad about it, of course. She wrote letters home that were never answered. We spoke about so many things. I spent a lot of time with her. She would sit and have tea with me just like this on many afternoons. There have been many times that Eve had to wait for Mrs. Stearns to return from an outing on the campus. As the wife of the college president, Mrs. Stearns is called away all the time to meet with dignitaries, the faculty wives, and anyone who is interested. Sometimes Eve would go home, but if Norah Rose was at school, more often than not, Eve would sit with me, and we would chat about Ireland and all we had left behind. However, even more than that, we discussed all that we gained by leaving. I didn't leave behind nearly as much as she did, but neither one of us regretted our decisions. She was happy. Never before did you see a man who loved his wife so well as Hugh Doolan. They were as poor as church mice, but there was so much love in that family. Norah Rose was their shining star. I know they wanted to have more children, but the money was tight. I personally thought that she would do better in a city like Boston or even New York, where there would be lots of fancy ladies to sew for. There aren't nearly as many women who need or want that here in Amherst."

"I do hope the Reillys will take Norah Rose in," I said. "I hate the thought of her going to an orphanage."

"As do I," Addy said. "I would take her in myself, but we are already strapped with four children. My husband would be furious with me if I did." She set her teacup down on the table. "I'm not sure the Reilly family is the best place for Norah Rose. The family that rejected her mother, one of the sweetest women I have ever met. I don't believe so. They will poison her against Eve's memory, and they will certainly have nothing kind to say about her father."

I understood her concern. But shouldn't Norah Rose be with her relatives instead of the alternative, which would be getting shipped off to an orphanage in a city she had never seen?

There didn't seem to be any good answers for Norah Rose, and that was the hardest part to bear.

"Did Eve ever mention that she was afraid or that Hugh was worried or in trouble?" I asked.

She sipped her tea and thought about this. "About a week ago she did say that Hugh was behaving strangely. He was leaving the house at all hours of the night and coming back in the early morning. He told her it was because of the cold. He had to continually check the wells and pipes on campus to make sure they were still flowing. At a time like this, everything could freeze over."

"Did she believe him?" I wrapped my hand tightly around my teacup.

She held her teacup suspended in the air. "I could tell that she wanted to believe him. She wanted to believe him very much. She loved him, and from what I know she had no reason to doubt him up to that point."

"But she didn't."

Addy nodded. "She didn't."

I had more questions for Addy, but Emily stuck her head into the kitchen. "Willa Noble, there you are. What are you doing here? You should be out in the parlor. We are having an interesting conversation and I'm learning so very much about you-know-what."

She raised her eyebrows at me.

I didn't have to be a detective to know that she was referring to Hugh and Eve Doolan's murder. There were times that Emily could be as subtle as a blacksmith's anvil.

CHAPTER TWENTY-FIVE

I THANKED ADDY THE cook for the tea and conversation. Addy promised to keep Carlo company until we came back for him. As I left the kitchen, she was cutting the dog another healthy piece from President Stearns's prized block of cheese. With the plume of his tail thumping on the floor, he watched the cook's every move. Carlo was right at home in the Stearnses' kitchen, and I wished that I could stay with him there. Chatting with Addy and sipping tea would be much more enjoyable than going to the parlor. The stand-in housekeeper, Mrs. Brubaker, for one, would not be happy that I was there.

"I don't know how you can be comfortable in those clothes. They are far too tight," Mrs. Weston said to Lucy.

Lucy sat on a chair by the fire. She had her legs crossed like a man, which I supposed was the most comfortable way to sit when one was wearing trousers.

"And a corset is loose?" Lucy scoffed. "Fabric around my legs cannot be compared to my internal organs being squeezed to a pulp in the name of women's fashions. Do you really think men would wear clothing that was constraining and uncomfortable in this day and age? If that is true, I don't know why women should have to."

Mrs. Weston frowned. "Trousers are not flattering on a woman's body. You look far too masculine in them. You might believe that you are spurring on some type of reform by what you are wearing, but you are only making a laughingstock of yourself and embarrassing your friends like Olive."

"First of all, they are called bloomers, and you would serve yourself well by remembering that, because I can assure you there will come a day that all women will wear them or some such variation. And you are right, I do believe in my reform." Lucy tugged on the cuff of her pant leg. "But it goes way beyond attire. I am wearing what I want to wear, simply because I want to wear it. I am not asking you to wear the same clothes, nor would I expect you to. If you would like to continue to confine yourself in a corset, that is your choice. I would not make that decision for you, or for any other man or woman."

"All right, ladies," Mrs. Stearns interrupted. "That is enough. It is clear the two of you aren't going to see eye to eye on this matter."

Mrs. Weston folded her arms. "Olive, do you find her clothing appropriate? I'm surprised that you allow her inside of your home wearing this ridiculous costume."

"Lucy is my friend, and she has always done things her own way even when we were just girls in the schoolyard together. I would not wear what she has on, nor let my daughters dress so. But she is not my daughter. What say do I have?"

Mrs. Weston patted at the side of her silky black hair as if to make sure every strand was still in place. "She is your friend. You must do what you believe is best."

"I do, and I will." The president's wife cleared her throat. "I believe that we should get back to the matter at hand, and that's the church," Mrs. Stearns said. "I have asked Mrs. Brubaker to go through the attics in search of extra blankets and pillows, but we will have to ask even more women of the community to be involved. We won't be able to supply everything the church will need to help the families who are going to the church for warmth.

"We also have to spread the word to the Irish community. Mrs. Brubaker has told a few choice people in her community and said that they will share about the warming mission, but chances are, someone will be missed. I believe it would be best if we canvass and hand out leaflets about the mission. Before too long, everyone will know what we have to offer."

Emily sat by the fire. "Willa and I can take those leaflets out into the Irish neighborhoods."

"Willa?" Mrs. Stearns asked.

"My maid. She's right here. She used to live in the poorer communities in Amherst. I thought her personal experience would be a great help in understanding how to spread the word about the warming mission."

I looked at the floor to hide my face as I listened to Emily speak. I wasn't comfortable with her sharing my past with these ladies I didn't know, but there was nothing I could do about it.

"The dog is not here in the parlor, too, is he?" Mrs. Stearns asked with alarm. "I—I have a fear of dogs, and yours is as large as a bear."

"No, ma'am," I said. "He is still in the kitchen with your cook."

"Spoiling him rotten with President Stearns's finest cheese, I am sure." Mrs. Stearns shook her head. "If this is what you would like to do, Emily, we would appreciate it. The leaflets are at the printer's. I can ask them to have them delivered to your home. They should be done by now."

"No, no, that's not necessary." Emily held her teacup under her chin. "Willa and I can pick them up on our way to the Irish neighborhood this afternoon." She sipped her tea.

"That would be lovely," Mrs. Stearns said. "I knew the Dickinson family would be helpful. Your sister, Lavinia, is a dedicated volunteer for the church's Ladies' League. She will make a fine wife someday, as she is proficient in running a committee. That is a great precursor to running a home."

"It may be a precursor," Emily said, "but it is not a mandate."

Mrs. Stearns wrinkled her brow as if she was confused by Emily's comment.

I had my own concerns to worry over. I bit the inside of my lip. I could tell Emily's mind was made up on the matter, and I would be going to the Irish neighborhood whether I liked to or not.

"I feel just so awful for the Doolans. If the church had organized the warming mission earlier, they might have gone there and still been alive." Mrs. Weston shook her head. "It's a terrible shame. Eve was so talented. She had fitted me, too, for many of my dresses." She glanced at Mrs. Stearns. "I don't have as many occasions to wear such clothing as Olive does."

"Believe me, Verona, I would much rather stay home tucked in bed with a book than follow my husband around at these fundraisers and galas. The conversations can be so tedious."

"I suppose I will learn that in my own good time," Mrs. Weston said. "My husband has dreams of running for office someday."

Lucy raised her brow. "He does. What is his platform? Where does he fall on slavery? Or women's rights? What about working conditions in the cities?"

Mrs. Weston opened and closed her mouth. "I don't know. Those are not the topics that we speak about."

"My husband and I talk about these sorts of issues all the time. It's important to understand your life partner's beliefs," Lucy said. "If you don't know what they are, how do you know if those beliefs are in line with your own?"

"Maybe for you." Mrs. Weston sniffed. "But we are well aware that you don't have a traditional marriage."

"Thank heavens for that," Lucy murmured.

Mrs. Stearns, who was trapped between her two friends, shifted uncomfortably in her seat.

"When was the last time you saw Eve?" Emily asked.

She had directed her question at Mrs. Weston, but Mrs. Stearns answered. "Eve was here, the day before the fire. Even though it does not feel like it, spring will be here before any of us know it, and I needed several new gowns for the spring formals and award ceremonies at the college. As the president's wife, I have to keep up appearances. I bought three gowns on my last visit to Boston, but Eve always has to alter them so that they fit me perfectly. I need to look my very best so that my husband looks his best."

Lucy stopped herself from taking a bite of a cookie that was mere inches from her mouth. "You are your own person. You are not an extension of anyone else. This type of statement is what has held women back for the last hundred years, and it has been fed to you by men."

Mrs. Stearns waved her comment away. "Oh, Lucy, let's not get into another discussion of the roles of men and women again. Verona is bound to march out of my door and never come back." Mrs. Stearns didn't appear particularly upset by Lucy's comments. It was almost like she had expected them and brushed them aside like she had many times before because they were old friends.

"Truly, how you speak to Olive is disrespectful," Mrs. Weston said.

"Verona, please don't think that. Lucy and I have had these squabbles since our school days. Even if we don't see eye to eye on everything, we are like sisters."

Lucy smiled at Mrs. Weston. "I couldn't agree more, Sister Olive."

Mrs. Weston set her teacup back on its saucer. "I will never hold you responsible, Olive, for having an eccentric childhood friend. I imagine that many of us have things from our childhood that we wish we could leave behind but simply cannot."

Emily's brow went up. If I knew anything about my mistress, she would not forget the last comment that Mrs. Verona Weston had made, and neither would I.

Emily stood. "Willa and I should head out if we would like to hand out some of those leaflets. At what time tomorrow will the church be allowing people to take shelter?"

"The minister's wife said people could start to arrive anytime after three in the afternoon. She hopes by then she will have enough donations of pillows, blankets, and food to care for everyone through the night." Mrs. Stearns cleared her throat. "I agree that you need to be on your way. There is no time to spare. Lucy and I will shortly return to the work of gathering donations. Verona, you are welcome to join us."

The pretty professor's wife hesitated. "I wish I could, but I believe my husband is ending his lab work early this afternoon and will want me home. If I am able, I will stop by the church."

Lucy wrinkled her nose as if she had caught something that smelled bad, and—not that anyone was paying any attention to me in the least—I had to look at the floor to hide my smile. I didn't know all of what Lucy lectured on, but in the short time I had been around her, I'd found her refreshing, especially compared to the likes of Mrs. Weston.

In some ways, Lucy reminded me of Emily, who was full of ideas and opinions. However, Lucy's ideas and opinions were firmly set on earth while Emily's many times floated in the clouds.

"How many people can the church hold?" Mrs. Weston asked, standing as well. "There will come a point when people have to be turned away. The church cannot just keep accepting people inside."

"When two hundred souls are reached that will be the end of it." Mrs. Stearns looked down at her hands. "I hate the thought of turning anyone away."

"The college has classroom buildings and halls that aren't used at night. Couldn't the overflow of people go to one of those places?" Emily asked.

Mrs. Stearns shook her head. "President Stearns would not

like it. The college has to consider the safety of the students first and foremost."

Lucy frowned. "The students would be in their dormitories. I don't see how they would be put in danger if a few classrooms were used for overflow. Is it not better than the alternative of a person freezing to death?"

"He would not like it," Mrs. Stearns snapped, putting a stop to the conversation.

Lucy's eyes were wide. "All right. I'm sorry if I upset you."

Mrs. Stearns regained her composure. "It's all right. As you can imagine, the last two days have been difficult for my husband. To lose an employee of the college in such an awful event—even if it was no fault of the college—tarnishes the reputation of the institution. People in this town talk, and with the cold weather, they have little more to do than gossip. My poor husband is up at night worrying about what they are saying."

"Gossip is just that—gossip," Lucy said. "I never pay attention to what people say about me."

"Not everyone has the iron backbone that you have carried through your life, Lucy." Mrs. Stearns smoothed the edge of her waistcoat.

Emily pulled the flannel sleeve of her dress. "Hopefully, it won't come to that, and the church will be able to house everyone seeking shelter from the cold. I would imagine that not everyone from Kelley Square will want to leave their homes, despite the weather," Emily said. "I don't know how any one of us could turn someone away who is shivering on our doorstep."

A strange look passed over Mrs. Weston's face, and I could not help but wonder if she had experience in this area.

Emily turned to me. "Willa, will you go and collect Carlo from the cook, then meet me at the front of the house?"

I nodded and left the room. I found the cook and Carlo just where I had left them in the kitchen. They seemed quite pleased with themselves. Their content expressions made me wonder just how much of President Stearns's prized cheese the dog had eaten.

"I just love dogs," the cook said. "I wish Mrs. Stearns didn't have such a fear of them. I would love for the president and his wife to adopt a dog. A home doesn't feel like a home without a pet. I have three cats and two dogs at our home."

I smiled. "The Dickinsons have lots of animals in and around the house. It's one of the many reasons that I enjoy working for them so much."

Addy wrapped the much smaller block of cheese in wax paper. "What is it like working for them?"

"The Dickinsons?" I asked, knowing full well that she couldn't be talking about anyone else.

She nodded. "Is the mother as cuckoo as they say she is?"

I bristled. Mrs. Dickinson was quiet and kept to herself, but she had always been kind to me. I had liked the cook from the beginning, but her question changed my opinion of her in an instant.

"I need to return to my mistress."

"I'm sorry if I offended you." Her cheeks flushed red. "I was just curious. My husband says my mouth gets me into more trouble than anything else."

I slapped my leg. "Carlo, come."

The large dog lumbered over to me.

"Please don't be upset. I enjoyed talking to you." Her brow furrowed.

"I'm sensitive when it comes to the Dickinsons," I said, and opened the door. "They have been quite kind to me."

"And from what I have learned of you in the short time we have been acquainted, you have been kind to them too. I am very sorry to have upset you."

"Thank you," I said. "I hope we will cross paths again."

"As do I," the cook said in return.

Carlo followed me out the back door of the house after one final forlorn glance at the block of cheese in the middle of the table.

CHAPTER TWENTY-SIX

EMILY CAME OUT the front door of the grand house just as Carlo and I rounded the corner of the building. Carlo let out a friendly bark when he saw his mistress and gave a little hop for good measure.

Emily beamed at him. I don't know if I had ever seen a person so connected to their dog before. I knew Carlo liked me, but he didn't love me or anyone else as much as he loved Emily. She was his whole world.

Emily came down the steps. She was bundled up in bonnet, cloak, scarf, and mittens. I was wearing the same, but my outer garments weren't nearly as fine as hers. Even so, I had purchased the bonnet in the fall from the milliner and was quite pleased of it. I wondered if it would be too presumptuous of me to pin a sprig of holly from the Dickinsons' garden on the brim.

"This is perfect," Emily said. "We can collect the leaflets from the printer and visit Kelley Square. It will be the best place to find out more about the Doolans. We might even find out who wanted them dead."

"Do you think it was someone from Kelley Square?" I asked.

"It's as good a guess as any, and I am just happy to have a direction to begin searching."

I swallowed. "I very much want to go with you, but Margaret—"

"Yes, yes, I, too, agree we have been away from home for far too long. Margaret will be upset, and Vinnie will be suspicious. The warming mission will be tomorrow. Let us go collect the leaflets from the printer and we can pass them out first thing in the morning. Is that a suitable compromise?"

I knew it was the best one I would get, and I hoped Margaret would be understanding.

The printer was uptown along with most of the shops, including the dressmaker whom Eve Doolan had been a seamstress for. It was already after two in the afternoon when we reached the printer. There were only a few hours of daylight left.

How I pined for the long days of summer when sunshine stretched into the early night. Those were the best days. Emily and I would work in the garden after dinner for hours with Carlo and a few of Miss Lavinia's cats looking on. Horace Church was always there to give his criticism as to how we were constructing the gardens. He was one of the few people working for the Dickinsons who could freely share his opinions without the chance of reprimand. Once I had even heard him correct Mr. Dickinson on a matter. Anyone else would have been dismissed on the spot, but not Horace. It made me wonder what he knew about the family that made him feel so secure. The only other person to challenge Edward Dickinson and not be scolded was Emily. This put both Horace and Emily in a very elite category.

The bell rang over the printer's door when we went inside. There was a short man behind the counter with a pencil-thin mustache over his upper lip and even thinner sideburns. He wore a white dress shirt and bow tie, and black bands at the forearms held his shirtsleeves close to his skin.

"Miss Dickinson!" he said. "This is a surprise. What are you doing out in this dreadful weather? I would have stayed home myself if I had the luxury of that choice."

"Hello, Mr. Jennings. I'm helping the Ladies' League from my father's church spread the word about the warming station for tomorrow night. I'm here to collect the leaflets that will be distributed to the families on Kelley Square."

"I did not know you were a member of the Ladies' League." He touched his minute mustache as if to make sure it was still in place.

"I'm not," Emily said in a clipped voice. "I can be a help with no religious motivation."

He swallowed. "Yes, well, I will get those leaflets for you. I think it is a fine thing you are doing, very fine indeed. I used to live in the Irish community, as my mother was Irish."

"You don't have an accent," Emily observed.

Mr. Jennings made a face. "I was born in this country. I am as Yankee as anyone else in Amherst. I wish everyone would see that."

Emily seemed to consider this.

He pulled at his stiff collar. "I will go gather the leaflets." He went through the curtain into the back room.

"He seems quite sensitive about the whole business," Emily said.

"I think you might have insulted him."

"Me?" She removed her bonnet and patted her hair. "How did I do that?"

"When you mentioned that he didn't have an accent," I said under my breath. "You made him feel different."

Emily seemed to consider this. "I have never seen being different as a bad thing. I am different myself. I am reminded of that constantly by family and friends. Different is the same as unique, and I am proud of being both."

I wasn't sure how to explain the issue to Emily, and before I could come up with an idea, Mr. Jennings returned.

"Mr. Jennings, I just want to apologize if I offended you in any way by commenting on your accent," Emily said. "Willa has told me that my wording might have been in poor choice. I meant no offense at all."

I grimaced at the mention of my name. I very much wanted Emily to leave me out of her apology.

His cheeks turned red. "It's all right, miss. I know you didn't mean anything by it." He cleared his throat. "Not everyone who comes in here and makes a comment like that is so innocent or has the decency to apologize, so I thank you for that. Being Irish is not a disadvantage." He sighed. "I just get frustrated at times that the Irish are seen as second-class citizens. I would have been counted in that number if I didn't have an English surname."

The packets of leaflets were tied up with twine, and Mr. Jennings handed them to Emily. "I will also be sure to spread the word to those who I can."

Emily thanked him, and we left the printer.

Carlo, who had waited for us on the sidewalk, jumped to his feet the moment we came out the door. It had begun to snow while we were inside. The large dog shook snow from his coat.

Emily stood in front of the printer's door, looking up into the snow. The flakes were large and floated to the earth rather than fell.

She murmured, "I counted till they danced so their slippers leaped the town . . ."

"Emily, we should hurry home before the snow becomes worse."

She blinked at me, and her face looked as if she had come up from a bottomless lake. For a moment, she didn't know me, and then recognition clicked into place. She was again with me in the here and now. "Yes, we should. I have a poem that must be written."

Margaret wasn't nearly as upset with me as I'd expected when I walked into the kitchen. I believe she was just relieved that the Dickinsons weren't expecting any guests that day. I could agree with the sentiment. Entertaining could be exciting for the family, but it was three times the work for the staff.

She handed me a wicker basket of dry laundry. "Here, the ironing is all yours."

Ironing was one of my least favorite tasks, but I knew better than to complain. I simply set the iron on the stove and got to work.

THE NEXT MORNING, my back ached from leaning over the ironing board for so long. It had taken me hours and hours to finish all of Mr. Dickinson's shirts and the ladies' dresses. Now all the garments hung in their wardrobes perfectly clean and ironed and waiting to be worn.

Even though my back was sore and I was tired, I got up an hour earlier than normal to go about my tasks. I knew that Emily wanted to do more detecting that morning. As I dressed, I felt the weight of the rose-engraved key that I found under the bed in the Dickinson home where Norah Rose slept her first night with the Dickinson family. I had been carrying it around in my pocket like a talisman all this time. I had not asked Norah Rose about it as we had not yet been alone since I found the key.

Still terrified by the prospect of fire, I thoroughly cleaned all the fireplaces in the parlors. I dusted the tables and mantels, and I polished the windows. While I worked, Baby Z, the black cat, followed me about, and when he rolled on his back while I brushed the rug, I stopped for a moment to scratch his stomach.

It was my goal to have the home in the best condition possible, so Emily and I could slip away again. I was also eager to find Matthew and tell him what I had learned from Mrs. Stearns and her cook, Addy. I had the name of Norah Rose's family in Dublin. Surely that would make the process of finding them that much faster. However, the question remained. If they were found, would they take her in, and if they did, was Addy the cook right that they would poison Norah Rose's young mind against the memory of her parents?

I had just finished brushing the rug and was gathering up my things, planning my return to the kitchen to start the family's breakfast, when Emily came into the parlor. She was still in her dressing gown and her long auburn hair hung in waves down her back. "Willa, I did not expect to find you up this early."

I stood up with my cleaning bucket in hand. "I wanted to do everything I could before we leave so that Margaret will be less stressed."

"That's very thoughtful and true. I have some good news too. I received a letter late yesterday. Dr. Weston has invited me to meet him at his lab on campus. He was very impressed with my knowledge of botany and asked if I could come to the lab at half past eight this morning. I immediately agreed, and you are coming with me."

"What about the pamphlets for the warming mission at the church?" I asked.

"Not to worry. We will go from the lab to Kelley Square." She folded her hands together. "I don't know about you, Willa, but I feel like we could be close to finding exactly what happened to Eve and Hugh Doolan."

I wished I shared her confidence.

CHAPTER TWENTY-SEVEN

When Emily and I left the homestead later that morning, she was again in the navy gingham dress, but as the temperature had dropped, she wore a warm sweater over her dress, and then wrapped the whole ensemble in her cloak.

I wasn't taking chances with the cold either. I wore two pairs of stockings, plus a cardigan and shawl over my housedress and under my cloak. Even so, as soon as we stepped outside, I felt frozen through. I was not looking forward to walking door-to-door around Kelley Square, passing out church leaflets, but it had to be done. I worried for the families who lived there that didn't have enough firewood to make it through the night.

I buried my nose in my scarf. Emily conversely looked up into the sky. Carlo stayed close to her, as if he was trying to protect her from the frigid blasts of wind.

"My poem eluded me last night, Willa, and my mind can't touch on what is wrong with it. I sense something is amiss, but it's just out of reach. It is the most frustrating thing in the world for a poet. I feel that I am on the cusp of discovery, but the words that I rely on to unlock it elude me, leaving me at a loss inside of myself."

"Can't you just bend the poem to your will?" I asked, not understanding at all how this could possibly be a struggle.

"The truth about writing, Willa, is that you are never in complete control of it. Words will lead you down new paths. Not all those paths you want to take, but sometimes those paths open your eyes to an understanding that you could never reach in the practical world. You must be willing to go where they lead, Willa. You need to understand that. If you do not follow them, they will not return to you another day."

I nodded. I would have to take her word on that since I had written nothing more than a letter in years, and I had certainly never felt like the words were taking over my letter or leading me along some winding path. It was another indication to me that writers thought differently. I had noticed it also during the past summer, when Ralph Waldo Emerson had visited the family. He wasn't a poet, but he was the first person who I had thought was most like Emily in terms of that faraway look she would get in her eyes when a poem took over.

We said little else on the walk to Dr. Weston's lab. The lab wasn't far from the maintenance shed where we had met Jimmy O'Malley the day before. I looked around for the janitor but didn't see him. I hoped that he was somewhere safe inside and staying warm. I would have thought this a good day to sweep all the classrooms.

As I'd overheard while serving breakfast to the family that morning, Amherst College planned to restart classes that very day, following numerous cancelations due to the blizzard, but President Stearns had decided to call classes off again because of the desperately low temperatures. If all went well, classes would resume at the end of the week. However, going well with the weather was proving to be a challenge.

"This is the building," Emily said, and walked up to the small brick building that read "Science Hall" on the side.

I half expected the door to be locked, but it opened easily. Emily, Carlo, and I found ourselves in a grand hall. There was a large rosette window across from where we stood. I imagined the light coming in through the window would be warm and lovely on the polished wood paneling all around us. But on this cold day the light from the window had a dull gray cast to it.

Footsteps echoed around us, and Dr. Weston came around the corner. "Miss Dickinson," he said. "Thank you so much for coming. Ever since you mentioned your interest in botany, I have been looking forward to your call. Since the college was closed again today, I knew this would be the best chance for you to visit without being bothered by my students."

"I would not have minded coming when your students were here. I used to love the vibrancy of the lab when I was at Mount Holyoke."

His eyes shone when he looked at her. "How long were you there?"

"Just one year. I may have wanted to stay longer, but my father felt like it was enough. I did miss my friends at first, but I found that staying home and furthering my education on my own was far more enlightening. I would say in this case my father made the right choice for me."

It seemed to me that Dr. Weston had eyes only for Emily, so I wasn't surprised in the least when it took him a moment to see Carlo and me standing behind her.

"Oh, you brought your dog and your maid," he said.

I tried not to take offense that yet again the dog was mentioned before me. Carlo was larger than life after all. It was something I was accustomed to.

"Yes, Willa works with me in the greenhouse and in my garden, so I thought it would be beneficial to have her here to pick up on anything that I might miss. She has a great attention for detail, and I rarely go anywhere in Amherst without Carlo."

Dr. Weston looked this way and that. "I can't have the dog in the lab."

"That is fine. He is very obedient and will gladly stay here in the hall."

"The dean would not like it," Dr. Weston said. "But that old man won't be coming out in this weather. Please follow me."

Emily told Carlo to lie by the door, and he plopped down with a great sigh. If he had his way, he would always be with his mistress.

Emily and I followed Dr. Weston into his lab at the back of the building. It was more of a greenhouse than a lab, and every last corner was full of plants. There was a black stove in one corner heating the room. It pumped out volumes of hot air that were a great benefit to the plants, but as soon as I stepped into the lab, I began to sweat.

Emily removed her bonnet. "It's quite warm in here."

"I should have told you to leave your bonnet and cloaks in the hall. I have to keep the temperature high in this room in order to protect the plants. There are days when it's eighty degrees in here and thirty outside. Now, since it's so far below zero today, the temperature is holding steady at sixty."

I removed my bonnet and cloak and took Emily's from her hands.

"That's much better," she said. "It must be a great deal of work to keep all these plants alive."

"It is, but I have had help until recently."

"Until recently?"

He tapped one of the waxy leaves of a snake plant. "Yes, Hugh Doolan came and looked after my plants when I wasn't able to. Now that he's gone, I have to spend even more time here, watering and pruning. It takes time away from my experiments."

"I did not know that Hugh worked for you. Neither you nor your wife mentioned that."

"I don't know that Verona even knows. She has no interest in plants, so I speak very little of my work to her."

Emily seemed to consider this.

"Now, let me show you what I am working on. This is the exciting piece of the tour."

He led us out of the greenhouse, while I continued to carry our heavy cloaks and bonnets. When we stepped over the threshold the temperature dropped a great deal. In all this cold, I was surprised to be so relieved at no longer being hot. It was a wonder to me that Dr. Weston wasn't ill all the time as he went back and forth through these shifting temperatures. My mother always said that was what caused fevers.

We found ourselves in a much smaller room. There was a wide wooden table in the middle. In one corner, the table was piled high with books and papers. The rest of the surface was covered with newspaper and seeds in different levels of dissection.

He walked over to the table. "If I can find out how the inside of the seed works, I believe I can make changes to the plant that will make it more viable."

"Why would you want to do that?" Emily asked. "I think every gardener knows that seeds are no guarantees of fruit or blooms."

"Yes, but I am trying to change that."

"How?" Emily stepped forward and picked up the magnifying glass that sat on the table. She held it over one of the open bean seeds.

"People have been propagating plants for specific qualities for centuries. I am looking for how to do that in a faster and easier way."

"With any success?" She set the glass back on the table.

"Not yet. I just need more time." He glanced back in the direction of the greenhouse. "The loss of Hugh is a great inconvenience to me."

I bit my lip. I knew that Dr. Weston was upset that he lost a reliable volunteer in Hugh, but it was nothing in comparison to what Norah Rose had lost. I had to hold fast to my tongue to keep myself from saying something.

"All of this must take a great deal of your time," Emily said. "Is the college funding your research?"

He frowned. "No. I asked them to help me, but they refused. When I make my discovery, they will be thrilled beyond words over it, but the college is no help."

"You are paying out of your own pocket?" Emily asked.

"I have a benefactor. Mr. Ward, whom you have met. He owns quite a lot of land out in Texas. He believes that it could be the breadbasket of the country, if not the world. The issue is water, which is scarce. He is putting a great deal of pressure on me to come up with drought-resistant crops that can flourish in the area."

"I do remember him saying something like that, but how can a plant live without water?"

"There are succulents and cacti that survive on little to no water. It's just a matter of using their properties to make it possible."

"Yes, but are those grown for crops?"

"Not yet, but maybe someday. I am trying to cross succulents with well-known crops to see if they are drought resistant. Mr. Ward is quite excited with my work, but it is a great deal of pressure." He rubbed the back of his neck.

"Is Mr. Ward here? I have not seen him since he came to our home."

"He returned to Mount Holyoke just yesterday. He braved the foul weather as he was eager to get back since his wife is expecting. To be honest, I was relieved to see him go. I work better without someone looking over my shoulder. With Mr. Ward here or not, I have and will be in the lab for many long hours. My wife is not happy about that."

"Verona is quite a striking woman," Emily said. "I am surprised . . ." She trailed off.

He finger-combed his black mustache and again the image of a broom came to my mind. "You wonder how she ended up with a man like me?"

Emily shrugged. "Well, yes, that is what I wonder."

I winced. There were times that Emily's bluntness caused me to cringe. This was one of those times.

He cleared his throat as if the conversation made him uncomfortable. "She was the sister of a friend of mine from university. Her brother, Simon, died in an accident. He was like a brother to me too. She didn't have anyone else. I thought the right thing to do was marry her and give her a good life. I had just been appointed to this position at the college and had begun working with Mr. Ward on his crop project. I believe that made me attractive to her. Being a professor's wife was prestigious in its way." He said that last part as if he wasn't entirely sure that was true.

"You married her out of pity."

"No. I did love her." He looked away. "She might have married me out of pity."

Emily wrinkled her brow, and I sensed that she was going to ask even more about this, so I was glad when Dr. Weston steered the conversation back to crops. "Where I am running into trouble is with grafting, which is an ancient method to propagate new varieties of plants, and which is not working between succulents and, say, some crop staple like corn."

Emily shook her head. "I know quite a bit about plants, and I don't know how this will work at all. Perhaps cross-pollination would be a better method."

"Perhaps," he said with a good amount of doubt in his voice.

"I wish you a great deal of luck on that, as it seems it would be a great challenge."

"It is, but you must understand that I am doing good work that will benefit the whole country, if not the whole world someday. Imagine if crops could be grown in the desert with little or no water for weeks at a time. What a wonder that would be." He wrung his hands. "But if I don't have help, it will never happen."

"Surely, there is someone on campus who would help you. A student?" Emily said. "Or what about Jimmy O'Malley? He is also a janitor, is he not? Can't he jump in and help?"

"I would not ask O'Malley for help with anything. I would be too afraid that my plants would not survive. He is not the most delicate of men, and this is a delicate operation."

It was true "delicate" was not the word I would use to describe Jimmy as I remembered how he threw the wrench at the hydrant.

"Your wife?" Emily asked. "Surely, she has a great deal of interest in your work now that you have been married for a little while."

"My wife has no interest in plants." He cleared his throat. "But since you have an interest in plants, I thought you might be willing to participate in the project."

Emily placed a hand on her chest. "Me?"

He nodded. "You're very knowledgeable about plants, and I would trust you."

Emily wrinkled her brow. "I'm flattered, but I don't—"

He held up his hand. "Don't answer now. Please think it over. I am desperate for help."

Emily frowned.

Shortly after that, we said our goodbyes and collected Carlo at the door.

The heavy wooden door closed behind us. "There was something about him that made me uncomfortable," I said, remembering how he spoke of his marriage and how he looked at Emily. "I know you have a great interest in plants, but I don't think you should take this offer of his."

She looked at me. "Not to worry, Willa. The only projects I work on are mine and mine alone." She glanced back at the hall. "But I think it's a good idea to let him think it's a possibility until we find out what happened to the Doolans. I have a feeling the Westons may have a part to play in all of it."

I did too.

CHAPTER TWENTY-EIGHT

As we walked to Kelley Square, I asked Emily, "Do you think Jimmy O'Malley knew that Hugh was doing all this extra work for Dr. Weston?"

"He must have suspected something. Didn't he say something about Hugh wandering off all the time?"

"And Eve wondered about Hugh too. Addy, Mrs. Stearns's cook, said that Eve was worried about him. He claimed to be working extra hours at the college to make sure the water pipes didn't freeze. However, Addy believes that Eve thought he was gone more often for another reason."

"What other reason?"

"She either didn't know or didn't tell Addy."

Emily spun the burgundy ribbon from her bonnet around her mitten-covered hand. "It was woman's intuition, then. Most of the time that is proven right."

"But why wouldn't he tell his wife if he was simply watering plants? Why would he lie and say it was something else entirely?"

She shook her head as if she didn't have the answer to that either.

The barometer's prediction about the plummeting temperatures had been right.

Yesterday, there had been a few people outside chopping firewood and hanging cloth over their windows with the hope it would keep the heat in the house, but today, there wasn't a soul about.

We had reached the edge of Kelley Square, and Emily stopped and sat on a boulder that marked the entrance to the community. She had little care that she was getting snow on the back of her cloak. Carlo lay on her feet as if he wanted to keep them warm.

Emily had a small satchel attached to her wrist. She opened it and removed a scrap of paper and a stub of a pencil. Hunched over on the rock, she scribbled onto the piece of paper. Standing in the cold, it seemed to me that she had been writing for a very long time, but it could have been only a matter of minutes.

She dropped the paper and pencil back into the satchel.

"There." She stood. "I had to get the words out before they strangled me."

"Strangled you?" I asked.

"Yes, of course, as any writer will tell you, you can choke on the words not written. They will nag you and claw at your mind if you ignore them. There is no ignoring the urge to write."

I frowned. I would have to take Emily's word on this. The only strong urge I ever had was to garden and dig into the earth. I wasn't sure if it was the same feeling she described. I certainly never felt I might be strangled by it.

The sound of someone playing the fiddle brought back childhood memories. We weren't Irish, but we were poor. My mother could only just afford to rent us a room in one of the small homes. When I was ten, she had found a small house in the woods where we lived until she passed.

The moment my mother was buried, the landlord made Henry and me leave the house, and we moved from place to place in the years that followed.

My little bedroom in the Dickinson home was the first time I felt like I had a place of my own. Margaret, for all her faults, rarely ever knocked on my door when we weren't working. I curled up on my bed with books borrowed from the Dickinson library, often with one or two of Miss Lavinia's cats beside me. I didn't know how Miss Lavinia would feel if she knew her cats liked my company, so it was a secret just between the felines and me.

They also liked to visit me because I would sneak them pieces of chicken or ham from the kitchen. It had come to the point that anytime I opened a book they expected a snack. That was especially true for the black cat, Baby Z, who was still a kitten in many ways.

When we reached the remains of the Doolan home there was a small cluster of people gathered there. A priest stood in front of them. His words rang through the square. "Hugh and Eve Doolan will be remembered as devout members of our congregation and community. All they wanted was to raise their daughter in the faith and contribute to the community. I know they didn't come to mass often, but it was not for the lack of wanting to be there. Let us pray."

The small congregation all lowered their heads, and the priest lowered his voice, so Emily and I could not hear the prayer. Even so, I felt its sentiment.

When the prayer came to an end, the priest reached into the canvas pouch at his hip and pulled out what appeared to be a vial and a stick. He dipped the stick into the vial and dashed water onto the remains of the home.

The group broke up, and the priest spoke softly to each person as they left.

"Was this the funeral?" Emily asked.

"I don't believe so," I said. Having lived in Kelley Square I had seen Catholic funerals before, and this appeared to be much different to me. Although it had been a very long time since I attended such a service.

"We should tell them about the First Congregational Church's warming mission," Emily said, taking a step forward.

I grabbed her hand. "No, wait until they speak with the priest. It seems wrong to break into something so solemn." I dropped my hand to my side.

Emily arched her brow at me. It wasn't often that I disagreed with her on such matters. She nodded.

The last parishioner spoke with the priest and shuffled in the cold presumably toward her home somewhere in Kelley Square. Emily jumped into action with Carlo at her side. I knew that it would be impossible to hold her back now, so I didn't even try.

Emily waved at the priest. "Reverend?"

He turned. "You can call me Father. I am Father Bryan. How can I help you, child?"

He said "child" to Emily, but as we drew closer to him, I realized that he could be no more than thirty.

"I am sorry if you missed the blessing," Father Bryan said.

"That's what you were doing? Blessing?" Emily asked.

He nodded. "Hugh and Eve were a fine couple. I wish that Norah Rose, their daughter, could have been here, but I have heard she's been placed with a Protestant family."

"That's my family," Emily said.

"Oh!" He held on to the side of his canvas satchel as if he feared Emily might snatch it from his hip.

"She is a lovely little girl, and it's been my family's honor to care for her."

The priest relaxed. "Good. Good. I have always been fond of her and her parents. They were honest hardworking people. Hugh just wanted to take care of his wife and daughter. He wanted them to have a better life."

"It's what any father would want, I imagine," Emily said.

Father Bryan sadly shook his head. "You would be surprised. That is not always the case."

I knew this was true from my own experience with my father.

"What is your name, so I can share with my flock that Norah Rose is safe?"

"I'm Emily Dickinson and this is Willa Noble."

I was gratified that Emily didn't introduce me to the priest as her maid.

"Oh, Dickinson, I'm familiar even though I don't live here in Amherst. I am a traveling priest, you see, I go from town to town where there is no church building to provide services and last rites. I know the name Dickinson well. I even heard your father speak once when he was on the campaign trail years ago." His brow wrinkled. "What has brought you back here to this sad place?"

"The First Congregational Church is hosting a warming mission tonight because it promises to be so cold. We are telling the families on Kelley Square that might be running low on firewood."

"That is very kind of the church. It is gratifying to know that Christian charity knows no lines when it comes to Catholic and Protestant."

"I believe that it should know no lines at all," Emily said.

"You are right, Miss Dickinson," Father Bryan said. "Sadly, that is rarely the case."

"You are welcome to come to the church tonight as well," I said, speaking for the first time since we met with the priest.

He shook his head. "I wish I could, but I have a very large parish over a great amount of land. A priest's work is never done, and I am expected in the next town. There are many people I need to minister to, and I cannot let the weather be a barrier to keep me from them."

"Where are you headed?" Emily asked.

"I'm off to Mount Holyoke next," he said, and lifted the hood of his cape over his head as the cold wind had picked up.

Emily brightened at the mention of Mount Holyoke as she always did. "We just met a man from Mount Holyoke. His name is Kelvin Ward. He owns a lot of land in the area, he said."

Father Bryan wrinkled his nose. "Yes, I know Kelvin. He is an ambitious man, and I have learned that he will do whatever it takes to move his agenda forward."

"Really?" Emily asked. "He seemed quite pleasant when we met him."

"Kindness is his first method. He has others."

Emily and I shared a look. We were both wondering what that could possibly mean.

"One of the professors here at the college is working for Mr. Ward to create a drought-resistant crop that can be grown on Mr. Ward's land in Texas."

"I imagine that this professor is under a great deal of pressure to succeed, then. Kelvin Ward will expect nothing more than success. If there is not success, he will want something in return." Father Bryan shook his head as if he didn't even want to think about all the possibilities.

The priest pulled his cape more tightly around his thin body. "As I see parishioners on my travels today, I will tell them of the First Congregational Church's warming mission."

"Thank you, Father," I said.

He nodded. "Now I must be on my way if I want to make it to Mount Holyoke by dark. It's a half-day's ride. My horse is at the stables at the end of town."

"Father Bryan," I said.

He looked to me.

"The Dickinsons will not be able to keep Norah Rose forever."

"This is a difficult time to ask someone to take another child on due to the weather," he said. "I know many who would consider it if the winter wasn't so harsh. Now they struggle to feed the children that they have."

I nodded. I understood his answer, but it still pained me to hear.

"Was that all?" the priest asked.

"I have one more question," Emily said. "Did Hugh have any enemies that you know of?"

He shook his head. "This I do not know as it is something that young men rarely tell their priest." He paused. "Please tell Norah Rose that I pray for her daily and for her parents' souls. She can take comfort in that they are at rest. I know this. I would like to stop by and visit her on my return travels if that would be all right."

"We would love that," Emily said.

"And it would mean a great deal to Norah Rose," I said.

He nodded. "I am glad. A child must be protected at all times. The Lord will look on you with favor for your kindness."

Emily stared at him but said nothing in return. I knew his words had stirred a poem deep in her heart.

CHAPTER TWENTY-NINE

FATHER BRYAN BID us good day, and after he left, there was no one on the street. Only a fool would be outside when it was this cold. I supposed that meant Emily and I were counted among the fools.

I held the leaflets in my arms. "What do we do now?"

Emily straightened her shoulders. "We just start knocking on doors."

It sounded simple enough, but I felt shyness wash over me. I wasn't one to just walk up to another person's home and knock on the door. Even when I had been interviewed by Margaret to work for the Dickinsons, I had been scared to walk to the house, and she had known that I was coming.

Emily didn't feel the same way at all. She confidently walked up to the first clapboard building and knocked on the door. Inside the house, barking broke out, and Carlo squeezed between the front door and his mistress. He pushed her three steps back with his large body.

"Carlo, behave."

"He's just trying to protect you," I said.

"From dogs barking?" Emily asked. "I am not afraid of dogs."

Having been chased by a dog myself in this very village as a child, I believed that having a healthy fear of a dog you didn't know was a good thing. They were unpredictable animals.

"Cut that out, you!" a man shouted in the house.

The dogs stopped barking, and Carlo relaxed some. However, he still had his eyes trained on the front door of the house as if he knew those barking dogs would jump out if given the chance.

A man with a full black beard came to the doorway. He wore a thick fisherman's sweater and a knit hat on his head. "What's this?"

"Hello. I'm Emily Dickinson, and this is Willa. The church in town would like everyone in Kelley Square to know that the church will be opening its doors at three this afternoon and throughout the night as a warming mission. There will be food, blankets, hot tea and coffee, and everything needed to get through what promises to be the coldest night of these last few weeks." Emily held one of the pamphlets out to him.

When he made no move to take it, she said, "Here, this is for you, and tell your friends and neighbors too."

He took the piece of paper but didn't even glance at it. I didn't know if that was because he was unable to read or the fact that he didn't want to give Emily the satisfaction of showing he was interested.

"You're with the church," he said.

"I'm not with the church," Emily said. "But we have volunteered to spread the word to avoid another tragedy. As you must know, there was a fire not far from here and a young couple was killed."

"Yes, I know all about it. Everyone in Kelley Square has been paranoid about setting a fire in their homes ever since. The chimney sweeps are working double time."

"I can imagine," Emily said. "My father is having all of our chimneys looked at today as well."

"It's dangerous work, especially when there is so much ice on the roof. I used to do it when I was younger. I work in the warehouse now. It's backbreaking work, but not nearly as dangerous as being a sweep. I've fallen from my share of roofs over the years and had always made it through. Now, at my age, I am no longer willing to take the risk."

Emily folded her gloved hands together in front of herself. "Have you worked at the warehouse very long?"

"It's going on four years."

"Then, you might know Willa's brother, Henry Noble. He worked at the warehouse for a long time, isn't that right, Willa?"

I nodded, but my stomach turned at the mention of Henry.

He looked at me. "You're Henry Noble's sister?"

I nodded. "Willa."

"Ahh, he spoke of you. I remember the name because it was my grandmother's, God rest her soul. She was always good to me. I'm Declan," he said as if I should recognize the name, but I didn't. Henry was always very secretive to me about his work because he didn't want me to know what he was up to. Had I known, I might have been able to save him. I pushed that thought away and reminded myself for the hundredth time that my brother made his own choices.

"He was a good lad," Declan went on.

I was grateful when he didn't ask if Henry had mentioned him to me.

Declan shook his head. "Most of them prefer to loiter rather than unload the train cars. We were all disappointed that he left and went to work at the stables. Didn't go well for him, since he was killed. What a shame."

I wasn't going to tell this man why Henry left. It would expose an underground operation in the town of Amherst, and I didn't know him or whether he could be trusted.

Instead, I said, "Thank you for saying that. He was a good brother." I cleared my throat. "You said everyone in Kelley Square is speaking of the fire. Did you know the Doolans well?"

"As well as any of us did. They had been married for a good while, and Eve was so talented with a needle and thread. They lived in a boardinghouse until just a few months ago. Hugh said that he came into some money to rent a proper house for his family." He shook his head. "It's a shame if you ask me. If they were still living in the boardinghouse, they'd be alive now, wouldn't they?"

I shivered. "Did he say how he came into the money?"

He tugged on his beard. "Said there was extra work for him around the college."

Could that extra work have been caring for Dr. Weston's plants? Had he paid him? Dr. Weston certainly didn't offer Emily any money to take on the duties.

"You'll want to go to Sean McGill's home, if it's answers you're looking for," he said. "He's—for lack of a better title—the busybody of Kelley Square. While you're there, if you tell him about the church, he'll make sure the word gets out. He'll tell you all the gossip there is about the Doolans—crying shame as to what happened to them. I hate to see young people pass on. It just isn't right."

Emily and I agreed that it wasn't right.

"Will you be coming to the church?" Emily asked.

The man shook his head. "I have two hound dogs and can't leave them here in the cold alone. I don't think they would be welcome." He nodded at Carlo, who leaned against Emily's side. "I see you have a dog of your own. Maybe you will understand."

"Yes, I do. I'm sure the dogs would be welcome. How could the church turn beloved pets away on these cold nights? Please come and bring your hounds. They will be most welcome."

"I'll see about that," Declan said.

Somewhere in the house, the hounds began to howl in tandem. The sound was piercing, and I wondered how much louder it would be when it was reverberating off the thick stone walls and high ceiling of the church.

I held my tongue, as I guessed the hounds would not be welcome at the church. I hoped Declan would choose to stay home.

CHAPTER THIRTY

As we made our way to Sean McGill's house, we stopped at every residence along the way and handed out flyers. Some people never came to the door, others took the paper and then slammed the door in our faces. Others thanked us and welcomed a bit of small talk. At every chance Emily got, she asked after the Doolans. Every time, her questions were greeted with suspicion, as if the person wondered whether she was up to something.

By the time we reached Sean McGill's home, the sun was beginning to set. Carlo whimpered at our sides. He knew that it was high time we began the walk home unless we wanted to walk in the dark.

Sean's house came into view. It was a railman's home. There were railroad ties on either side of the front door just peeking out of the snow. From what I could tell, the ties marked off Sean's garden. If he was a gardener, he would get along with Emily just fine. When she wasn't writing, she spent most of her time working in the greenhouse and gardens. It would be good for this conversation that she could talk with a kindred spirit who also loved plants as much as she did.

Like all the other doors in Kelley Square, she knocked on this one with no hesitation at all.

No one answered, and the sun sank behind the trees. Shadows lengthened all around us, and I knew very well that Margaret was seething back at the homestead for me being gone so very long. I did not begrudge her that; I would have felt the same in her place.

Emily knocked again, and when no one came to the door a second time, I touched her arm. "Let's come back tomorrow in the light of day. He must not be home. Your parents will be getting worried for you."

She sighed and clapped her hands to signal Carlo to stand, as it was time to leave. We were just a few yards from the house when the door opened. "What is all this racket out here?" An elderly man in a wool coat asked. His silver beard hung to the third button of his coat, and a pair of spectacles perched on the tip of his nose.

Emily turned with a big smile on her face. "Are you Sean McGill?"

"Who wants to know?" He spat a stream of black chewing tobacco into the snow.

I stepped back and looked away so that he would not see the disgusted expression on my face.

Emily was undaunted by his crude behavior. "I'm Emily Dickinson, the daughter of Edward Dickinson. I am sure you have heard the Dickinson name often in Amherst."

"So, what if I have? Am I supposed to be impressed by that?

I've also heard the name of the livestock at the Mitchell farm. Does that make the cows noteworthy?"

Emily removed a leaflet from the stack in her arms and held it out to him. "We were told that you were the one to spread the word in Kelley Square. The church is having a warming mission tonight since the temperatures promise to drop well below zero. We are telling everyone we can about it."

"Are you telling us because we are poor?" He squinted at her. "You don't think we can take care of ourselves? The rich have a lot of nerve to make such assumptions, but I suppose that is what the rich do."

"Yes, we are concerned that you will not be warm enough as the temperatures promise to drop to dangerous levels. This is especially dangerous to children and the elderly, such as yourself," she said in her matter-of-fact way.

"Good grief, girl, did you just call me old to me face?" He grabbed his stomach and gave a great belly laugh.

"You are, aren't you?"

"You are right about that, lass." He smiled. "I like a person who isn't afraid to state the facts."

"Then, you and I will get along famously," Emily said. "And the facts are your walls are not as thick as some of the other homes in town, and it's difficult to keep up with firewood at this time, since so much of the forest is buried in snow. We want the people in Kelley Square to have an option to go someplace a bit warmer for the night."

"You make quite a convincing argument for just a little sprite." Sean held out his hand. "Let me see that."

Emily smiled as she handed over the leaflet. "I am a poet, sir, not a sprite."

"Sprite? Poet? Are they not the same? Both are ethereal in their way."

"I can see that," Emily said.

Sean's lips moved as he read over the leaflet, and then he looked up at Emily again. "I'll spread the word. I know some families very low on provisions, and this will be a great help. There will be food there?" he asked.

"Yes, hot food, blankets, and warmth. Everything that anyone in your community will need to get through the cold night," Emily said.

"Very good." He made a move as if he was going to close the door.

Emily waved her hand. "One more thing."

He waited.

"The church has thought to do this because of the terrible tragedy that befell the Doolan family."

His cheeks flushed.

"They don't want an accident like that to happen to another family in Amherst. When it's this cold, a house fire is, of course, a very real concern."

"An accident," he snorted. "The murder of Hugh and Eve Doolan was no accident. I can promise you that." With that he slammed the door closed. It seemed like any rapport that Emily had fostered with Sean had vanished the moment she mentioned the Doolans.

The sunlight was all but gone now, and I was able to pull Emily away from Sean's house. "We have to go."

"Yes, I suppose you are right, Willa. I hate to leave when we are so close to answers. You can't tell me that Sean McGill doesn't know something about Eve's and Hugh's deaths."

"I agree with you," I said. "But it's too late in the day and getting far too dark and cold to stay out much longer." I squeezed her hands. "Your hands feel like ice, even with gloves on. You will put them in hot water when we get home so you don't get frostbite." I removed my hands.

"To any happy flower, the frost beheads it at its play," she said.

I did not know if she was speaking of herself or the Doolans in this case. I did not believe that she intended me to know of whom she was speaking. At times, I thought Emily's words were to be interpreted as how the receiver wished, nothing more, nothing less.

She smiled. "But you are right. We have passed out dozens of the pamphlets. We should return home before we freeze."

We began the walk home that wasn't very far at all, but in the cold, it felt like miles and miles. I tried not to think about how cold I was, but that made me feel only colder.

"Willa, I must say," Emily said, seemingly undaunted by the temperature. "We have to consider everyone attached to the Doolans as suspects in this crime."

"Like who?" I asked, doing my very best to keep my teeth from chattering as I spoke.

"First of all," she said, "there is Olive Stearns. Eve was her seamstress, so she would be privy to much that was being said in the college president's home."

"You think Mrs. Stearns could have done this? Or President Stearns, for that matter?"

"No, of course not, but they are connected to the Doolans. It would be irresponsible to leave them off the list."

"Then, you will have to include Mrs. Verona Weston as well," I said.

Emily's bonnet bobbed up and down. I took that to be a nod, as I was beside her and couldn't see her face around the wide brim. "Yes, I think that she is far more of a viable suspect than Olive, and she has the added connection that Hugh was doing extra work for Dr. Weston, who looked quite anxiety-ridden if you ask me."

"According to Father Bryan, he has reason to be. It sounds like Kelvin Ward is putting a great deal of pressure on him."

She nodded. "Pressure like that can be detrimental to a marriage."

Miss Susan and Austin's young marriage came to my mind. It had not quite been a year, and there were signs already of the edges beginning to fray.

"That crude man Danny Boyle is on the list," Emily said. "Maybe for the mere fact that I don't care for him, but he does have proximity to the Doolans' home as a neighbor. He could have set the fire very easily without being seen and waltzed right back to his bed."

"I don't like Danny either," I said. "But why would he take the risk of setting a fire so close to his own home? His house with his wife and children in it was just a few yards away."

"You make a very good point as always, Willa."

"If we are thinking of everyone connected to Eve and Hugh, we have to include the other college janitor, Jimmy O'Malley, as well. He does look like he has a violent temperament," I said, again remembering Jimmy throwing the wrench. "And he was very angry that Hugh was leaving him with most of the janitorial work while—we know now—Hugh worked for Dr. Weston in his lab."

"Yes, he's on the list. I must say, Willa. You are getting quite proficient at assessing suspects."

"I'm not sure that is a good thing, miss. I am now suspicious of everyone I meet."

"It's better than being naive, Willa, much better than that," she said.

As we walked out of Kelley Square, Mrs. Turnkey came from the opposite direction. Behind her, I could see the back of a man hurrying away from Kelley Square. I might have been mistaken, but I could have sworn it looked like Danny Boyle.

Mrs. Turnkey stopped in the middle of the street and waited for us. "Miss Dickinson, I am surprised to see you out in this weather. Are you here to look in on the Boyles again? I'm quite impressed that you have come out again so soon and on a much colder day."

"We may stop by to see how the Boyles are doing but are actually here to pass out leaflets about the First Congregational warming mission." Emily gave her one of the pamphlets. "Mrs. Stearns is spearheading it with the help of the church's Ladies' League."

Mrs. Turnkey looked over the piece of paper. "What does the church think it's doing? The Ladies' Society of Amherst are the ones who have been reaching out to help the residents of Kelley Square during this difficult time."

"The church is not limiting it to Kelley Square. Anyone in Amherst who needs to escape the cold is welcome. Is it wrong that more than one group is willing to help the residents of Kelley Square in this cold?"

"Don't put words in my mouth," Mrs. Turnkey snapped. "I want to help as many people as I can, but it would be a great courtesy if the First Congregational Church would have at least let me know. I have very many connections in Kelley Square. I could have been telling the residents about this for days."

"You can still help. The church needs people to serve soup, hand out blankets, and visit with the people who will be staying there tonight."

Mrs. Turnkey sniffed. "That is not usually what I do. My job covers the wider picture of supporting those in need." She paused. "But I will stop by if time allows."

"What brings you to Kelley Square today?" Emily asked.

Mrs. Turnkey bristled and the fox head of her wrap bounced on her shoulder. "I am here for the same reason you are, to check on the people who are living here. I have some calls to make. I have been disappointed in the commitment of the women of Amherst to visiting and bringing provisions to families in Kelley Square. Because of that, I must pick up the slack. It is my duty, being the president of the society."

"We won't keep you, then," Emily said.

Mrs. Turnkey nodded and continued on her way.

Emily clapped her hands again, and Carlo ran ahead of us on the cold walk home.

CHAPTER THIRTY-ONE

"YOU HAVE ABSOLUTELY no respect for me or for my position in this home," Margaret said. She stood at the stovetop stirring the warm custard that would be served to the family for dessert. "You have put me in a terrible position. I had to do all of my duties, all of your duties, and make dinner for the family."

"I know. I—"

She waved her wooden spoon at me. "I am not finished. When Mrs. Dickinson asked where you were, I had to say that you were with Miss Dickinson, and you would be back soon. That was hours ago. Because you were not here, I had to press Mrs. Dickinson's dress for dinner tonight. You know anytime Austin and Miss Susan come to dinner she wants to look her very best to prove to Miss Susan that she is still the matriarch in the family. When she asked me where you were to press the dress, I said that you were making the dinner. I could not tell her that you were still out with Miss Dickinson, off heaven knew where, doing heaven knew what. By that time, it had been hours and hours since you both had been gone. She would have worried. She would have alerted Mr. Dickinson. Miss Dickinson would have been reprimanded, and you!" She waved the spoon like a wand. "You would have been sacked." She took a breath.

My hands were shaking. Margaret had been angry or frustrated with me many times since I had started working with her. She was especially aggravated when it came to my relationship with Emily. She did not understand our friendship and made it very clear in her statements that she didn't believe family and staff could ever be true friends. I believed that she was right to a point. I could never be as close to Emily as Miss Lavinia or Miss Susan were. I wasn't and never would be their equal or a member of the family. I was not a Dickinson; I was just a maid.

Even so, Margaret had never yelled at me so harshly before. It was just more proof to me how upset she really was about my absence. Truly, she had every right to be. I wasn't in a place to make excuses. I could not tell her that Emily wanted me to go with her to Kelley Square and that we went to the village with the intention to tell the families in the community about the warming mission in the church that night. It would not matter to her or how she felt about the position I had left her in.

I certainly couldn't tell her that we went to Kelley Square to learn more about the Doolans because Emily was convinced that the couple's death was no accident, but murder.

"Margaret, I am deeply sorry. You have every right to be angry, but you don't need to protect me. I would not want you to put your own place in the homestead at risk on my behalf."

"I don't need to protect you because Miss Dickinson will do so for you. As far as she is concerned you can do no wrong." She glared at me. "Do you know she treats you with the same dignity and affection that she bestows on her dog? If you want to be counted in that number with pets, so be it. That is what you are, her pet."

Her words came as a slap across the face, and it took everything within me not to snap back. Lashing out would only hurt both of us even more.

"I am ready to take up the next course," I said.

She turned and looked me in the eye. There must have been something in my gaze that caused her to bite her tongue. "The ham is ready to go up."

With thick towels on my hands, I removed the ham from the oven, where it sat in a stone dish to stay warm. It was uncut. That would be the duty of Mr. Dickinson, who liked to make a great production of carving the meat at the head of the table.

I didn't make eye contact with Margaret as I carried the dish from the room. I would need to make amends with her and soon if I wanted our days to be civil, but I wasn't ready yet. What she had said about me being Emily's pet cut me to my very core because I feared it was the truth.

"There we are!" Mr. Dickinson said. He stood as I set the stone dish on the two trivets on the table.

"That looks lovely," Mrs. Dickinson said. "Please thank Margaret too. I know how hard she works." She gave me a pointed look.

I felt a little weak in my knees. The last thing in the world I wanted was for Mrs. Dickinson to begin to doubt my work ethic. I had gotten up early and completed all the morning duties before Margaret was even awake, but it seemed that went unnoticed because yet again I was absent during the day.

I glanced at Emily. I did not want to take credit for preparing the meal, but I also didn't want to deny that I had made it, as that was what Margaret had said I'd been doing when she had pressed Mrs. Dickinson's dress.

I stepped back to stand near the sideboard while Mr. Dickinson made the first cut. Plates were soon filled and passed around the table. They were eating family style that evening. There truly was no reason for me to stay in the dining room other than I dreaded going back to the kitchen and facing Margaret again.

The entire Dickinson family was present. Miss Susan and Austin sat across from each other, and every few seconds Austin looked up at his wife with a hint of worry on his face. I could not help but wonder what was bothering him. I hoped it had nothing to do with Norah Rose. We were no closer to finding a friend or relative to take her in. I knew Austin would tolerate the child in his home only so long, and although she was strong, Miss Susan would eventually give way to her husband's wishes of dismissing Norah Rose in the name of being a dutiful wife.

Miss Susan selected a small piece of ham and set it on her plate before passing the serving dish to Emily. "After the meal, I intend to go to the church and help with the warming mission. I know the reverend's wife is overwhelmed. Many of the members of the Ladies' League will be there."

"I will come with you," Miss Lavinia said. "It's the least that we can do to help those poor souls."

"We have done enough," Mr. Dickinson said. "Your mother donated all the blankets and coverlets in the home. We will be lucky if she did not snatch the quilts off each and every one of our beds to hand over."

"Edward, that is not true, nor is it fair for you to say that," Mrs. Dickinson said. "I only gave things that we weren't using. If the church can make use of them to help others, I see nothing wrong with that."

The whole family turned and looked at Mrs. Dickinson. It wasn't often that she made such a strong statement, especially to her husband.

Mr. Dickinson was quiet for a moment, and everyone was frozen as they waited to see how he would react.

"I know you did it out of kindness, Elizabeth. I would expect nothing less from you," Mr. Dickinson said.

The tension went out of the room like air out of a deflated balloon.

Emily cut her potatoes. "I will be going to the church as well."

"But you don't attend church," Miss Lavinia said.

"I am well aware of that, Sister, and this doesn't mean that I am going to start. However, I can be charitable without the backing of religion." Emily cut a small piece of ham from her serving and ate it.

Mr. Dickinson pressed his lips together. "It seems that I have been outvoted here." He nodded to Austin. "Let this be a lesson to you, Son. When women band together, they can be a powerful lot."

Austin glanced at Susan. "I believe, Father, they can be powerful all on their own."

I had loitered long enough in the dining room. If I stayed much longer, it would appear that I wasn't there to assist with the meal but to eavesdrop on their conversation. That wasn't entirely false. Any domestic would tell you that eavesdropping on his or her employer was a part of the life for good or for ill. However, it was also the best way to be in tune with the household and aware of any big changes that might be coming to the family or to the staff.

Margaret and I were both proficient in the craft, and despite our differences, we shared what information we gathered. The only things I didn't share with her were the things that Emily told me in confidence. Margaret might be right, and Emily might have viewed me as a beloved pet, but I viewed her as my mistress and my friend. No matter what Emily's true opinion was of me, there was trust there I would not betray.

I left through the doorway and stopped just out of view from the family when I heard Mr. Dickinson ask, "What are you planning to do about the child?"

Miss Susan spoke up. "The police are looking for her family or perhaps a family friend to take her in. Apparently, most of her living family is in Ireland. That does make it a bit difficult to correspond with them as it will triple the time to send and receive responses. I have told Austin that we must have patience and allow the authorities the time to make the necessary connections to secure the child's future."

"Why don't they ship her back, then, and let the Irish authorities sort it out?" Mr. Dickinson asked.

"It is not as easy as that. Do you want a child to travel to the other side of the world alone where she doesn't know a single person?" Miss Susan asked. "Just because someone is of the same blood as you does not mean that you have a relationship with that person. They might not even welcome her, and then what is she to do? She was born here and does not have an Irish accent. She would be seen as an outcast."

"Those are all very good points, Sister," Emily said. "I think we should take Norah Rose with us to the church tonight. I believe members of the Kelley Square community will have compassion, and there must be one family willing to take her in. She's such a tiny little thing. How much can she really eat?"

My stomach turned. Taking Norah Rose to the church was a terrible idea, one of the worst that I had ever heard.

"I don't think that is wise," Miss Susan said. "The poor sprite is already traumatized. Taking her to the church will not improve her well-being."

"It wouldn't be for long, and it might be the best way to find her a suitable home. I don't think any of us want her to be sent to the orphanage, but it might come to that." Emily patted a napkin to the corner of her mouth.

"Emily is right," Austin spoke up. "I think that it is a good idea."

"Agreed," Mrs. Dickinson said.

"This is a horrid idea," Susan said.

I couldn't agree more.

CHAPTER THIRTY-TWO

I HURRIED TO THE kitchen to collect the family's dessert. I wanted to take it to them right away, so I could clean the kitchen and dishes before the family left for the church. I had every intention of going now that I knew Norah Rose was being taken there.

Just outside of the kitchen, I stopped because I heard sniffling like someone was crying. I didn't know who it could be. The whole family was in the dining room.

I stepped into the kitchen to see Margaret staring out the window. Her back was to me, but she sniffed and dabbed at her face with a tea towel.

"Margaret?" I asked.

She turned to face me. Tears were in her eyes. I had never seen Margaret cry before. Not even when she dropped an iron pot on her foot and bruised it to the bone. I would have been curled up in a ball of pain. Margaret simply looked down at her shoes and said, "That hurts. I should probably see the doctor."

The doctor was called, and everyone was relieved that it was only a bruise and not broken. Had she not been wearing her sturdiest pair of shoes it would have been a different story altogether.

She wiped vigorously at her eyes. "Are they ready for dessert?"

"Just about," I said. "Are you all right?"

"I'm fine. Why wouldn't I be fine?" She cleared her throat and tucked the tea towel into the waist strings of her apron. "The custard is ready to take up. The bowls are already on the sideboard."

"Are you sure nothing is wrong?" I knew she wouldn't like it, but I had to ask again. It was disconcerting to see her this upset.

She glared at me. "What is wrong is that I get taken advantage of while you are off gallivanting with Miss Dickinson. I have worked in this home for years longer than you and am treated so differently than you are. Is it because I am Irish and you are a Yankee?"

I opened and closed my mouth. "I don't think that is the reason. But I am sorry to cause you any hurt at all."

"If you truly were sorry, you would tell Miss Dickinson that you were hired to cook and clean, not accompany her on her fool errands." Her face flushed red. "You do not have to go on these rambles with her, and if you began to say no that would be the end of it. She would go alone or find someone else to go with her. She has no shortage of friends and acquaintances."

Everything Margaret said was true, and maybe in part that

was why I never said no to Emily's requests of me, because I was afraid that she would stop asking.

"Please," I said. "Take the rest of the night off. I can clean up the kitchen, wash the dishes, and stoke the fires for the night."

"Are you sure that you will do it all even if Miss Dickinson comes here to ask you to wander off with her? I know how the two of you are."

I thought about my plan to go to the church to make sure that Norah Rose was treated well, but I didn't know how I would be able to go now.

I licked my lips. "Yes, I will stay and take care of it all."

She removed her apron and threw it on the stool. "It's about time."

With that, she marched out of the room.

I carried the dessert upstairs and found Emily, Miss Lavinia, and Miss Susan getting up from the table.

"Won't you at the very least stay for the custard?" Mrs. Dickinson asked.

"No," Miss Susan said. "If you insist that we take Norah Rose to the church, I would like to go as early as possible. She is just a child and should be put to bed at a decent hour."

I stood at the sideboard, and Emily walked over to me. "Are you coming to the church?" she whispered into my ear.

I shook my head. "I promised Margaret that I would care for the house so she could get some rest." I kept my voice low.

"That shouldn't take you too much time at all. Come over when you are finished," Emily said as if it were nothing to worry about at all. She didn't understand that as I was doing all the evening chores alone, it would take me two hours, give or take, to complete them, and that was if I worked at a sprinter's pace.

NEARLY THREE HOURS later, I placed a fresh log on the fire in Mrs. Dickinson's room. She was at her dressing table brushing her long hair for the night. I stood up. "Is there anything else you require, Mrs. Dickinson?"

She made eye contact with me through the mirror. "No, that will be all."

I nodded and gathered up my extra kindle, log carrier, and poker with the intention of moving to Emily's room to stoke her fire for the night next. I knew she wasn't there. She, Miss Susan, Miss Lavinia, and Norah Rose were at the church. It pained me that I wasn't there as well, but I knew I had made the right decision to stay behind and complete my duties. I was still holding out hope I would have time to go to the church and see Norah Rose. She needed all the support she could get.

I was about to step out of the door when Mrs. Dickinson spoke again. "Willa, what is your relationship with my daughter?"

I turned. "Ma'am?"

She was no longer looking in the mirror but had fully turned in her seat to look at me. "What is your relationship with my daughter?"

I adjusted the heavy logs in my arms. "I work for her and the whole family, ma'am."

"It is something more, isn't it?" she said. "There are times when I believe Emily prefers your company above all else. She used to be like this about Susan, but I know it broke her heart when Susan married, even if she joined our family forever."

I stood there because I didn't know what to say or what she wanted me to say.

"Emily is different. We all know that. There are times when she acts before thinking it all through. She lives in her writing where she can behave in such a way without being hurt or causing hurt. Real life is much different. I expect you to protect her from harming herself or someone else."

Before I could respond, she turned back around and resumed brushing her hair.

CHAPTER THIRTY-THREE

When I tucked the last spoon into the cutlery drawer, my shoulders sagged. All I wanted to do was go to bed and sleep. I couldn't do that though. I would never have been able to sleep a wink until I knew Norah Rose was safe. Through all my tasks that evening, I had worried about her. How was she feeling? Did a family take her on? Was one of her relatives found? Were there any relatives in Amherst?

It was just half past eight when I left through the back door of the homestead and followed the path Horace had cut in the snow to the street. I crossed the road and made a short walk to my right in the direction of the church.

Fires set in barrels peppered the churchyard, and young men stood around them warming their hands. Declan, whom Emily and I met at Kelley Square, was among them, and he had two red hound dogs at his feet. I could see only the dogs' heads, as they were wrapped in blankets. Declan stood out from the group not only because of his dogs but because he was twice the age of the other men.

"You there," he said as I was trying to pass. "You and that other girl told me that my dogs would be allowed in the church to stay warm. Now we are standing out in the freezing cold to see if we will be let in. We would have done much better staying home."

"I'm sorry. We thought animals would be welcome. Let me go into the church and find out."

"You had better because I am holding you and that other one responsible if anything happens to either one of my dogs."

"I—I will find out, sir."

They all watched me as I walked by, and a chill ran down my back. I didn't recognize any of the younger men, but I wondered how many of them Henry had played with when we were small and lived in Kelley Square.

I walked to the church door, and it opened before I set my hand on the handle.

An elderly woman with a hooked nose and wool coat looked me over. "We are full for the moment and only taking mothers with small children." She looked at me up and down. "Do you have a child with you?"

I shook my head.

"Then, go and stand with the men. If we can find space, we will invite you in." She started to close the door.

"I'm not here to get warm." I lowered the hood of my cloak. "I'm here to help. I'm the Dickinsons' maid."

She eyed me. "You are not the first one to make such a claim and then sneak inside for a warm meal. I told the reverend's wife that this idea of letting folks sleep in the church would backfire. How does it make us look to turn people away? It would have been better if we had never started this in the first place." She clicked her tongue in disgust. "What are the chances these people would die in the cold like everyone is afraid would happen? Rare, I tell you."

"I'm not lying," I said. "And I believe it is a great thing that the Ladies' League and church is doing."

"That is what they all say." She slammed the church door in my face.

I stood there for a long moment unsure what to do next. Behind me, I could feel the dozen or so young men and Declan watching me.

With as much dignity as I could, I lifted my chin and walked down the steps, and without looking at the men I walked around the back of the church.

There was no path to the rear of the building, and I trudged through the snow. The snow was over the top of my boots, and I felt it slip into the boots and fall to my feet.

Before too long my feet were wet and had nearly frozen. It would have been wiser of me to give up and go back to the homestead, where I could soak my feet in hot water and snuggle in bed.

However, the thought of Norah Rose being inside the church and being frightened hurt me more than any pain in my feet.

Behind the church, Horace's small cottage stood where he lived alone. Along with it was the church garden that in many ways was his garden. He was the gardener for the college, the church, and for the Dickinsons. He had told me once that the church's garden was his favorite because he had full autonomy. Both on campus and at the Dickinson homestead, including the Evergreens, he had to contend with many opinions.

In January, the garden was buried under several feet of snow, and I longed for the summer days when I could walk back here at the same time in the evening. The sun would still be in the sky, and there would be a blanket of colors in front of me. Right now, all I saw was a field of white.

I went to the back door of the church, and I expected it would be locked. To my surprise, the door opened easily, and I found myself in the back storage room.

I wove through the barrels and boxes and out the door into a back hallway of the church. Voices floated around me, and I was disoriented because I didn't know which direction they came from. Whenever I entered the church, it was through the front entrance. I had never been in these back rooms before.

I went to this church every Sunday because Mr. Dickinson insisted that anyone in his household would. That everyone did not include Emily. Mr. Dickinson had given up trying to convince his elder daughter to attend church years ago. Instead, on many Sundays Emily went for a walk in the woods with Carlo and a paper and pen.

The hallways were narrow and dark. I had to take a breath and calm myself. I did not like narrow dark spaces. I blamed it on the fact that I wasn't a small woman. My mother had told me as a child that my body was made for work and that would serve me well. I was taller than most men I met and had broad shoulders.

I believed that every girl wished from time to time that she was a dainty little thing. I was not. My mother was right; my height and width served me well in my work. However, in tight passageways like this one the characteristics betrayed me.

After a few moments, my eyes adjusted to the dim lights, and I made out the shapes around me. Most were crates filled with ribbons, candles, and fabric. Everything around me was red and green. I realized that they were the Christmas decorations for the church, which would have been removed just a few short weeks ago after Epiphany on January sixth. I didn't know if this passageway was the items' permanent home for most of the year or if it had just been a stop on the way there.

I stepped around a crate filled to the brim with half-burnt candles.

As I did so, I heard a screeching sound, and there was a flash of light as if a door at the end of the passageway was opening. I gave a sigh of relief to know the way out.

I didn't immediately move that way because I didn't want whoever opened the door to catch me creeping in the back of the church. If it got back to Mr. Dickinson that it even appeared that I was up to anything nefarious he would be furious and want to sack me. Over the last two years, he had wanted to fire me so many times, but Emily always intervened on my behalf. I didn't want to give Emily a reason to have to do that again.

I crouched and tucked myself behind the crate of candles. I usually found the scent of beeswax soothing, but so close to it and with so many candles just next to my nose, the aroma made me a bit queasy.

The door closed with a thud, and I started to stand until I heard voices.

"You are going to be found out. If I learned of it only being here a few days, others will know in short order," a harsh voice said.

"You don't know what you're talking about."

"I do know. I know how gossip can ruin a life."

"Is it gossip if it is true?"

"You admit it."

"I'm not admitting anything, and you need to keep your mouth shut."

"Olive is my friend."

"Leave her out of this. She has nothing to do with it."

"Her reputation does," the first voice argued.

"Reputations are worth little."

"Maybe to you because you sacrificed yours long ago."

"You can't possibly know how much I have sacrificed or how much I have lost," the second voice snapped.

"You haven't lost as much as that little girl. What does she have left?"

"She is none of my concern."

"You have made that very clear," the first voice snapped. "I will speak to Olive."

Although I could not tell if the first voice was a woman or man, the second voice was certainly that of a woman.

There was a yelp, and the second voice snarled, "You won't say a word if you know what is good for you."

I shivered in my hiding spot. I couldn't take it any longer. My stomach was turning from smelling the beeswax for so long and my legs began to cramp.

The "little girl" they spoke of had to be Norah Rose. I was sure of it.

I started to stand and the door at the end of the passageway opened. One of the people went out, but I sensed one stayed in the passageway with me. The sound of footsteps made me slide noiselessly back into my hiding spot.

The person walking by wore trousers, but it wasn't a man. She made her way past me and went out another door in the opposite direction.

In my crouched position, I pressed my back against the cold stone wall while she walked by. There was only one woman I had ever seen so openly wear trousers, and that was Lucy Stone.

As Lucy passed me my heart dropped. I had liked her very much when I had met her, but if she was involved in the death of Norah Rose's parents, I knew any admiration for her was doomed.

I didn't know if she was the first voice or the second. Was it her reputation that was lost or the other person's?

I crouched on the floor for a few more minutes for fear that Lucy or her companion would come back to the passageway for some reason. When I heard not a noise save for the dull sound of people talking somewhere deep in the recesses of the church, I stood a second time.

I waited beside the crate of candles, unsure which direction I should go. Lucy's companion had exited to the right, but she herself had exited to the left.

Since Lucy was the only one of the pair I could identify, I went in her direction. The door was dark varnished wood, and the handle was made of iron. I pushed the door open and found myself behind the narthex. The reverend's study was to my right. The room was dark, and the door was closed. I was grateful for that. If I had run into the reverend, it would have surely gotten back to Mr. Dickinson that I was creeping around the church and somewhere I didn't belong.

The noise of the people in the church reverberated through the sanctuary. I peeked out through a door. There had to be more than one hundred people in front of me. They were wrapped in extra coats and blankets.

Women from the church walked around passing out bowls of soup and cups of tea. Everything looked to be in order.

Mrs. Stearns was among the women. She held a pile of scarves in her arms and handed them out. With each person, she bent down and said a kind word to them. Did she have any idea that her houseguest Lucy Stone was talking about her behind her back? I could not believe such a kind woman could know that and allow Lucy to remain in her home. When she did find out she would be scandalized. I considered the ways that she could be told and none of them was appealing.

Through the window in the door, I saw Miss Lavinia. She stood in the far corner of the sanctuary and handed out what appeared to be tracts of some sort. I wondered what they said.

As far as I could tell no one was looking in the direction of where I stood. Now was the time to slip out the door. I put my hand on the iron handle when someone grabbed my arm from behind and yanked me back from the door. I was too shocked to scream.

CHAPTER THIRTY-FOUR

EMILY RELEASED MY arm and clapped her hands together. "Wonderful detective work, Willa. You found me."

"I found you?" I gasped, surprised that I even managed to form the words.

"Yes, of course. You were looking for me, were you not? I came back here to take a moment. We are doing good work, but I don't care to be around so many people at once. It's quite overwhelming for me. How did you know that I would be back here?"

I felt like my heart would beat right out of my chest. "Emily, you nearly scared me out of my skin."

"You didn't know I was there?"

"No, not until you yanked me back by the arm." I rubbed the arm in question.

"I am sorry for that. Next time, I will tap you on the shoulder to get your attention."

That would have frightened me, too, under the circumstances, but at least it would be better than feeling like I was in the middle of my own kidnapping.

She folded her arms. "If you are not looking for me, why are you back here?"

I swallowed. "I came through the back because one of the ladies from the league wouldn't let me in through the front door."

"Oh, that must have been Mrs. Hawkins. She is a tough old bird and doesn't believe anything anyone says about anything. She also has the eyesight of a mole. Even if she had seen you at church with the family, she would not know it because she can't see your face. Truly, I cannot think of anything worse than losing one's eyesight. I would do whatever it takes to get mine back if my vision was ever threatened. I would not be able to write if I lost it, and that would be a cruel existence. I would choke on my words.

"Now that you are inside, let us get down to business. There are many people here that know the Doolans. I believe that we will have greater success here in the church than we did at Kelley Square. It is like shooting fish in a barrel as they say. I feel confident that we will be able to convince several people to reveal something new about the case. I have even taken it upon myself to start asking questions without you. I have learned nothing of interest yet, but I know that will change now that you are here."

She put her hand on the door handle and motioned to open it. She didn't wait to assess that no one was looking at the door the moment she opened it. She opened the door with the confidence of a Dickinson, or a person who never thought they weren't permitted to go and do whatever they wished whenever they wished.

I stopped her this time. "There is something that I need to tell you."

"Is it more important than seeing Norah Rose? She is in the sanctuary helping Susan pass out tea. She asked about you earlier."

"She asked about me?" My heart did a little flip-flop at the very idea.

She nodded. "And I think that was the only question that she asked. When I told her that you would be here just as quick as you could, she seemed much happier. Speaking of that, why did you take so long to get here? Dinner has been over for hours."

"I told you that I had to clean the kitchen and stoke the fires."

"I thought you would rush through the task in order to be here sooner. If we want to find out what happened to Norah Rose's parents, you must be here." She went out the door.

Emily entered the sanctuary like she had every right to be behind the narthex near the reverend's study. I slipped into the massive room with my head down, trying my very best not to be noticed.

There were times I wished that I could walk into a room with the confidence and brashness of Emily, but I had learned being a servant going about life being unnoticed has served me better. The upper class forgets servants are near and reveals things they would not want a living soul to know.

Around the large space, mothers and grandmothers sat with their children, and many of the young children lay prostrate wrapped in blankets like a caterpillar cocoon on the pews trying to sleep while their mothers rubbed their backs.

It took me back to the many times I had been ill or upset as a child, and my mother rubbed my back. There was no more comforting thing in the world than a mother's touch. Thinking of that, I realized that was something that Norah Rose would no longer know as her mother was no longer on this earth. At the ripe old age of eight, she was utterly alone.

At least when I lost my mother, I had Henry to lean on. He was younger and more mischievous than me, but he was family, and it gave me purpose to care for him and make sure that he had everything that he needed.

Norah Rose stood in the middle of the aisle just a few steps behind Miss Susan. Her muff, that Emily had insisted she needed, hung around her neck and she had her hands tucked into it.

Miss Susan smiled at a tall man as she filled his cup of tea.

Instinctively, I started toward Norah Rose. There was so much that I wanted to say and so many questions that I wanted to ask. I was so relieved to see her, and she appeared to be all right. But I was stopped again.

Mrs. Stearns walked up to Emily and me, and Lucy was at her side. I studied Lucy's face to see if there was any hint as to what she was up to. Was she going to tell Mrs. Stearns and Emily what she had been doing just a few moments ago? I strongly doubted it.

"Emily, it is so kind that you are here to help with the warming mission. I must say the Dickinson family showed up for this event. I just had a very nice chat with Mrs. Susan Dickinson, and I saw Miss Lavinia across the sanctuary pitching in where she can."

"We are happy to help."

"We certainly need it," Mrs. Stearns said. "We have about thirty families here. They were all ones who weren't able to sufficiently heat their homes. Their chimney is not clean enough, they sleep outside in a barn or warehouse, they can't afford to buy wood from someone else. Nor can they cut down their own timber." She shook her head. "Not one of them wished to be here. The Irish are very proud people."

"Are they all Irish?" Emily asked.

"Most, not all. We have a few other families in the mix. Three Black families are here too. As a church we are open to everyone."

"Why are all those men outside?" I asked. "It's far too cold to be out there for any amount of time."

Mrs. Stearns looked at me as if she didn't understand why I dared ask a question. "The church has decided to take in children, women, and the elderly first. If there is space, they will let the men inside as well."

I shook my head. I understood the church's need to save the more vulnerable first, but it seemed to me that those young men, not to mention Declan, would have been better off if they had stayed in Kelley Square.

"What about Declan?" I asked.

She looked at me again. "Who?"

"He is an elderly man who is standing out by the fire with the younger men. Shouldn't he be allowed to come in?"

She narrowed her eyes. "You mean the man with the massive dogs. We can't let beasts like that in the church, and he refuses to come in without them. There is nothing more that I can do to help him. He made his choice."

"I'm sure that Horace would let the dogs into his cottage behind the church," Emily said. "Knowing that they were cared for by Horace, I think Declan would come inside."

Mrs. Stearns pursed her lips. "If you can convince Horace of that, it is fine with me, but for absolutely no reason should those beasts darken the church's doors." She narrowed her eyes at Emily as if to make certain that she understood. "As for the other men, they are hearty stock. Once all the women and children have found places to sleep, we will let them inside. They might have to rest in the hallways of the church, but it's much better than the alternative."

"I would imagine so," Emily said, and then nodded at Lucy Stone. "It is nice to see you again. It's kind of you to help with this as well."

"What was I to do? Sit in Olive's home and eat cake until she returned home? That is not me at all." She folded her arms. "I always have a heart for helping others and most especially women."

I bit the inside of my cheek to keep myself from saying anything that might tip her off that I overheard her conversation behind the narthex.

She claimed to help others, but I knew very well that she might be a killer or at least know who the killer of the Doolans was.

"That's admirable," Emily said. "Willa and I are here to work. What should we do?"

"If you could go around the room and see if anyone needs anything, that would be welcome. I think by and large we have settled into a routine," Mrs. Stearns said.

Emily's eyes lit up, and I knew what she was thinking. Being assigned to go around the room and offer assistance would be a perfect cover for finding out more about the Doolans and how they died.

Someone waved at Mrs. Stearns. She shook her head. "There is always someone needing help. Lucy, will you come with me?"

Her friend nodded, but before Lucy walked away she looked me right in the eye and it felt like a block of ice had been pressed at the back of my neck. I held still until she faced the other direction, and when she turned away, I shivered.

"Are you cold?" Emily asked. "Maybe you need one of those blankets."

I swallowed. "No, miss, I am fine."

CHAPTER THIRTY-FIVE

When I turned around Miss Susan and Norah Rose were gone. "Where did Norah Rose go?"

Emily patted my arm. "Do not worry so, Willa. She's with Susan. All will be well. Until we stumble upon them again, we need to ask some questions. I feel like we are on the cusp of cracking this case wide open. Mark my words, the culprit is here among us tonight."

I wanted to protest but knew it was no use with Emily.

"Come with me," Emily said.

I bit my bottom lip. She was right. We would find Norah Rose eventually.

Emily stopped in front of an elderly man wrapped in a blanket. He leaned his head on the side of the church pew in what looked like an extremely painful position.

As if he sensed Emily standing over him he opened one eye. "You can't sit here. This is my spot."

"I wasn't going to sit with you, sir. I am one of the volunteers."

She nodded at me behind her. "Willa is, too, and we are just walking around asking folks if they need anything."

He licked his dry, cracked lips. "I could use a pillow. That's for sure and certain."

"Willa, could you grab a pillow for this gentleman?" She turned back to him. "I'm Emily. What is your name?"

"Keagan McCallister," he said.

"Willa will find you the perfect pillow." She shooed me away.

I didn't for the life of me know where to find a spare pillow in the church. Across the room, I spotted Miss Lavinia. I supposed she was as good to ask as anyone else.

Miss Lavinia handed a glass to a young woman sitting on the floor with two small children in her lap. "This warm milk will help them sleep. It always makes me tired."

The young woman smiled up at her. "Thank you. Thanks to all of you for what you are doing here tonight. I was so worried over what would become of us. My husband works for the railroad and has been called away to help clear the tracks so the trains can start running again. We were all out of firewood. He chopped so much before he left. I don't think any of us knew that this cold would go on for so long."

"That's very true." Miss Lavinia patted the little girls on the head. "Get some rest, little ones."

She took a step back and bumped right into me. I wanted to kick myself for standing so close. I didn't need to give Miss Lavinia an extra reason to be irritated with me.

"Willa, why are you underfoot at all times even away from home? Are you trying to knock me over?"

I felt my cheeks turn red. "I am so sorry, Miss Lavinia. Your sister sent me in search of a pillow. Since you know the church so well, I thought you might know where I can find one."

"It is always expected that I know where everything is and know how to take care of everything. It's exhausting, and I don't even know why you're here. Shouldn't you be off doing all of Margaret's chores since you left her in the lurch today? Yes, I know all about that." She waved her hand at me, and I took a step back.

"I know all about you and Emily wandering off again because you think that you can solve a murder." She looked heavenward. "The outlandish ideas she gets into her head."

I thought it was best not to remind her that Emily and I had solved a murder more than once before, so it would not be irrational at all to believe that we could do that again. I held my tongue because I had learned long ago that arguing with Miss Lavinia never ended well for me.

"No matter what you do it's not going to bring Norah Rose's parents back. The child is still an orphan. What is to be gained by asking all these questions?"

The truth, I thought, but I didn't think Miss Lavinia would accept that answer. Instead, I asked, "How is Norah Rose?"

"She seems fine." Her face softened. It wasn't an expression that I saw on Miss Lavinia's face all that often. It happened only when she was in the garden with Emily or cuddling one of her cats. "She is with Susan. Susan is nothing if not efficient. She will know how to watch over the child." She tilted her head to one side. "You really care about Norah Rose, don't you?"

"I do. There is something about her that reminds me of myself, if I am being honest. I just want to protect her from the lessons that I had to learn the hard way. I lost my mother, too, when I was young. The blessing for me was I was old enough to take care of Henry and me."

"How old were you?"

"Twelve."

"That's not old at all," she said.

"It was old enough to work."

A strange look crossed Miss Lavinia's face, as if she had a new respect for me. If I was being honest with myself, I was shocked that I told her that much.

I might have thought she respected me, but what she said next reminded me of my place. I believed that was its purpose all along.

"If you need a pillow go look in the Sunday school room, that's where all the donations are." She narrowed her eyes. "I hope the pillow is for someone in need and not for yourself."

I didn't even respond to her snide comment and in some ways was happy that we were back on more familiar turf. I thanked her for telling me where to find the pillows.

In the Sunday school room, there was a large basket of pillows. I selected one that looked like it was the softest and went back into the sanctuary in search of Emily and Keagan. Thankfully, I found them right where I had left them.

Emily was seated next to Keagan, and the two of them were speaking like they were old friends.

"It's just the plight of the Irish, you see. It always has been. We work on the land of English lords in our homeland and come here and do the same for American businessmen. The Americans may not have a title, but they have the same level of greed. I can promise you that."

"Hugh thought he was getting away from that?" Emily asked.

"He didn't want to work the farmland any longer," Keagan said. "I believe that he knew that he would never reach the point where he would be able to purchase land and even more than that to pay the taxes on it. The government always has to get its share no matter what side of the Atlantic Ocean we are on. I told him that a job was open at the college, and he took a chance. Eve took up work as a seamstress, too, so that they could live close to the college and pay the rent. They were so proud of that little house." He shook his head. "It's a shame. A terrible shame. Now I kick myself every day for ever telling him about that job. I thought I was helping a young man from my homeland. Instead, I was setting him up to be killed."

CHAPTER THIRTY-SIX

I HUGGED THE PILLOW to my chest. Could it be that we were about to learn how Hugh and Eve Doolan had died? Did this old man sitting under a pile of blankets in the middle of the church know who killed them?

I wasn't the only one who was wondering that, based on Emily's question, which was direct as always. "You know who killed him?"

Keagan shook his head. "I'd tell you if I did, and I would have gone to the police by now to tell them too. That is saying something because I hate the police. I had a run-in or two with them back in Ireland. It's been my lesson that the coppers aren't to be trusted." He wrapped the blankets more tightly around himself as if he suddenly got a chill. "I might not know who did, but I know that it was because of that college. Before he started working there, he was happy and carefree. He and Eve were as poor as church mice, but they were happy."

"What changed?" Emily asked.

He ran his tongue over his yellow, crooked teeth. "The job was the only thing that changed, so it had to be because of that. He was moving in different circles with the new work. He was among those who felt very highly of themselves and did all they could to impress others, so those others thought highly of them too."

"I met one of the men he worked with as a custodian of the college. He was Irish too. I don't think he cared much at all for Hugh," Emily said.

"Would you?" Keagan wanted to know. "You work at the college for years and this young handsome man comes and gets all the attention of the faculty. They never paid a lick of attention to Jimmy; I can tell you that right now. He would come back to Kelley Square at night and complain about everyone he came across that day. Is it any wonder that a friendly chap like Hugh would have done better?"

"Do you think Jimmy would be jealous of him enough to kill him?" Emily asked.

I gasped. I wasn't surprised that Emily came right out and asked the question like that, but I didn't know how Keagan would receive it. Not many people were used to young women of Emily's stature speaking in such a way.

"I pray he didn't, but you can ask him. He's outside with the other young men."

Emily's eyes gleamed at this news. "Indeed, we will."

I gave Keagan the pillow, and Emily thanked him for his time.

Emily grabbed my arm as we walked away. "Willa, this is it! We are on the heels of discovering the killer."

I did try to stem Emily's enthusiasm. "Do you think a man would kill another man and his wife in such a horrible way just because he was more well-liked?"

She released my arm and frowned. "When you say it like that, it loses some of its appeal. Oh, Willa, at times you are too practical."

"I don't think this is a matter of practicality, miss."

"We still need to speak to Jimmy again. He would have been the one to spend the most time with Hugh on campus. I must believe that he might know more than he told us already. Keagan seems certain that Hugh and Eve were killed because of Hugh's job. If that is so, Jimmy must know more. Bundle up, Willa, we are going out into the cold again."

If I thought it was cold when I first arrived at the church, it was nothing compared to the temperature outside now. It was shocking to me that these men could stand it despite the many layers that they wore and their closeness to the fire in the middle of the churchyard. Before we ventured outside, I had the good sense to fill a tray of coffee tins for the men. The coffee was scalding hot and just what they needed. Even if it was too hot to drink, just holding the boiling tins in their hands would improve their plight.

When I came into the church an hour or so ago, there had been close to a dozen men, and now, in the dark of night, there were a lowly five that were still there. Declan and his hound dogs were among them.

I prayed that they all found shelter and wished that Mrs. Stearns had let them in. She could have always asked them to leave if too many women and children arrived.

The men didn't even look at us as we approached. Perhaps

they were frozen into place. I held the tray as steadily as I could as Emily removed two tin mugs of coffee.

"Good evening," Emily said. "We brought you some coffee to warm up. It's blistering cold out here. How are you standing it?"

One of the men slowly turned his neck in our direction. All we could see of his face were his dark eyes that looked like pools of day-old tea. "As you can see, not all of us made it. Many of the chaps went back to their cold homes as it would be better than standing out here in the elements."

Emily held out a coffee tin to the man. "I did not agree with the church's decision to hold the men at bay, and now I am worried for those who made the long walk home in the cold."

"Thank you, miss, for understanding." He raised his tin to her. "And for this, as it is just what we need. I plan to stay until I am allowed in the church. I am far too stiff to make the walk home and at the rate I am moving at this point, I would not be there before sunup."

I walked around the fire, giving coffee tins to other men. Each one thanked me. I heard their teeth chattering as I went. Just being around the men who were so terribly cold made me feel even colder myself. I felt like my cloak was doing nothing to keep out the draft, and now that the wind was picking up again, it seemed all the worse.

"What we really need is to go into the church," one of the men said. "It's wrong of them not to let us in. We would leave if it became too overcrowded with women and children. What kind of men do they think we are?"

"Jimmy, we all know this," our friend said. "Complaining

about it for the last hour hasn't made it any better. Instead, you have made us all miserable."

"That reverend and the president's wife are the ones who have made you miserable, it isn't me."

The other men took their tins from my tray and moved as close to the fire as they could without being singed. All the men but Declan hovered closely together, but Declan was on his own on the other side of the fire. I thought that was telling. I needed to find Horace soon to see if he would take in Declan's dogs.

"I agree with you," Emily said.

Jimmy's eyes slid in her direction.

"Didn't I meet you at the college yesterday?" Emily asked.

Jimmy pulled his hat down over his prominent ears before taking the tin from Emily's hand. "You were the one with that big dog." He looked around as if he was scared that Carlo might pop out from behind a tree. "He was larger than some men I know."

"Oh, he is, and that's why my father selected him. He is part companion, part bodyguard."

"Is he here now?"

She shook her head. "Carlo had a very long day, so he is back enjoying the fire at home. My mother is sure to be slipping him a treat or two while I am away as well."

"I don't care much for dogs," Jimmy said. "They don't like me."

Across the fire Declan scowled at him.

"I have found that dogs are excellent judges of character," Emily said.

"Hmm," Jimmy murmured as he held the tin in his mittened hands under his chin. The steam from his cup turned into ice crystals on his beard.

"Have you thought any more about Hugh?"

He looked at her. "Why do I need to be thinking about a dead man?"

"You worked with him every day," Emily said. "It would make sense if you wondered why he died."

Jimmy held the tin in one hand and held the other just over the flames. "I do not wonder. I'm just glad I don't have to deal with his foolishness. So many times, we were working, and he simply would wander off. When I complained, I was told that I should get back to work and not worry about another man's job."

I shifted back and forth on my feet. Discomfort pricked the back of my mind as it was reminiscent of the place I was in with Margaret, but in that case, I was Hugh.

"It's very much like the story of the prodigal son if you ask me," Jimmy went on. "I stay and do all the work, and he does nothing but gets all the recognition and praise."

"You're happy he has passed?" Emily asked.

He glared at her. "I don't like what you're suggesting. I had nothing to do with his death."

"But you might know who did."

"If I had to guess, it would be all his extra duties."

"What extra duties?" Emily asked.

"Whatever it was he was doing when he left me in the lurch."

"What did he do when he disappeared for a time? What did he say that he was doing?" Emily asked.

"I have theories."

"And what are those?"

"Gossip isn't always free."

Emily reached into the satchel on her wrist and pulled out several bills.

"He was always with a woman."

"His wife?" Emily asked.

"Not his wife. Another man's wife."

His words seemed to seep into Emily and me as we processed the gravity of them. Had Hugh been having an affair? While Jimmy's motive was sketchy at best, an affair was high at the top of the list of motives for murder.

Could it have been the mistress's husband who killed them when he found out the truth?

Another more disturbing thought came to my mind. Could it have been Eve when she found out? She killed her husband and herself. I felt ill at the very idea, but then I was comforted when I remembered that Matthew had said that the doors were barred shut from the outside. Eve could not have done it. For Norah Rose's sake, I was happy that I could rule that out.

Emily reached into her satchel and removed more bills. She held out the money to Jimmy. "For the name of the woman?"

He took the bills from her hand, folded them, and tucked them into the pocket of his coat. "That, I do not know."

"You must give me something about her. You can't just take my money and tell us nothing at all. Or would you like to get a call from the police and let them take a crack at getting the information from you?"

He scowled at her. "I don't know the name, but she's the wife of a professor."

CHAPTER THIRTY-SEVEN

EMILY AND I were both taken aback by Jimmy's news. It changed everything that we had thought about Hugh. If he was having an affair, then that would negate all the good we had heard about him as a husband and father.

Would Mrs. Stearns, who took it upon herself to be friendly with all of the faculty wives, know who the woman in question was? I guessed that she would have an inkling even if she didn't know for certain. The ladies had interwoven lives. They all went to the same parties and the same church, and even from the little I knew about them, they gossiped to and about one another incessantly.

And I could not forget the gossip the clothier owner Mrs. Feely had said about Mrs. Weston. Could she be the woman whom Jimmy meant?

"You all come inside," Emily said to the men. "You have been out here long enough. It is inhumane."

The men looked at Emily, and a man with dark eyes spoke.

"We don't want to upset the church. We do take kindly to the fact they are taking in the women and children."

"In the name of their Christian charity, they should be doing nothing less," Emily argued. "If the reverend or Mrs. Stearns has issue with it, they can take it up with me. You are all close to frozen and will come down with hypothermia if you stay outside a moment longer."

It seemed that was all Emily had to say to the young men and they marched toward the door. Declan held back. "If I can't go in with my dogs, I'm not going in."

"Please go in," I said. "You all will catch your death of cold if you don't."

He shook his head defiantly.

"The church sexton Horace Church has agreed to take the dogs into his little cottage. Horace is a good man. They will be safe there," I said, even though I knew nothing of the kind as I hadn't asked Horace for permission yet to spring the hounds on him. However, I knew Horace and his kind heart under his curmudgeonly exterior. I knew that he would not turn the hounds away when I showed up on his doorstep.

Declan looked hopeful. "He said this?"

I nodded, praying I would not be struck down for lying on church property.

Declan looked at the church. "I will take your word as a promise." He handed the dogs' leads to me. "Normally, I would walk with you to the caretaker's house, but my legs are too stiff and threaten to give way at any moment."

"Go inside. I will take good care of them." I tugged on the leads and was happy that the hounds dutifully followed me around to the back of the church where Horace's cottage sat.

"You are as well-behaved as Carlo," I told the hounds. "And believe me when I say that is quite a compliment."

They wagged their tails in appreciation.

Thankfully, Horace had dug a path from the church to his cottage, and the dogs and I walked single file to the little house with smoke pumping out of the chimney. I knocked on Horace's door with the side of my mittened fist.

"I said that I don't want anything to do with the chaos at the church tonight," was the angry shout that came through the door.

Horace flung the door open. "And no. No one can stay here, and—" He stopped midsentence when he saw the hounds and me on his doorstep.

"Can you make an exception for a couple of hounds?" I asked.

He squinted at me. "You can come in, Willa."

Horace Church was a man of around forty with a full beard and sour disposition, but I had learned over the years working with him in the Dickinsons' garden that he had a soft heart and cared deeply for people and nature. Nature especially, I would say.

As soon as I was inside Horace's home, I felt warm. So much so that I had to remove my mittens right away for fear that my hands would begin to sweat.

The two red hounds went over and lay down in front of the fire.

"They made themselves right at home," I said with a smile.

"Where did you find these beasts?"

I told him about Declan.

"Well," he said gruffly. "I don't want any old dodger to

freeze to death, and you made the right choice to bring me the hounds instead of the old man himself. I wouldn't have stood for that. Old men like that talk too much and I like my quiet time."

I knew this well. Horace was a man of few words. When we worked in the garden together, he rarely spoke, and I had long since given up trying to make small talk with him.

"I was surprised that I didn't see you inside the church," I said.

"I can't stand to be inside there and see what damage is happening to my lovely church. It will take me days and days to set it back to rights." He shivered.

"Well, I do thank you for taking these beasts in, and Declan is thankful too."

He nodded.

I turned and made my way to the door.

"Willa," he said as I put my mittens back on, preparing to leave.

I looked at him and waited.

"There was a man here today asking about you."

I frowned. "A man? Who was it?"

He shook his head. "He wouldn't tell me his name, but he asked about you. He wanted to know if you were happy."

I shivered, but it wasn't from the cold.

As I made my way back to the church on the path that Horace had so expertly made, I could not help but wonder who would come to the church asking about me. Who would want to know if I was happy? My father came to mind, but I shook the thought away. Danny had made the story up about my father purely to torment me.

One of the young wives of the church was at the door when I approached. I was very grateful to see it wasn't Mrs. Hawkins, who turned me away the first time. "Are you Miss Dickinson's maid?" she asked.

I nodded.

"She brought all those men inside the church, and I don't know what to do. I told her that Mrs. Stearns didn't want them to come in for another quarter of an hour, but she would not listen."

"What difference will a quarter hour make to the church?"

"I'm just trying to follow the rules." She wrung her hands.

"Not to worry. If it comes to it, Miss Dickinson will take all the blame. She will not bring you into it at all."

Her shoulders sagged. "I am relieved. Miss Dickinson would not take no for an answer."

"She never does," I assured her. "And that is no fault of yours."

I did have sympathy for her. When Emily was forceful and you weren't used to it, her determination was daunting. I know it took me months and months to realize she didn't mean anything by her tone.

As if on cue, Mrs. Stearns came to the door. "Melinda, I thought I told you to let them inside at eight on the dot. Why are there men already inside the church?"

Melinda looked as if she was about to cry.

"Don't blame her, Olive," Emily said, walking over to us. "I let them inside. Willa and I were giving them coffee, and we could hardly stand the chill in the air. They have been out there for hours. They needed to come in and warm up. There are only five men who entered the church."

Mrs. Stearns stepped back. "Well, I suppose it is fine now there are only the five. What happened to the others?"

"What do you think happened?" Emily snapped. "They were far too cold and took their chances by going home to their unheated homes in Kelley Square. At least there they would be out of the wind."

Mrs. Stearns blinked at Emily's directness. "I didn't want to put anyone at risk, but the women and children are more vulnerable."

"*Everyone* is vulnerable in these temperatures," Emily said before she walked away.

"I did what I thought was right," Mrs. Stearns said. "We only have so much space."

I simply nodded. There was no reason to rake this woman over the coals. The church warming station was helping many people that night.

Mrs. Stearns pressed her lips together in a thin line. It seemed that she had met her match in Emily Dickinson.

CHAPTER THIRTY-EIGHT

Poor Melinda was no longer up to watching the door after being reprimanded by the college president's wife, so I volunteered to take her post. She quickly agreed and disappeared into the church. I would have been surprised if I caught sight of her again at all that night.

It was quiet at the front door, and I was grateful for that. I must have dozed off at some point because I was awakened by a knock on the door. I opened the door and let a man inside. His coat was encrusted with snow and ice, and I could not help but wonder if he had been sleeping outside. If that was the case, he was lucky to be alive.

He stopped just a few feet inside the door. I closed the heavy church door behind him and was relieved to push the cold air outside. I would not say the church was toasty warm. The walls were cold stone, and the ceiling was too high for that, but it was far better than what these men had been exposed to for hours. I still didn't know how they withstood it.

"There is soup and hot coffee inside. Just follow the other men. They will show you the way."

He turned around and removed his hat and wrap. "You look just like your mother."

I jumped back as if I had seen a ghost. I knocked my shoulder painfully against the heavy wooden door in the process. Frantically, I looked around for Emily, but we were the only ones left in the entry. All the other men had made a beeline for the warmer places in the church.

"Willa, it's me."

I licked my lips. "I don't know you, sir. As I said before, there is soup and hot coffee inside. You must be hungry."

"You don't remember me? I'm your da."

I felt like I was falling into a pit. It was like staring at an older view of Henry, what Henry would have looked like if he had lived beyond his eighteen years and had the kind of life that had beaten him down. The realization came like a stab in the chest. How dare this traitor still be alive and my mother and my brother, the two people I had loved most in this world, are dead? It was a great injustice. And how dare he reveal himself to me now? After so many years away?

He was right about one thing; I didn't remember him. He had left my mother when I was a very small child. There were no renderings of what he looked like, and I never asked my mother about his appearance because I knew I would never see him again. I was happy to never see him again. The only resemblance was to Henry. It was because I knew even now, two years after he died, every line and every divot on my brother's face that I could see the same on this man who claimed to be my father.

"I was told that you would be here tonight, so I came."

"The warming mission is for those in need. If you are taking a spot that would better serve someone else, that is cruel."

He waved his hands, which were far drier and more wrinkled than they should be at his age. It was like his hands had washed a thousand dishes. I knew this because my own hands looked much the same. They were hands of a life of labor.

"I do need to stay here. I have nowhere else to go. I was traveling when the foul weather hit and passing Amherst at the time. I had not planned to stop. I knew I would not be welcomed here by you and many others because of my choices." He licked his lips. "I had to find safety from the storm, so I took shelter in the train station. Now that they are working to clear the railroad, I have been brushed away and am staying anywhere I can lay my head until it's safe to move on."

He had not come to Amherst to find me. I was an afterthought because he was stuck here. I wished learning that didn't pain me so. I should not care for his motives.

"Who told you I would be here?" I asked even though I thought I knew.

"Danny Boyle. My, that boy has grown up. I remember when he was just a little lad, and here he is today with a family of his own." He studied my face. "You are very grown up too. I have heard that you are working for the Dickinsons. What good fortune that is for you."

"Did you hear that from Danny Boyle again?" I asked. "What he says I would not trust."

"I did. He knows a lot about what you have been up to." He looked down. "He told me about Henry as well."

Tears came to my eyes. I would not talk to him, who abandoned Henry when he was just an infant, about my brother.

"Willa," Emily said as she came back to the entry. "Whatever has held you up for this long? Norah Rose is waiting for you."

Norah Rose? She was more important to me than this man I didn't know. Blood was not thicker than water. Real love and affection were. Loyalty and thoughtfulness were. The family I chose was.

"I'm coming." I turned to leave the man where he stood.

However, Emily was curious. "Who are you?" she asked.

"I'm her da. I came here to see her."

Emily cocked her head. "Don't you think you are a decade or two too late?" She slung her arm through mine and pulled me away. It was the best reaction to my father I could ask for from my friend.

"Take three deep breaths before you see Norah Rose. You need to be pulled together for her," Emily whispered in my ear as she took me to the same Sunday school room that I had been in earlier that evening.

I took the breaths as instructed. "I don't know what to do about him being here. I don't know what to do about him still being alive."

She looked me in the eye. "That's the beauty of it, Willa. You are in control. You don't have to do anything at all about it. It's your choice to move forward any way you see fit. You can speak to him again or you can pretend you never saw him. He has no say in it. You forgive or you don't. The choice is yours."

"He looks so much like Henry."

"But he's not like Henry. He's not like the Henry whom you have told me about so many times. He's not like the brother who was so loyal to you and to your mother."

"He's not."

"Good. Now that we are agreed, my dear heart, we will forget him."

I nodded.

She nudged me in the direction of the Sunday school room. As soon as I walked through the door the child wrapped her arms around my waist and buried her face in my middle. A feeling I could not describe washed over me, and I knew that I had to protect her at all costs. I knew family had a different definition for me. It included Emily, Margaret, Baby Z the cat, and even Carlo. And Matthew was my family. In his steadfastness, he had been my family much longer than all the others. And now I included Norah Rose. Above all, Norah Rose. I could not be parted from her.

My heart ached as I remembered I knew the name of her mother's family in Dublin. Reilly. I knew I had to tell Matthew. They had to be asked the question that I selfishly wanted them to say no to. But I had no alternative for her so how could I even wish that?

"I have been waiting for you. They told me that you would come. You took a very long time," she spoke into my middle.

"I know. I'm sorry. We have been trying to help all the people who are here. Do you know any of them?" I asked.

She looked up at me. "They are neighbors or friends of my

parents. Some of the children were my friends, too, but their mothers tell them to stay away from me now that I am an orphan."

Her words sliced my heart in two.

Miss Susan was standing by the window. It was pitch-black outside now. "No one has spoken up as a relative or close family friend that might be willing to take her . . ." She trailed off. We both knew what that meant.

Miss Susan stepped out of the room, and as she went, I saw tears in her eyes. She loved Norah Rose too. How could we possibly part with her?

I knelt in front of Norah Rose as I remembered the rose-engraved key in my pocket. This might be my one and only chance to ask her about it. I removed the key from my skirt pocket and showed it to her. "Do you know what it is?"

"You found it. I thought it fell out of my nightdress pocket in the woods. I knew I would never find it in the snow."

"What is it to?" I asked.

She shook her head. "I don't know. My father gave it to me just before he set me out the window during the fire. He told me to keep it safe for him." She took it from my hand and pressed it against her chest.

"Do you want to keep it?" I asked. "Your father gave it to you. It is yours."

She bit her lip as she considered this. "No, you keep it. I think my da would want you to keep it safe for me."

"I promise to keep it safe," I said.

She wrapped her arms around my neck. "I trust you."

My heart sank and I held Norah Rose a little more closely

to me. How could she trust me when I would play a part in her going away?

"Can I live with you?" she whispered. "I would be no trouble. I promise."

I held her close and did not answer as I was unable to speak.

CHAPTER THIRTY-NINE

Miss Susan took Norah Rose back to the Evergreens shortly after our meeting, and it pained me to see her go. The truth was I did want to take the child under my wing and care for her. But how could I possibly do that as an unmarried maid? Matthew came to mind. To marry him for the child was not genuine.

My head hurt from all the thoughts and emotions coursing through me. I went in search of Emily and wondered why she hadn't come into the Sunday school room with me to see Norah Rose. I had not realized that she wasn't there until the child left.

To my surprise, I found Emily in the corner of the sanctuary speaking to none other than Matthew. The way that the two of them had their heads bent toward each other set me ill at ease.

I cleared my throat, and they jumped back from each other as if they each had been stung by a bee.

"Willa, it's wonderful that you are here."

"It is?" I looked from one to the other.

"Yes," Emily said with her usual confidence. "I was just telling Officer Thomas all that we had accomplished today."

"You learned the name of her family in Dublin is Reilly?" Matthew asked.

I relaxed some. They were talking about Norah Rose. Of course, they had been talking about Norah Rose.

"I will send them a letter first thing tomorrow. The post is doing its very best to run in this cold. Postmen have been coming in and out of town on horseback as the railroad is still being mended. It should be up and running at the end of the week, I have been told."

"That is very good news," Emily said. "I could use some coconut."

Matthew wrinkled his brow at her as if she spoke another language.

"Miss Dickinson really loves coconut," I explained. "With the rails down, the market has been out of it for a long while."

"I see," Matthew said. He looked around the room.

The lights in the church had been dimmed and people had settled in on pews or mats on the floor to sleep for the night and keep warm the best that they could. I thought of my bed back at the homestead in my warm little room with a hot brick at my feet. I had never been more thankful for all that I had. Could I really give that all up?

"It is late," I said. "We should return home."

Emily nodded. "Yes, tomorrow will be another long day. Don't forget we have that lecture at Mrs. Turnkey's house tomorrow given by Lucy Stone. Willa, I really think you should come with me."

That reminded me of the conversation that I had overheard Lucy Stone have with another person behind the narthex. Did I mention that to Matthew?

"I left my bonnet in the hall. I will go get it and we will leave," Emily said, and she hurried off before I could even offer to fetch the bonnet for her.

She left Matthew and me alone.

"I don't think that it's wise for you and Miss Dickinson to be walking around Kelley Square asking questions. People will become suspicious of you," he said. "Not everyone will welcome you."

"That is fine because we are already suspicious of them."

Matthew sighed.

"I am worried for Norah Rose. If the Reillys don't take her, what will become of her?" I held my mittens in my hands and twisted them as if in a vise.

"We have already discussed what would happen."

"What if I take her?" I asked. "I know I don't have much, but I could scrape by. My mother was able to do that with two children and she was sick. I am in good health."

He stared at me. "Willa, you can't be serious."

I looked him in the eye. "What is the alternative?"

"We could care for her as a family." His voice was low.

"I don't want to put that on you. I don't want you to have to take on a wife and a child so quickly. It would not be fair."

"I don't care as to what is fair. You wouldn't be putting anything on me. I love you. You know this. I have waited for you. You, Norah Rose, and I could be a family. We could make it work. It would be a chance for all three of us to begin a new life together."

I bit my lower lip. It sounded tempting. I would be doing it for Norah Rose, not out of love for Matthew, but I wasn't completely sure that was true. I loved Matthew. I realized tonight that he was family to me. In truth, I had known that all along. I realized it now that I was running away from my love of Matthew because I was afraid he would just be one more person I would lose, but the chance of love was worth the risk of loss. I wanted to say all of this to Matthew, but the words lodged themselves in my throat. I could not speak.

He touched my arm. "You don't have to make a decision now. Until we hear from the Reillys, we can't even think about it."

Emily returned. "Willa, are you ready to leave?" Her bonnet sat squarely on her head.

I nodded.

CHAPTER FORTY

Again, the next morning I got up early before anyone was awake, but instead of jumping into my chores, I donned my cloak and bonnet in the laundry room before venturing outside.

I was just about to go out the door when I noticed a scrap of paper on the laundry room floor. I recognized it immediately as one of the little bits of paper that I found around Emily's room after a feverish night of her writing. I had so many of these pieces tucked under my mattress in my little room. I have never told her that I have kept them. I do not think she would have approved that I had, as she had not found them worthy of keeping and had tossed them away.

I picked it up, knowing that I would add it to my collection. I smoothed the small paper on my palm and read.

I died for Beauty—but was scarce
Adjusted in the Tomb

When One who died for Truth, was lain
In an adjoining Room—

He questioned softly "Why I failed"?
"For Beauty", I replied—
"And I—for Truth—Themself are One—
We Brethren are", He said—

And so, as Kinsmen, met a Night—
We talked between the Rooms—
Until the Moss had reached our lips—
And covered up—Our names—

I shivered. Never before had one of Emily's poems shook me so deeply. I could not help but believe that those two poor souls speaking to each other in the tomb were those of Eve and Hugh Doolan. She died for beauty. She was an artist. He died for truth. He was trying to find answers in Dr. Weston's lab. But were those truly the reasons they were killed, or had they just inspired a poem both morbid and lovely?

I neatly folded the poem and tucked it into the pocket of my cloak. I would save it to show to Norah Rose one day, so she could know the true meaning of Emily's words. I realized knowing Emily's words, whether fully comprehended or not, was important.

I walked to the church holding the rose-carved key and Emily's words inside of my pocket.

It was still dark out and bitterly cold. I prayed that the sun would bring some warmth when it rose over the horizon.

To my surprise, the church door was open, and unlike

the day before, there was no one blocking the door and keeping me out.

It seemed whoever wanted to leave the church was welcome to do so in their own time.

Several men shuffled out the door as they were on their way to work at the warehouse or perhaps the stables. Like me, their workday began before sunup.

It made me wonder if my father was among them because I had asked no questions the day before. I knew nothing of his life, if he was working, or where he was living. Did he even have a home? All I knew was he had been trapped in Amherst by the weather.

The sanctuary, where most of the people had spent the night sleeping or trying to, as I imagined that both the pews and the floor were equally hard, was in the process of waking up.

I searched the faces of the people quietly shuffling through the room. They were all taking care not to wake the babies and children who seemed to have the ability to rest on any hard surface and in any position.

I looked for my brother's face. It was an older more worn version, but still what my brother's would have been if given the chance. I finally spotted him tucked into the corner of the first pew at the front of the church.

He was awake. I was glad that I didn't have to wake him.

"I didn't think I would see you again," he said.

"I didn't think you would see me again either." I removed my bonnet and held it in front of me.

"I'm glad that you are here."

"Why did you leave?" I asked.

If he was startled by my abrupt question, he didn't show it. "I married your mother before I was ready to marry. I loved her, but I was afraid of being trapped as a husband and a father. I allowed myself to fall in love with another woman. She was young and exciting and wanted to see the country like I did. We left Amherst together. We went to New York."

"What happened to her?" I asked.

"I don't know. She left me for another chap with more money just as soon as she could." He stared at his hands. "I know now she just used me as her ticket to get out of Amherst."

"Why didn't you come back when she left you?" I asked.

"I couldn't do that. I thought if I came back, I would have made it worse for your mother. I didn't want to force her to make the choice of taking me back or not. I knew I wasn't worth being taken back. I wasn't meant to be a husband or a father. I would have made her life more difficult—of that, I am sure."

I squeezed my bonnet so hard that the brim was beginning to bend. I set it on my knee. "Did you know she was sick?"

He looked away. "Yes. I ran into a neighbor from Kelley Square in Philadelphia, and he told me."

"But you still didn't come back."

He shook his head. "But I came back now."

"Because of the storm," I said. "I was an afterthought."

"No, no, that is not true. You and Henry were never an afterthought to me. I thought and prayed for you every day. I was heartbroken to learn what happened to Henry. I still can't believe it." He licked his lips. "When Danny told me, I knew I had to see you."

"To comfort me?" I asked. "The time for comfort has passed. Henry died two years ago."

"I would have come sooner if I had known."

"Why?" I met his eyes for the first time. I swallowed as they were the same light blue color as Henry's, as my own.

"To see if you were all right."

"I am all right. You can see that now with your own eyes." I stood. "What will you do now?"

He licked his lips. "That depends on you."

"It doesn't, because I've forgiven you. I forgave you a long time ago. That's what I came here to say to you, for you and for myself, but that does not mean we have to move through the remainder of life as father and daughter. I am not expecting that. I have no expectation where you are concerned." I stood and stepped out of the pew. "I am grateful to have seen you again though. It closes a chapter for me so that I can start a new one."

I did not wait for his reply and left the church not knowing if I would ever see him again.

CHAPTER FORTY-ONE

I SAT WITH EMILY, Miss Lavinia, Miss Susan, and Norah Rose in the back of the carriage. Jeremiah was driving Terror as usual. It felt strange not to be seated up in the front with Jeremiah. Emily had insisted that I sit in the back with the ladies and Norah Rose due to the cold.

Honestly, it had been too cold to argue.

It was evening, and we were headed to Mrs. Gertrude Turnkey's home to hear a lecture given by Lucy Stone. I still didn't know how I felt about Lucy. After overhearing that conversation behind the church's sanctuary, I lost trust in her. I did not know if she was who she said she was. I hadn't told Emily about overhearing the conversation yet. She had been so enamored with Lucy that I wanted more proof before revealing what I knew.

"Emily, I don't know why you thought it was so important that Willa come with you," Miss Lavinia said.

"I think it's important for all women in Amherst to hear

what Lucy Stone has to say. I would have invited Mother if I thought that she could bear the cold. Besides, Vinnie, it does you good to leave the house from time to time."

"This from the person who likes to leave the house the very most," Miss Lavinia said. "But why did we bring Norah Rose?"

"Education can start at any age," Emily said.

"Please," Miss Susan said. "Will the two of you stop squabbling? You're giving me a headache."

Norah Rose looked up at me from where she sat on my lap while the women quibbled. She then leaned back and rested her head on my breast. The pang I felt whenever I was around her returned in full force.

When we arrived at the Turnkey home, we saw that we weren't the only ladies at the lecture. In fact, the street was lined with parked carriages and horses stamping their feet, doing their very best to stay warm in this bitter cold.

Emily looked out of the carriage window. "I did not realize she was expecting this many people, and they are all women from what I can tell."

"What do you expect?" Miss Susan asked. "We have all been trapped in our homes for weeks. Of course, we would be chomping at the bit to get out even to hear a crackpot lecture."

"We do not know it's a crackpot," Emily said.

"Emily, she wears men's clothes. How are we to take a woman seriously who wears trousers in public?"

Emily tilted her head. "I have been thinking of trying on a pair."

"Father would drop dead," Miss Lavinia said.

"I believe you don't have the faith in our father's constitution that I do," Emily said.

Miss Susan rubbed her temples. "Being stuck in a carriage with the two of you is a very close thing to torture."

Jeremiah opened the carriage door, and we disembarked and hurried into the house. The Turnkey home was grand, much grander than the Dickinson home, and I wondered what Mr. Turnkey did for work. I realized that I knew very little about Mrs. Gertrude Turnkey other than her involvement in the Ladies' Society of Amherst and her affinity for her fox wrap.

All of the furniture had been removed from the large parlor, and in its place were rows and rows of wooden chairs and a lectern at the front. Mrs. Turnkey and Lucy Stone stood at the lectern.

Mrs. Turnkey smiled at her audience as if she was very pleased with the turnout. "Ladies, ladies, please take your seats so we can get started."

The women filed into the chairs and when the murmurs died down, Mrs. Turnkey spoke again. "The Ladies' Society of Amherst is pleased to have this opportunity to host Lucy Stone. She is here to speak to us on the important topic of women in society and our rights and the rights we deserve. Now, I know Lucy's visit to Amherst was a surprise due to weather, but we are so happy she's here." She nodded at Lucy.

"Thank you, Mrs. Turnkey," Lucy said. "I am happy to have this chance to speak to the women of Amherst. I am here to speak on marriage specifically. Not many people know that I am married, very happily in fact. However, for me, it was about marrying the right man. A man may say that he believes women are equal to him, but when it comes to his wife, it's another matter entirely. In my case, my husband and I are partners, and I married under my terms. My husband knew I would not agree to it otherwise. He cared for me enough to accept me for who I am."

A woman in the back of the room spoke up. "It seems to me that you are controlling your husband. Then, why marry at all if you want to be in charge?"

"I'm not in charge. We are equals. Just because I believe I am equal to any man does not mean I have to give up the love and joy of being a wife and a mother. I should be able to have both."

A ripple of whispers ran through the room.

I glanced at Emily. She was staring at Lucy intently, as if she had never seen anyone like her in her life. It was very likely she hadn't. None of us had.

"I want to be married in the church," another woman said. "It does not sound like that is possible with what you want."

"We did marry in the church. My longtime friend Thomas Wentworth Higginson led the service."

"He must have been a forward-thinking man to do that."

"He is. He's a good man. There are times that I wished he had more political aspirations because we need more men like him in office, but he much prefers to write and edit."

Emily reached into the little satchel at her right for her paper and pencil and began scribbling away.

Miss Susan touched my arm. "Willa, I'm going to take Norah Rose out. She needs water. The poor thing has the hiccups."

"I can take her," I whispered back.

She shook her head and took Norah Rose by the hand and left our row.

Lucy Stone continued to speak for another half hour, and all that time Norah Rose and Miss Susan were gone. How long would it take them to find water? I couldn't listen to the lecture because I was consumed with waiting for them.

Finally, I couldn't wait any longer and whispered to Emily that I, too, needed water. I slipped out of the row.

At the front of the room, Mrs. Turnkey glared at me.

In the hallway, I looked left and right and guessed like most homes the kitchen would be in the back of the house. I walked to the kitchen and found it empty. Where could they be?

I knew I wouldn't rest until I found them, so I went from room to room, opening each door a crack and peering inside. The third room I came upon was a private sitting room. I pulled up short as I cracked the door as there was a man and woman inside. They were in a tight embrace. I saw the woman's back, but I would have recognized that striking raven-colored hair anywhere.

"Herschel, you are being so bold," Mrs. Weston said. "Your wife is here with all her guests."

I stifled a gasp. I not only recognized Mrs. Weston's hair but her voice. It was the same voice I had heard speaking in the back of the church with Lucy.

The man laughed, and the guffaw rumbled in his ample belly. Round spectacles sat on the small bridge of his red nose. He was easily old enough to be Mrs. Weston's grandfather.

"What does it matter to me?" he asked. "She already knows, and there is little that she can do about it." He tried to kiss her neck.

She pushed him away. "Not now, my love, not now. Your wife might know, but I will not be caught by one of these uppity professor's wives in the act. I would rather they be vague and uncertain of their gossip."

This made Mr. Turnkey laugh again. "I love how you think."

He kissed her on the mouth, and when she pulled away, she had a look of utter disgust on her face. The expression was gone by the time Mr. Turnkey opened his eyes.

"I hate to bring it up again, but when are you going to leave that old hag and marry me?" she asked. "It is what I have been waiting for all this time."

"You know we can't marry. It would hurt my reputation in the town to leave my wife and look poorly on the children."

She turned her back to him. "Then, what are we doing here?"

He laughed, and while her back was turned away from him walked over to a side table. He opened the small drawer and pulled out a long velvet box. Mrs. Weston was still looking away from him. He removed a gold necklace from the box and put it around her neck from behind her.

She turned and touched the gold necklace at her throat. "If you continue to spoil me like you do, I can live with that."

He laughed and pulled her close.

I stumbled back from the door. What had I just seen? Verona Weston was having an affair with Mrs. Turnkey's boar of a husband.

"I must get back to the lecture. I want Gertrude to think I am paying at least a little bit of attention." She laughed. "I also want Lucy Stone to know that I am watching her."

"Do you think she will tell the Stearnses about us?" Mr. Turnkey asked.

"I don't care if she does. As long as I have you, what do I care what those college wives think of me?"

Before she could come out of the sitting room, I threw open the next door I saw and jumped inside the dark room. I closed my eyes for a moment. I was certain that they heard me and would throw open the door at any moment. When no one came, I opened my eyes. An oil lamp sat on a table by the door, and I lit it so I could have a better look at the room.

I was inside a private study and it was clear to me with the ornate desk, ivory-handled letter opener, and cabbage rose wallpaper that it was Mrs. Turnkey's study, not that of her husband.

No one was in the room, and I was about to leave when the desk caught my eye again. All around the edges little roses were carved. I stepped closer to it. There was a rose on the lock of the single drawer in the middle of the desk.

I had seen that rose before.

I reached into the pocket of my skirt and the small key was still there. I slipped the key into the drawer, and it turned with ease. Frowning, I pulled open the drawer and found two ledgers inside. They both had the title of the Ladies' Society of Amherst written on the covers.

I opened the first ledger. It was numbers and figures of donations to the society and where the money went. I opened the second ledger, and it seemed like it was the same thing but the donation numbers were different. They were much lower.

Why would Mrs. Turnkey steal from the Ladies' Society?

As I looked around me it seemed to me that she had everything that she could want or need.

I heard a noise behind me.

"Willa!" Miss Susan said as she threw open the study door. "There you are. Have you seen Norah Rose?"

I jumped up from the desk, tucked the ledgers under my shirtwaist, and slammed the drawer shut with my hip. I tucked the key back in my pocket.

"Norah Rose?" I asked.

"Yes! She's missing."

CHAPTER FORTY-TWO

I PRESSED MY HAND against my waist to reassure myself the ledgers were secure before running out of the room with Miss Susan.

The lecture appeared to be ending in the parlor, and Emily and Miss Lavinia came out.

"Where have you two been?" Miss Lavinia wanted to know.

"Norah Rose is missing." Miss Susan wrung her hands. "I was talking with another woman in the kitchen while Norah Rose was getting water from the cook. Norah Rose must have overheard that she might go to an orphanage and ran off."

I felt sick. I should have never let Miss Susan leave the parlor without me.

"Where would she go?" Miss Lavinia asked.

"I know!" Emily said. She grabbed my hand. "Willa and I will go look for her. You two stay here and search just in case she is somewhere in the house. She could be hiding. She's a small girl and there are many nooks and crannies a small child could tuck herself in, in such a big house."

Before Miss Susan and Miss Lavinia could protest, Emily pulled me to the door and gave me just enough time to grab our bonnets and cloaks from the parlor.

Emily and I ran out to the carriage. Jeremiah sat inside of it wrapped up in a blanket. He jumped up when he saw us. "I'm so sorry, miss! I was just taking a break from the cold."

"There's no time to apologize, Jeremiah. You have to take us to Kelley Square and take us to Kelley Square now!"

Jeremiah looked at me.

"Norah Rose is missing," I said.

Jeremiah leapt out of the carriage, and Emily and I climbed into the carriage.

In no time, the carriage rattled on the icy dirt road as it bounced in and out of ditches and crevices in the frozen mud before its wooden wheel. I prayed that the axle or wheel would not break.

We arrived at Kelley Square in record time.

Emily and I jumped out of the carriage and ran to the Doolan home. I pulled up short. Norah Rose with her muff stood in the middle of the rubble of her home.

Emily held back and I walked up to the child. She turned to me with tears in her eyes. A sob shook her whole body. She had cried before in the time I had known her, but not like this. This was mourning. I knew it well. I took her in my arms and held her with all my might.

I didn't know how long we stood there when a second carriage appeared, and Mrs. Turnkey was let out by her driver. "I expected that you all would be here," she said. "I would like my ledgers back, Willa."

The ledgers felt tight where they pressed against my waist.

I guided Norah Rose out of the rubble to stand next to Emily.

Norah Rose cried uncontrollably. They were big heaving sobs that shook her whole body.

"I don't know what you are talking about," I said in a shaky voice.

"Don't lie to me, Willa. Susan Dickinson said that when she found you, you were standing behind my desk and looking very nervous. I knew then and there what you had done, and when I went to my desk and found the ledgers missing, my suspicions were confirmed."

"What is she talking about?" Emily asked.

"I discovered tonight when looking for Norah Rose that she is stealing money from the society. It is money that should be going to those in need." I locked eyes with Mrs. Turnkey. "Are you using the money to support your lavish life?"

She snorted. "I do not own that home or anything in it. My husband and his family have lived there for generations. I am a guest and will always be so. When my husband dies, I will be the guest of my own children. It is always the way for the one who marries into money." She glanced at Emily. "I have told Susan Dickinson this. I believe she is the only one in your household who could understand my meaning."

"Susan is my sister. I do not treat her differently because she is not my blood."

"Then, perhaps she disagrees with you on that point."

Emily frowned and worry creased her forehead. I knew

how much she cared about Miss Susan. She would never want Miss Susan to believe that she thought less of her.

"Is it wrong that I want my own independence and money?" Mrs. Turnkey asked. "I want to buy what I want, do what I want. Instead, I have a miserly and unfaithful husband whom I must go to for a handout and count the days until he passes so I can control my own life then."

"Was it worth killing the Doolans for?" I asked.

Beside me, Norah Rose suddenly stopped crying. She was listening. That could not be helped.

Mrs. Turnkey laughed. "It was worth escaping my husband, who does not love me. Verona Weston is a terrible flirt and was having an affair with my husband. They both knew I knew about it, and my husband knew I couldn't do anything about it. If I left him, what did I have? I had to start socking away money of my own. It was the only thing to do in order to leave him."

"I don't understand what the Doolans have to do with this," Emily said.

"Hugh Doolan was a fool and went to work for Dr. Weston, who knew his wife was having an affair with someone. He actually thought it was your brother, Miss Dickinson. I would have been convinced of that too. Austin Dickinson does seem to have the wandering eye. I would warn Susan about that."

"How dare you?" Emily balled her fists at her sides.

"Hugh confessed to me that he was following Verona for Dr. Weston, and she often came to my home when I was away working for the league. I knew this too. As I said, I knew of the affair. Verona was only doing it for access to my husband's money. How do you think she afforded all those fancy clothes and to have Eve Doolan on call as her seamstress? It is not a young professor's salary; I tell you that. My husband gave her the money to buy those things. He's willingly handed it out to a woman he didn't know, and I have to beg for enough money for a new cloak."

"When did you learn of the affair?" Emily asked.

"A few weeks before Christmas. My husband said that we could not throw our usual Christmas gala because it was too expensive. It had never been an issue before. In fact, I thought that he enjoyed the galas we hosted. I was so angry. When he was away on business, I searched his office for proof that money was tight and he wasn't canceling the party just to spite me. That is when I found the correspondence between Verona and my husband. I was furious. Not in the way a wife should be maybe. I didn't care that he loved another woman. We had long fallen out of love with each other. Marriage is like that, you know. You're all bright-eyed in the beginning and then it dulls. As a woman, you are lucky if you are with an honorable man who is willing to stick out his commitment to you. If you are unlucky, they stray or worse, divorce you."

I raised my brow in surprise that Mrs. Turnkey would believe divorce was worse than an unfaithful husband. I'd much prefer that the man end the marriage before he moved on to someone new as I saw how much my father's affair hurt my mother even a decade after he was gone.

"I am not a withering violet. When my husband came home, I showed him the letter and told him to explain. He confessed to all of it. He wasn't remorseful one bit. If anything, he seemed proud. He claimed he finally found a woman who loved him for who he was." Her voice shook with anger.

"What a fool he was. He was a means to an end for a black widow like Verona Weston."

I shivered. In my mind, both Mr. Turnkey and Mrs. Weston were to blame for the affair, but I remembered how she looked at him back in the Turnkeys' sitting room when he wasn't looking at her. She hated him; that was clear to me.

"Why did you not expose your husband and leave when you learned the truth?" Emily asked. "Why would you stay?"

"It's clear to me that you're not married, and considering your family, you are in a position that you don't have to marry for security. I suggest you pose that question to your sister-in-law, Susan, in a decade or two. You will be surprised to learn that she will have the same answer as I do." She tapped the head of the dead fox on her shoulder. "In the best-case scenario, he and Verona would have ended their relationship, and I would still be trapped in a loveless marriage. I had to find a way not to depend on my husband, and the only way I would be able to do that was with money of my own."

"And when you had the money, did you plan to leave?"

"No, but I would be comfortable again. I have nowhere else to go. Why should I leave? I was here for decades longer than Verona. Why should I give up everything that I earned by putting up with him for so long and for being his wife? If I leave him, I leave my children as well. They are adults now, but as a mother, separation from them at any time would break my heart. However, if and when it was time to choose between their father and me, they would go with their father. They need to have that safety and the funds from being his children just as much as I need it as his wife."

"He could divorce you. Why does he not do that?"

"And suffer the embarrassment? He would never." She laughed as if this was the most ridiculous thing that she had ever heard. "In a man's eyes, it is better to be a married man having an affair than an unmarried man with a young lover."

I shook my head, not understanding how that could be true, but then again, I was not from their class and certainly was not wealthy like the Turnkeys were.

"It would make more sense to me that you killed Verona or even your husband. I don't understand why you would go after Hugh Doolan. Could you not explain away what he had found?"

She laughed. "You think I am here because I am the killer? You are as foolish as my husband. I have never killed anyone. I simply want my ledgers back and will continue on my way."

"But we now know of your husband's affair and your thievery," Emily said. "Aren't you afraid that we will say something? Aren't you afraid that we will reveal this to the Ladies' Society?"

"No, because who will be believed more? A girl who is known to have her head in the clouds and her maid? Or me? Now, please hand over the ledgers, so we can put an end to this nonsense."

But Emily was not done with her questions. "Why not steal from your husband? Why from the Ladies' Society?"

Mrs. Turnkey narrowed her eyes at Emily. "I knew from years of experience that the Ladies' Society of Amherst was lax with the bookkeeping. It was something that I planned to rectify when I took my position as the society's president. When I realized how easy it would be to take some of the funds as my own, it was the perfect plan."

"But you could have gone to Dr. Weston and told him of Verona's betrayal too," Emily said.

"In hindsight, I wish that I had. If I had, Hugh Doolan would never have been involved. At first, Dr. Weston was too absorbed in his research to even notice the change in her clothing and her demeanor. However, something must have turned him on to the fact that his wife was unfaithful, and he was paying Hugh to find the man she was having an affair with. My husband and Verona weren't as secretive as they thought about this affair, and before long, Hugh was spying on my home. When my housekeeper told me that she found him looking through my desk, I knew he'd learned not only my husband's dirty little secret but mine as well."

"So, you killed him," Emily said.

She laughed. "I didn't kill anyone. Danny did."

"Please don't forget, Gertrude, you paid me to do it," Danny Boyle said as he came out from the alley behind his house. "Your hands are as bloody as mine are."

In the window of his little house, Moira's small face and the top of her baby's head glowed in candlelight.

Mrs. Turnkey glared at him. "You were happy to take the money."

"'Course I was, you old bat." He walked toward her with a wooden staff in his hand. Pulling out a piece of flint, he lit the end of the torch. It ignited.

Danny Boyle waved the torch back and forth.

"Danny," I said as calmly as I could. "What are you doing?"

"I'm tired of being used by the rich. I need to teach this old bat a lesson."

He waved the torch closer to Mrs. Turnkey, and she

stepped back and slipped on the ice as she ran and hobbled to her carriage.

The driver's eyes were the size of dinner plates.

Before Mrs. Turnkey could climb into the carriage, Danny threw the torch inside of it, and the interior burst into flames.

She fell back into the snow. "My leg!"

The driver leapt from the seat. By this time, the neighbors were all out, and the driver and two other men released the horse from the burning carriage.

They just about had him free when fear took over and he ran, half pulling, half dragging the burning carriage behind him.

The poor creature was completely lost and ran to the alley, and in doing so, he hit the carriage on the side of the Boyle home. He broke loose and kept running, but now the Boyle's small house was on fire.

Men threw snow on the flames, but it was no use.

"Moira and the children are in there!" I cried.

Danny Boyle looked back at his house and instead of running to it to help his wife and two small children, he ran the other way. Two of the men on the street knocked him over and held him down.

"Willa, go tell Jeremiah to run for the police," Emily said.

"What are you going to do?" I asked.

"I'm going in after them."

"I should be the one to run into the fire," I said.

"We can't argue about this." She ran to the door of the Boyle home.

I ran to the carriage, dragging Norah Rose along behind me. Church bells began to ring. The smoke had been noticed just like it had the night the Doolans died.

"Jeremiah, go get the police."

He stared at me.

"Please. And take Norah Rose with you. Keep her safe." I tucked the child in the back of the carriage. "Please stay in here for me," I whispered.

I looked up at Jeremiah. "Go!"

He flicked the reins and turned the carriage around.

I ran back to the Boyle house, which was now ablaze. Mrs. Turnkey lay on the ground crying about her back. I didn't have any sympathy for her. Danny was nowhere to be found.

Jeremiah had gone for help. Norah Rose was safe. The firemen and police would be here soon, but would it be too late for Emily?

I ran back to the house that was in flames now. Moira and the children stood outside shivering. They were wrapped in blankets given to them by neighbors.

"Where's Emily?"

"Who?" one of the men asked.

"The young woman!"

"She fell," Moira said. "In the back bedroom where we were hiding. She told us how to get out."

I didn't wait to hear anymore. I ran into the alley past the burning carriage. The heat was unbearable.

I peered into the back window of the house and could not see anything. I yanked on the back door, and the doorknob burned my hand. I kicked the door open instead and threw my cloak down for fear it would catch aflame.

The house was black with smoke. All I could think was this is what Hugh and Eve Doolan saw before they died.

"Emily!" I choked on my own scream.

I heard the faintest squeak to my left and found Emily in the doorway of a bedroom.

Not stopping to see what injuries she had, I grabbed her by her wrists and pulled her out the back door of the house. The snow, rocks, and ice tore into her cloak and skirts. I pulled her down the alley until I thought we were safe.

I dropped to the ground beside her.

She rolled on her side and spat out black muck.

"Emily! Emily!"

"Willa?" Her voice was hoarse. She smiled at me. "I've saved you and now you have saved me."

"We saved each other," I whispered, and for that moment I truly forgot that she was my superior and hugged her with all my might.

EPILOGUE

SPRING FINALLY CAME in May. March and April were at times as cold as the darkest days of January. The rivers flooded the fields. For the farmers that year, the growing season would be late if it was possible to happen at all.

Norah Rose had been with Miss Susan and Austin all that time. I knew Miss Susan had grown as attached to her as I had. Austin still wanted the child to leave but he had agreed to wait until we heard from her family in Dublin.

Emily and I were clearing leaves and debris from the flower beds in the front of the homestead when Matthew came up the walk to the house.

Planting was late this year, and there was still much to do.

Across the yard, I saw Norah Rose following a bunny around, and I smiled.

By the way Matthew walked I knew he was here in his official capacity. He had the same gait when he came to the homestead to collect the Ladies' Society of Amherst's ledgers from me the day after the Boyles' home burned. The ledgers would be returned to the society. Mrs. Turnkey was stripped of her title and dismissed from the group, but the society wished for it to end there. They asked the police not to arrest her as they wanted to minimize the scandal. Danny Boyle, on the other hand, wasn't so lucky and sat in prison. He would be there for years to come. He continued to claim Mrs. Turnkey paid him to kill the Doolans, but it fell on deaf ears. I tended to believe him on this one point, but there was little I could do about it. At least now Moira and her children would be free of him.

Matthew wasn't just making a call on Norah Rose. Over the last several months, he had visited the Evergreens often to check in on Norah Rose. He trusted Miss Susan that the girl was safe and well taken care of, but he had also taken it upon himself to be her guardian.

Whenever she saw him, she leapt into his arms. She had fallen in love with him like a child who loved their parent. I, too, had fallen in love in a much different way. It wasn't until Norah Rose came into our lives that I realized the walls I had built around my heart over my father's abandonment, over losing my brother and mother. Norah Rose broke through those walls and made me realize that I loved Matthew all this time since the moment that he took Henry under his wing to try to keep him out of trouble. And now the three of us could be a new family.

I stood up and dusted dirt from my hands. "Emily," I said.

She was on her hands and knees pulling weeds. She looked behind her and sat up.

As Matthew grew closer, I saw that he had a letter in his hand. My stomach churned. I knew it was the letter that we had been waiting for all these weeks.

He gave me the letter and it read, *Please stop writing. We do not acknowledge the child. We have no daughter by the name of Eve Doolan. If you write again, we will be forced to take legal action.*

I handed the letter to Emily. I felt a strange mingling in my gut of relief and horror.

She read it quickly. "Legal action? What do they mean by that? Is it illegal in Ireland to write someone who will not take the letter?"

"We can't send her there if she is unwelcome," Matthew said. "She has been through enough already."

"She has," I agreed.

"I wish she could stay here in Amherst," Emily said. "I just don't know how that's possible."

"There is one way," Matthew said.

I looked up at him. "No, there are two ways."

Emily frowned.

"What are those?"

I turned to Emily and took her hands in mine.

"Willa, you are scaring me."

"The two ways are: I take her on as my daughter or Matthew and I take her on as our daughter together."

She looked from Matthew to me and back again. "Have the two of you been planning this the whole time?" She picked up her trowel and stomped away.

I squeezed Matthew's hand. "Let me speak to her alone."

He nodded and called Norah Rose's name. She yelped with glee and ran to him. I was making the right choice.

Emily stood to the side of the house under the large oak tree. She sat in that spot so many times writing and daydreaming, but now she stood there with a frown etched on her face as she stared off into the direction of Kelley Square.

I didn't say anything. I just stood beside her. I wondered how many times in the last two years we had stood just like this, side by side under the tree, gazing at the gardens and watching passersby walk up and down the street.

Finally, she spoke. "I am happy for you. You will not have the life that I want, but it suits you. You, Officer Thomas, and Norah Rose will make a happy family. You can heal one another."

"And who will heal you?" Perhaps it was too intrusive a question to ask her as I was still just a maid.

"My poems. My poems will heal me as far as I let them. And someday they will heal others when I let them go." She clapped her hands together and Carlo came running to her from across the yard.

She started to walk away and then she turned back to me. "Remember, Willa, my friends are my estate. You are my estate. The estate cannot be broken." She paused and looked up into the blue sky. "Long years apart can make no breach a second cannot fill—the absence of the witch does not invalidate the spell."

And then she and Carlo went into the homestead. It was the place she loved most and knew best. It was the place she chose never to leave.

AUTHOR'S NOTE

JANUARY 1857 HAD some of the worst weather on the east coast of the United States in recorded history. It began in early January and lasted through the end of the month. There was a record snowfall, causing trains to stop running and the temperature plummeted to well below zero. In New England alone, there were reports of snowdrifts from the driving wind being eighteen feet high. It is referred to as the "Cold Storm of 1857."

At the time, fire in either a stove or a hearth was the source of warmth for any home, and with fires running around the clock in such weather, an out-of-control blaze was a constant fear.

The Cold Storm would have hit Amherst, Massachusetts, dead-on, so I knew Emily Dickinson and her family would have lived through it. In their large home with numerous fireplaces, they would have been better off than many in town during this time, but the struggle to get supplies, mail, and other essentials would have been a very real concern. Also, fear of a house fire would be prevalent.

Kelley Square, the Irish community in Amherst at the time, was just a short walk from the Dickinson homestead and near the railroad tracks. It was a close-knit community and where many of the Dickinsons' employees lived. In the 1850s in the United States, because of the Great Famine in Ireland, there was a large influx of Irish men and women emigrating into the United States. These immigrants were not always welcomed with open arms and were many times looked down upon. In Massachusetts at the time, they were primarily servants and day laborers. Emily Dickinson was surrounded by Irish servants most of her life. In fact, she cared about many of them. She died on May 15, 1886, and left instructions for her family to have six Irish workmen be her pallbearers. Her family honored this request.

Lucy Stone was a suffragist who traveled around the country speaking on abolitionism and women's rights. She is less known than other women activists at the time, such as Susan B. Anthony and Elizabeth Cady Stanton, but was just as influential in the movement. She married and had a child but never took her husband's name, saying, "A wife should no more take her husband's name than he should hers. My name is my identity and must not be lost." She was known for wearing trousers or bloomers instead of long skirts, which she found convenient in her travels but were seen as controversial by the public. There was no direct connection between Lucy Stone and Emily Dickinson; however, they were both friends with Thomas Wentworth Higginson. Higginson even officiated Lucy Stone's wedding to Henry Blackwell. Later in life, Emily would build a friendship with Higginson, who wrote for the *Atlantic Monthly*, through letters as she consulted him about her poetry.

Austin Dickinson, Emily Dickinson's brother, has a wandering eye in this novel to signal what is to come. Although he is not romantically involved with the fictional character Verona Weston in this novel, he did have a well-known affair with a young professor's wife, Mabel Loomis Todd, years later. He and Susan Dickinson never divorced, nor did Mabel divorce her husband, but all parties knew what was really going on. It is unknown how Emily felt about her brother's affair, but it had large ramifications on her life and after her death, on her work, as her sister, Lavinia Dickinson, separated Emily's poems in two. She gave half to Susan Dickinson to edit and have published, and when Susan was, in Lavinia's opinion, taking too long to publish Emily's works, Lavinia gave the other half to Mabel Loomis Todd to edit and have published. One could only imagine how Susan felt about that choice. With the help of Thomas Wentworth Higginson, Mabel got her portion of Emily's poems published first in 1890.

Lavinia's decision has ramifications on Emily's work to this very day. Because her work was divided between the two women, half of Emily Dickinson's original works are at Harvard University and the other half are at Amherst College. Amherst College owns and operates the Emily Dickinson Museum, which consists of the Emily Dickinson Homestead and the Evergreens.

ACKNOWLEDGMENTS

It's been one of the highlights of my career to write this series about Emily Dickinson. If I would have told my fifteen-year-old self, who fell in love with Dickinson's poetry decades ago, that I would one day transform my favorite poet into an amateur sleuth, I would have never believed it. So first and foremost, I must thank Emily Dickinson for her life, her work, and her inspiration. Truly, beauty and truth were the legacies she left behind for countless generations.

I also must thank those who believed in this series: my amazing agent and friend, Nicole Resciniti, and my wonderful editor, Michelle Vega. Without the support of both of you these books would not have been possible.

Thanks, too, for the support of the Emily Dickinson Museum, which not only recognized but embraced this interpretation of Dickinson. A very special thank-you to Jane Wald and Brooke Steinhauser at the museum.

Thank you to Kate Schlademen and the Learned Owl Book Shop, for their continued support over my career and especially for this series.

Thank you to reader Kimra Bell, for her thoughtful comments, the team at Berkley for their hard work, and my family and friends.

A very special thank-you to my husband, David Seymour, who not only traveled around the country for this series with me but is my number-one supporter and biggest fan. I love you, David.

And finally, thank you to God for allowing me to write this. Dickinson and I might have had very different views on religion, but I believe in the end we both might have come to the same right answer.

DAVID M. SEYMOUR

Amanda Flower is the *USA Today* bestselling and Agatha Award–winning mystery author of more than fifty novels, including the nationally bestselling Amish Candy Shop Mystery series, Magical Bookshop Mysteries, and, written under the name Isabella Alan, the Amish Quilt Shop Mysteries. Flower is a former librarian, and she and her husband, a recording engineer, own a habitat farm and recording studio in Northeast Ohio.

VISIT AMANDA FLOWER ONLINE

AmandaFlower.com
AuthorAmandaFlower
AmandaFlowerAuthor
AFlowerWriter